"INTRIGUING, CLEVERLY PLOTTED, AND SKILLFULLY WRITTEN . . .

Penman's clear prose and engrossing plot, the skill with which she brings the politics, people, and ambience of medieval England alive, and her engaging characters make this a must-read, must-have mystery."
—*Booklist*

"A fantastic historical whodunit that profoundly brings to life all of the scheming and intrigue that surrounds yet is abetted by John. The characters are all genuine with many of them stepping out of the history books into an exciting murder mystery. Only someone with the talent of Sharon Kay Penman could have penned this spectacular story . . . an amazing trip back to the twelfth century."
—*Feminist Mystery Reviews*

"Penman has a good feel for the period. . . . [She] ably links two main story lines, the one about ordinary folk caught up in a drama of passion and power effectively echoed by the second, about aristocrats maneuvering for power at the highest levels. . . . [*Cruel as the Grave*] delivers atmosphere, plotting, and nicely modulated characters."
—*Publishers Weekly*

"The historical detail is luscious."
—*Library Journal*

Also by Sharon Kay Penman

THE SUNNE IN SPLENDOUR
HERE BE DRAGONS
FALLS THE SHADOW
THE RECKONING
WHEN CHRIST AND HIS SAINTS SLEPT
THE QUEEN'S MAN

CRUEL
AS THE
GRAVE

A Medieval Mystery

Sharon Kay Penman

FAWCETT BOOKS • NEW YORK

A Fawcett Book
Published by The Ballantine Publishing Group
Copyright © 1998 by Sharon Kay Penman

www.ballantinebooks.com

ISBN 0-345-44144-3

This edition published by arrangement with Henry Holt and Company, Inc.

Manufactured in the United States of America

Cover art: Two scenes from the life of Richard I, taken from *Effigies regium Angline*, c. 14th century. British Library, London, UK/Bridgeman Art Library, London/New York.

First Fawcett Edition: November 2001

10 9 8 7 6 5 4 3

TO MOLLY FRIEDRICH

Jealousy is cruel as the grave.

—Song of Solomon 8:6–7

1

TOWER OF LONDON ENGLAND

April 1193

They were intimate enemies, bound by blood. Here in the torchlit splendor of the Chapel of St John the Evangelist, they'd fought yet another of their battles. As always, there was no winner. They'd inflicted wounds that would be slow to heal, and that, too, was familiar. Nothing had changed, nothing had been resolved. But never had the stakes been so high. It shimmered in the shadows between them, the ultimate icon of power: England's royal crown.

Few knew better than Eleanor of Aquitaine how seductive that power could be. In her youth, she'd wed the French king, then left him for the man who would become King of England. That passionate, turbulent marriage of love and hate was part of her distant, eventful past; if Henry's unquiet ghost still stalked the realm of marital memory, she alone knew it. Now in her seventy-first year, she was England's revered Dowager Queen, rising above the ruins of her life like a castle impervious to assault. If her fabled beauty had faded, her wit had not, and her will was as finely honed as the sword of her most celebrated son, Richard Lionheart, the crusader king languishing in a German prison. But she was much more than Richard's mother, his invincible ally: She was his only hope.

1

The torches sputtered in their wall sconces, sending up wavering fingers of flame. The silence grew louder by the moment, thudding in her ears like an army's drumbeat. She watched as he paced, this youngest of her eaglets. John, Count of Mortain and Earl of Gloucester, would-be king. He seethed with barely suppressed fury, giving off almost as much heat as those erratic torches. His spurs struck white sparks against the tiled floor, and the swirl of his mantle gave her a glimpse of the sword at his hip. This might be her last chance to reach him, to avert calamity. What could she say that he would heed? What threat was likely to work? What promise?

"I will not allow you to steal Richard's crown," she said tautly. "Understand that if you understand nothing else, John. As long as I have breath in my body, I will oppose you in this. As will the justiciars."

"You think so?" he scoffed. "They held fast today, but who knows what may happen on the morrow? They might well decide that England would be better served by a living king than a dead one!"

"Richard is not dead."

"How can you be so sure of that, Madame? Have you second-sight? Or is this merely a doting mother's lapse into maudlin sentimentality?"

Beneath his savage sarcasm, she caught echoes of an emotion he would never acknowledge: a jealousy more bitter than gall. "Bring us back incontrovertible proof of Richard's death," she said, "and we will then consider your claim to the throne."

John's eyes showed sudden glints of green. "You mean you would weigh my claim against Arthur's, do you not?"

"Richard named his nephew as his heir. I did not," she said pointedly. "Must I remind you that you are my son, flesh of my flesh? Why would I not want the kingship for you?"

"That is a question I've often asked myself."

"If you'd have me say it, listen, then. I want you to be king. Not Arthur—you."

He could not hide a flicker of surprise. "You almost sound as if you mean that."

"I do, John," she said. "I swear by all the saints that I do."

For a moment, he hesitated, and she thought she'd gotten to him.

"But not whilst Brother Richard lives?"

"No," she said, very evenly, "not whilst Richard lives."

The silence that followed seemed endless to her. She'd always found it difficult to read his thoughts, could never see into his soul. He was a stranger in so many ways, this son so unlike Richard. His eyes locked upon hers, with a hawk's unblinking intensity. Whatever he'd been seeking, he did not find, though, for his mouth twisted into a sardonic, mirthless smile. "Alas," he said, "I've never been one for waiting."

Justin de Quincy paused in the doorway of the queen's great hall. Never had he seen so many highborn lords at one time, barons of the realm and princes of the Church and all of the justiciars: Walter de Coutances, Archbishop of Rouen; William Marshal; Geoffrey Fitz Peter; William Brewer; and Hugh Bardolf. These were men of rank and privilege, milling about now like so many lost sheep, agitated and uneasy. What was amiss?

William Longsword was standing a few feet away and Justin headed in his direction. He felt an instinctive sense of kinship to the other man, for they were both outsiders. Will was a king's bastard, half-brother to Richard and John, raised at court but never quite belonging . . . like Justin himself. He hadn't been as lucky as Will, had grown up believing himself to be an orphan, the unwanted child of an unnamed wanton who'd died giving him birth. Only several months ago had he learned the truth. He was no foundling. The man who'd taken him in as a much-praised act of Christian charity was the man who'd sired him, Aubrey de Quincy, Bishop of Chester.

That stunning revelation had turned Justin's world upside down, and he was still struggling to come to terms with it. He had no right to the name de Quincy, had claimed it at the whimsical suggestion of the woman who'd become his unlikely patroness. That act of prideful defiance had given him no satisfaction, for it was like paying a debt with counterfeit coin. He had a new identity, a new life. He was still haunted, though, by the life he'd left behind, by the father who'd refused to acknowledge him.

"Justin!" Will had an easy smile, an affable manner, and none of his half-brothers' unsated hunger for lands, honours, and kingship. "When did you get back from Winchester? Come here, lad, there is someone I want you to meet."

William Marshal, Lord of Striguil and Pembroke, was a very wealthy man, holding vast estates in South Wales by right of his wife, a great heiress. A justiciar, sheriff of Gloucestershire, a baron who cherished hopes of being invested with an earldom, Marshal was one of the most influential men in the kingdom, and Justin greeted him somewhat shyly, for he was not yet accustomed to breathing the rarefied air of the royal court. Just a few brief months ago, he'd been a nobody, a bastard of unknown parentage serving as a squire with no hopes of advancement, and now he was . . .

"The queen's man," Will said heartily, clapping Justin playfully on the shoulder. "De Quincy is the lad I told you about, William, the one who brought Queen Eleanor the news that Richard was captured on his way home from the crusade."

It seemed strange to Justin to hear it spoken of so openly now, for the secret of that bloodstained letter had nearly cost him his life. He could only marvel at the random nature of fate, at the improbable series of events that had been set in motion by his decision to ride out of Winchester on a snowy Epiphany morn. Because he'd stumbled onto the ambush of the queen's messenger, he'd found himself entangled in a conspiracy of kings, matching wits with the queen's son John and a murderous outlaw known as Gilbert the Fleming, sharing his bed with a seductive temptress who'd broken his heart with her betrayal, and winning a prize greater than the Holy Grail—the queen's favor.

Will was praising him so lavishly now that Justin flushed, both pleased and discomfited to be hailed as a hero. For most of his twenty years, compliments had been rarer than dragon's teeth; he could remember nary a one ever coming out of his father's mouth. "My lords, may I ask what has occurred here? I've been to wakes that were more cheerful than this assemblage." He hesitated briefly then, but he'd earned the right to ask. "Has there been bad news about the king?"

"No—as far as we know, nothing has changed; Richard remains the prisoner of that whoreson emperor of the Romans. The trouble is closer to home."

Will's face had taken on so unhappy a cast that Justin realized the trouble must involve John, for he knew the man harbored a genuine fondness for his younger brother. It was William Marshal who confirmed his suspicions, saying brusquely, "John summoned the justiciars to meet him this morn here at the Tower. He then claimed that Richard is dead and demanded that we recognize him as the rightful king."

Justin was startled; he hadn't expected John to make so bold a move. "They did not agree?"

"Of course not. We told him that we have no proof of

the king's death and until we do, the only king we will recognize is Richard."

Justin felt a surge of relief; he hadn't been sure the other justiciars would be as resolute as Marshal and the Archbishop of Rouen. The bleak truth was that they could not be utterly sure that Richard still lived. If he had sickened and died in confinement, the crown would be John's for the taking, for few were likely to support his rival claimant, a five-year-old boy dwelling in Brittany. So it was only to be expected that the justiciars would be loath to antagonize the man who might well be their next king, a man who forgot little, forgave even less.

"What happened then?"

"John flew into a rage," Will said sadly, "and made some ugly threats. The queen then insisted that they speak in private, and they withdrew to her chapel. If anyone in Christendom can talk some sense into John, for certes it will be the queen." Will did not sound very sanguine, though, and Marshal, a man known for speaking his mind plainly, gave a skeptical snort.

"Would you care to wager on that, Will? I could use some extra money." He went on to express his opinion of John's honour in far-from-flattering terms. By then Justin was no longer listening, for Claudine de Loudun was coming toward them.

The men welcomed her with enthusiasm—the young widow was a favorite with both Williams. All three engaged in some mildly flirtatious bantering, while Justin stood conspicuously silent, dreading what was to come.

Even as she teased the other men, Claudine's dark eyes kept wandering toward Justin, her gaze at once caressing and questioning. Finally she cast propriety to the winds and linked her arm through his, murmuring throatily that she needed a private word with Master de Quincy. Both Wills grinned broadly and waved them on, for Claudine's clandestine liaison with Justin de Quincy was

a poorly kept secret in a court in which only Eleanor's secrets seemed secure.

Steering Justin toward the comparative privacy of a
window seat, Claudine began to scold him lovingly.
"Why did you not let me know you were back from
Winchester? If I'd had some warning, I could have
coaxed the queen into giving me a free afternoon. But
she's not likely to be in any mood to grant favors now,
for this latest exorcism of hers is bound to fail."

Others might not have understood the joking refer-
ence to exorcism. Justin did, though, for she'd confided
to him that her private name for John was the Prince of
Darkness. As he looked upon the heart-shaped face up-
turned to his, the thought came to him, unbidden and
ugly: What did she call John in bed? He drew a sharp
breath, not wanting to go down that road. He knew that
she was John's spy. Was she John's concubine, too? He
pushed the suspicion away, to be dealt with later. Now
he must concentrate upon the danger at hand. How
could he conceal his knowledge of her treachery? Surely
she must see it writ plain upon his face.

Apparently not, for her smile did not waver. Those
brown eyes were bright with laughter and temptation.
Justin was shaken to the depths of his soul as he realized
how much power she still wielded over him. How could
he still want this woman? She'd betrayed him without a
qualm. Even worse, she'd betrayed her royal mistress
and kinswoman, the queen. And she'd almost seduced
him into betraying the queen, too. For more than a fortnight, he'd kept her guilty secret, at last unburdening
himself to Eleanor in a surge of self-hatred, only to find
that she already knew of Claudine's perfidy. But Claudine must not know that she'd been exposed. If John
learned that his spy was compromised, he'd look elsewhere. Eleanor had been able to act as if her trust was

still intact, but his role was far more precarious, for he was Claudine's lover.

Claudine beckoned to a wine bearer, claiming two cups for them. "Did all go as you hoped in Winchester, Justin? Was that outlaw hanged?"

He nodded. "I'll tell you about it later. What has happened at the court whilst I was away? Will just told me that John is back from France." He tensed then, for John's name seemed to sink like a stone in the conversational waters, sure to stir up ripples of suspicion between them.

Claudine appeared to take his curiosity as natural. "Did Will tell you, too, that John has laid claim to the crown?" Lowering her voice, she said in a conspiratorial whisper, "Do you think he found out what was in that bloodied letter? The one claiming that King Richard drowned when his ship was wrecked in a storm? We know now that it was not true, but mayhap John thinks he can make use of it somehow?"

This was the tale Justin had spun, entrapping her in her own web of lies. The memory was still so raw that he winced, reluctant to relive one of the worst moments of his life. Claudine saw his disquiet and squeezed his arm in puzzled sympathy. "Justin . . . is something wrong?"

"No," he said swiftly. "I . . ." Groping for a plausible response, he found it in the sight of the knight just coming into his line of vision. Tall and swaggering, he moved with surprising grace for so big a man, impeccably garbed in an eye-catching scarlet tunic with a dramatic diagonal neckline and tight-fitting cuffed sleeves. But Justin knew that his fashionable courtier's clothing hid the soul of a pirate. "I did not realize," he said flatly, "that Durand de Curzon was here."

"He came with John." Seeing his surprise, she said quickly, "You did not hear, then? Rumor has it that he was John's man all along . . . as you suspected. The queen dismissed him from her service."

Justin did not have to feign his shock; it was very real. "When did this happen?"

"Within the last few days. He—"

Claudine got no further. The door to the queen's chamber had swung open, and John paused for a moment in the doorway, for he had an actor's innate sense of timing. The hall hushed, all eyes upon him. He let the suspense build, then gestured to his household knights and strode toward the stairwell, leaving a trail of conjecture and speculation in his wake.

Durand de Curzon started to follow his lord, then stopped abruptly at the sight of Justin. Swerving toward the younger man, he flashed a smile as sharply edged as any dagger. "Lady Claudine," he murmured, reaching for her hand and bringing it to his mouth with ostentatious gallantry. Claudine snatched her hand away, scowling. Her distaste for Durand seemed genuine to Justin; she might conspire with Durand on John's behalf, but she had consistently rebuffed his every overture. Durand appeared oblivious to her recoil. "For the life of me," he said, "I cannot imagine why a woman like you bothers with this callow milksop. You could surely do better for yourself."

Claudine was a distant kinswoman of the queen and it showed now in the mocking arch of her brow. "You? I'd sooner join a nunnery."

"And you'd make a right handsome nun. But I believe, darling, that nuns are expected to take a vow of chastity."

That was too much for Justin. "You need a lesson in manners," he said angrily, taking a threatening step forward. Claudine thought so, too; her hand tightening around the stem of her wine cup, she flung its contents in Durand's face. At least that was her intent. Durand not only anticipated her move, he thwarted it, reaching out and grabbing her wrist. Wine sloshed over the rim of her cup, splattering her gown and Durand's stylish tunic. Unable to break free of the knight's grip, she turned to Justin for aid. He was already in motion, slashing down upon Durand's arm with the stiffened edge of his hand. Durand at once let go of Claudine and lunged for Justin's throat. As Claudine screamed and heads swiveled in their direction, they crashed backward into the window seat.

Before either man could inflict any real damage, others intervened. Will Longsword and William Marshal pulled the combatants apart, and Justin and Durand were forced to stand, panting and flushed, as the Archbishop of Rouen rebuked them indignantly for daring to brawl in the queen's chambers. Daubing at a cut lip with the back of his sleeve, Durand offered Claudine a laconic, highly suspect apology, shot Justin a look that should have been aimed from a bow, and stalked out. Finding himself the unwanted center of attention, Justin allowed Claudine to lead him into the queen's chamber to escape the stares and whispers. There she ignored his protests and insisted upon bathing his scraped knuckles in a laver of scented water.

"The least I can do is tend to your wounds," she chided. "After all, they were gotten on my behalf." She tilted her face up toward his, her lips parted invitingly. Her breath was warm on his throat and the familiar fragrance of her perfume evoked involuntary erotic memories of their past lovemaking. Justin was never to be sure what would have happened next, for it was then that Eleanor emerged from the chapel.

The queen's gaze was cool and unrevealing. "Claudine, would you find Peter for me?"

Eleanor's chancellor was right outside, but Claudine was astute enough to recognize a pretext for privacy when she heard one. "Of course, Madame," she said. "I'll see to it straightaway." Closing the door quietly behind her, she left them alone.

Eleanor moved to the window, beckoning for Justin to join her. Below in the bailey, John was waiting for his stallion to be brought. As they watched, he and his men mounted and rode off. "John will not back down," Eleanor said at last. "We must find out what he means to do next. Can you get word to Durand?"

Justin rubbed his sore jaw ruefully. "It has been taken care of, my lady."

"Do I need to know what you and Claudine were doing in here?"

"Yes, Madame, you do. I'd just gotten into a brawl with Durand. He baited me into it and I wish I could say that I realized what he was up to, but I did not. Not until we were grappling in the floor rushes and he muttered in my ear, 'The alehouse on Gracechurch Street, after Compline.' "

"I see." Her face remained impassive, but he thought he could detect a glint of faint humor in those slanting hazel eyes. "Could he not have found an easier way to get that message to you?"

"I was wondering that myself," Justin said dryly.

"I did not get a chance to tell you that Durand would be joining John's household knights. The closer he is to John, after all, the more useful he can be to me." Eleanor's eyes flicked toward the bloodied basin, then back toward him. "I have need of Durand," she said. "John trusts him . . . at least a little. But you were right about him, Justin. Bear that in mind in your dealings with him."

"I will, Madame," he said somberly, remembering the night he'd learned the truth about Durand de Curzon. He'd called Durand "John's tame wolf," and she'd smiled grimly, claiming Durand as hers. In reminding him of that now, she was also warning him. But there was no need. He already knew how dangerous it was to hunt with wolves.

* * *

Justin had been living on Gracechurch Street for barely
two months, but he was beginning to think of it as home.
His neighbors were hardworking, good-hearted folk for
the most part, unabashedly curious about the tall dark
youth dwelling in their midst. Secrets did not fare any
better on Gracechurch Street than at the royal court, and
only the very old and the very young did not know by
now that Justin de Quincy was the queen's man. But he'd
been befriended by two of their own—Gunter the smith
and Nell, who ran the alehouse—and their friendship
was Justin's passport into their world.

Gunter was alone in the smithy, sharpening a file upon
a whetstone. A lean, weathered man in his forties, he was
taciturn both by inclination and by experience, and he
greeted Justin with a nod, then went back to work. Justin
led Copper, his chestnut stallion, into one of the stalls, set
about unsaddling him. He would usually have gone on
then to the cottage he rented from Gunter, but the wind
now brought to him the muffled chiming of church bells;
Compline was being rung. "Stop by the alehouse later,"
Justin said, "and I'll buy you a drink." Getting one of
Gunter's quick, rare smiles in acknowledgment, he hastened out into the April night.

He crossed the street, then ducked under the sagging
alepole, entering the alehouse. It reeked of smoke and
sweat and other odors best not identified, and was deep
in shadow even at midday, for Nell was sparing with her
tallow candles and oil lamps; she had to account for
every half-penny to the parsimonious, aged owner. As
Justin paused to let his eyes adjust to the gloom, a dog
erupted from under a bench, barking joyously.

Grinning, Justin bent to tussle playfully with the ca-
pering animal. "I should have known I'd find you over
here," he said, and Shadow wriggled happily at the
sound of that familiar voice. He was the first dog Justin

had ever had, a young stray he'd plucked from the River Fleet and taken in temporarily. Although Justin still talked occasionally of finding the pup a good home, Shadow knew he already had one.

"I ought to be charging you rent for that flea-bitten cur," Nell grumbled, sidestepping Shadow as she carried a tray of drinks toward some corner customers. "He swiped a chunk of cheese when my back was turned, then nearly knocked over a flagon with his tail. And if he had, I'd have made a pelt out of the wretched beast!"

"I ought to be the one charging you," Justin countered. "How many alehouses have the free use of such a superior watchdog? If not for Shadow, the place might be overrun with cutpurses, prowlers, and vagabonds."

Nell cast a dubious eye upon the dog, sprawled belly-up in the floor rushes. "I think I'd take my chances with the prowlers." Justin had found an empty table by the hearth and she came over, set an ale down, then took the seat opposite him. "How did that happen?" she asked, pointing toward the fresh bruise spreading along his cheekbone. "And do not tell me you ran into a door!"

Justin hid his grin in the depths of his ale-cup, amused as always by the contrast between Nell's delicate appearance and her bold, forthright demeanor. She was barely five feet tall, with sapphire blue eyes, flaxen hair that invariably curled about her face in wispy disarray, and freckles she unsuccessfully tried to camouflage under a haphazard dusting of powder. With Nell, nothing was as it seemed. She looked as fragile as a child, but was tough-willed enough to run an alehouse—and to have helped Justin catch a killer. For all that she had a sailor's command of invective, her bluntness was armor for a surprisingly soft heart. A young widow with a small daughter, she was of a life that had not been easy, but then she had not expected it to be. She had little patience with fools, no sentimentality at all, and no education to speak of, but she did have courage, common sense, and a pragmatic realism that made her a sister under the skin to England's aging queen. Justin could well imagine Nell's disbelief if ever he told her that she reminded him of the elegant, imperious Eleanor. But in truth, she did, for both women had a clear-eyed, unsparing view of their respective worlds, and neither one wasted time or energy on futile denials or self-delusion. Justin would that he could do likewise. He kept looking over his shoulder, though, unable to outrun either his memories or his regrets.

"Well?" Nell demanded when he didn't answer. "Are you going to tell me how you got that bruise or not?"

"Not," he said, smiling, and then tensed, for Durand was coming in the door. He had to stoop to enter, for he was taller than most men. Justin had always been proud of his own height, but Durand topped him by several inches. He wore a mantle of finely woven wool, fastened with an ornate gold pin. Spying was clearly a profitable profession, Justin thought sourly. Durand looked out of place in such shabby surroundings, but Justin doubted that he'd be a target for cutpurses or robbers; his eyes would chill even the most obtuse of felons.

Spotting Justin, he crossed the common room, dismissing Nell with a terse "Leave us."

He'd misjudged his woman, though. Nell stayed put, looking up at him with an indifference that could not have been more insulting. "Justin?" she queried, and he nodded reluctantly.

"Will you excuse us, Nell?" He did not offer to buy Durand an ale, for he was damned if he'd drink with the man. "Sit," he said, as soon as Nell had risen, switching from English—Nell's tongue—to French, the language in which he would normally converse. Since most of the alehouse patrons were English-speakers like Nell, Justin could feel confident he'd foil would-be eavesdroppers; he strongly suspected that this was a conversation he'd not want overheard.

Durand seemed in no hurry to begin. He pulled up a bench, claimed a candle from a nearby table; the occupant was about to protest, then thought better of it. As the flame flared between them, Justin was pleased to see that the corner of Durand's mouth was swollen. Rarely had he ever taken such an instantaneous dislike to another man, but he'd distrusted Durand de Curzon from the first moment they'd met. It was a hostility returned by Durand in full measure, for Justin had outwitted the other man in the past. And then there was Claudine, who'd spurned Durand and taken Justin into her bed. Add to the mix their rivalry for the queen's favor and it was a very unstable brew, one likely to boil over at the least provocation.

"Jesú, what a pigsty." Durand glanced around the alehouse with contempt. "I do not know what I was thinking to pick this hovel for our meeting."

Justin knew exactly why he'd chosen the Gracechurch alehouse: to send a message—that he knew far more about Justin than Justin did about him. "You're not here for the pleasure of my company. You have word for the queen?"

"Yes . . . I do." Durand looked into Justin's half-filled ale-cup, grimacing. "How can you drink that swill?"

"Do you have something of value to tell me or not? I've already played one of your tiresome games with you this day, and am in no mood for another."

Durand laughed. "Are you complaining about our little joust in the hall? I had to get word to you, and that seemed the safest way to do it. All know we like each other not, after all. But if it eases your mind, next time I'll take a gentler approach."

Justin was determined that he'd not take the bait

again. "Say what you came to tell me. I assume it involves John?"

Durand's grin faded. "Be outside the priory of St Bartholomew's by dawn. John is sending a messenger to France on the morrow. He leaves at first light."

Justin leaned across the table. "What does this message contain?"

"If I knew that, would I not tell you?"

"I do not know. Would you?"

Durand's smile was mocking. "All I know is that the message is meant for John's allies in Normandy and bodes ill for the king. John does not confide utterly in me—no more than the queen does in you."

Justin ignored the gibe. "How will I recognize this courier?"

"His name is Giles de Vitry. He is French-born, not as tall as you, with hair the color of wheat, a scar under his right eye. And he'll be riding a rawboned bay stallion. Is that enough detail for you, lad? Should I come along and point him out as he passes by?"

"I'd manage better without you," Justin said coolly. "At least then I'd not have to be watching my back."

Durand had the bluest eyes Justin had ever seen, and the coldest; a blue-white flame flickered now in their depths, reminding Justin that ice could burn. Rising without haste, Durand smoothed the folds of his mantle, adjusted the tilt of his cap; his shoulder-length auburn hair gleamed where the candle's light caught it, brushed to a bronzed sheen. "It is now up to you, de Quincy," he said. "Try not to make a botch of this. The queen is depending upon us both."

As soon as Durand pushed through the door and out into the street, Nell returned to Justin's table. "Here," she said, bringing him, unbidden, another ale. "If ever I've seen a man born to drink with the Devil, it was that one. Who is he, Justin?"

Justin smiled, wryly. "Would you believe me if I said he was an ally?"

"With an ally like that, what need have you of enemies?"

Justin shrugged, but he agreed with Nell. What, indeed?

2

LONDON

April 1193

The sky was overcast and a damp, blustery wind had swept in from the south. The few hardy souls up and about in the predawn chill cast a wary eye skyward, knowing that spring too often carried a sting in its tail. Drawing his mantle closer, Justin shivered and yawned. He'd bribed a guard to let him out of the city before the gates opened, and for the past hour, he'd been keeping watch upon the Augustinian priory of St Bartholomew.

It was an uncomfortable vigil, made more so by the surroundings, for the priory overlooked the meadows of Smithfield. These open fields played an important role in the daily life of Londoners; the weekly horse fair was held here every Friday, and it was the site, as well, for numerous games of sport: jousting, wrestling, archery, javelin hurling. Now it lay deserted and still in the muted light, and Justin was alone with his memories. It was here that he had confronted a soulless killer. The trap had worked and Gilbert the Fleming had answered for his sins on a Winchester gallows. Eleanor had feared John's complicity in the murder of her messenger, relieved and grateful when Justin had been able to clear her son's name. Yet Justin doubted that there'd be any exoneration for John this time. The scent of treason was in the air.

Justin had no trouble in recognizing John's courier. A stocky, hard-faced man in his thirties, muffled in an inconspicuous dark mantle and wide-brimmed pilgrim's

18

hat, Giles de Vitry was dressed to blend in with his fellow travelers. They were astride placid mules and sway-backed geldings, though, and he was mounted upon a spirited bay stallion who was obviously eager to run. Justin tensed as the courier rode by his hiding place, for much depended upon what de Vitry did next. If he headed for Newgate and entered into the city, that would mean he meant to sail from Dover. If he took the road west, he intended to catch a ship at Southampton. Justin had a personal preference and he smiled as de Vitry urged his stallion on past Newgate. Easing Copper out into the stream of travelers, Justin let his mount settle into a comfortable canter, keeping a discreet distance behind his quarry.

The road was very familiar by now to Justin, for since January he had ridden it no less than seven times, going back and forth between London and Winchester in his hunt for the men who'd slain the queen's messenger. In winter, the trip had taken four or five days, but travel in April would be easier and quicker. If de Vitry pushed his mount, he could reach Winchester in two or three days' time, with Southampton just twelve miles farther on. The urgency of his message would dictate his speed.

It soon became apparent to Justin that John's message was very urgent, indeed. Most travelers would start at dawn, stop for dinner in the hour before noon, rest until midafternoon, and then resume their journey until dusk. Giles de Vitry's stops were few and far in-between. Not for him a leisurely meal at a roadside inn. He ate sparingly and hastily of the food he'd packed in his saddle-bag, and within a quarter hour was on his way again. Justin had expected him to stay over at Guildford, thirty miles south of London. But the courier raced the deepening shadows another ten miles, before finally halting for the night in the market town of Farnham.

Justin was not overly worried about attracting the

other man's attention, for the road was well traveled and
the choice of lodgings was limited. Even if de Vitry noticed him, he was not likely to read any sinister significance into their presence at the same inn. He was more
concerned that de Vitry might rise before dawn and gain
an insurmountable lead while he slept on, unaware. In
consequence, he got very little sleep at all, dozing uneasily upon a lumpy, straw-filled pallet surrounded by
snoring strangers, awakening to the dismal sound of rain
splattering upon the roof shingles.

De Vitry, undeterred by the day's damp start, was on
the road again at first light. Justin followed soon thereafter, grudgingly conceding that John was well served by
his messenger. What was in that letter, that it would send
a man out into the rain without breakfast or a decent
night's sleep?

Fortunately, the rain proved to be a spring shower, and
the sky cleared as they left Farnham behind. The day
brightened and the road ahead beckoned. Barring some
mishap—a thrown shoe, an encounter with outlaws—
Justin calculated that they should reach Winchester by
nightfall. But Justin had determined that de Vitry would
not be continuing on to Southampton on the morrow.
The reckoning would be in Winchester.

Stars were floating above his head. Clouds sailed across
the moon, briefly blotting out its light. The street was
shadowed and silent, for curfew had rung some time
ago. Justin knew the way, though, even in the dark.
Keeping his stallion to a walk, he saw before him the pale
outlines of the cottage. Thatched and whitewashed, it
looked well tended and peaceful, and he regretted having
to intrude into this secluded small Eden with yet more
snakes.

He and the man he hoped to find within the cottage
had a checkered history. They'd begun as enemies. Justin

had initially suspected Luke de Marston of having a hand in the murder of the queen's messenger, and then of being John's spy. Eventually they'd forged a truce, tentative and wary, as they united in the search for Gilbert the Fleming. Justin could think of no better ally in his looming confrontation with Giles de Vitry than Luke, Hampshire's under-sheriff.

After hitching Copper to a tree, he approached the cottage. Even before he could knock, the barking began, deep and booming, followed by an equally loud burst of sleepy cursing. Justin grinned; Luke was home. Motivated by a sense of mischief, he pounded mercilessly on the door until it opened a crack, revealing a thick thatch of tousled fair hair and a glaring green eye.

"What do you—Holy God!" Opening the door wider, Luke grabbed Justin by the arm and pulled him inside. "What are you doing here, de Quincy? I thought you were supposed to be in London, spying and lurking or whatever it is you do for the queen."

Justin, occupied for the moment in fending off the enthusiastic welcome of a gigantic black mastiff named Jezebel, let the gibe go unanswered. He didn't blame Luke for being testy. What man, after all, would want to be pulled out of Aldith Talbot's bed?

"Justin?" The voice sounded drowsy, delighted, and sultry. Aldith poked her magnificent auburn head through the bed hangings, her face lighting up in a smile that no man would soon forget. "Wait there," she directed, "whilst I dress," and disappeared behind the bed curtains.

Luke was in need of clothes, too, wearing nothing but a towel hastily snatched up and strategically draped. Fixing Justin with an accusatory gaze, he said, "What are my chances of getting back to bed tonight?"

"Not very good," Justin admitted, and Luke swore, then retreated behind the bed to pull on his discarded tunic and chausses, returning to prowl the chamber in search of his boots, all the while grumbling about a sheriff's lot and how rarely he got to pass a full night in his own bed. Justin paid his harangue no heed, for the deputy's irascibility was more posturing than genuine ill will. Sitting down wearily upon the settle, he closed his eyes.

"Got it," Luke said triumphantly, holding up a boot. "I do hope you have a damned good reason, de Quincy, for making me put these back on."

Justin opened his eyes. "I followed one of John's men from London. He is bearing a message I must see. Can you help me?"

"I assume there is more to this than satisfying your curiosity," Luke said wryly. "Do you know where this messenger is or must we scour the city for him?"

"I trailed him to a bawdy house in Cock's Lane, and since he told their groom to bed down his horse in their stables, it is safe to assume he plans to spend the night there."

Luke had to concede his reasoning. "There are several bawdy houses in Cock's Lane. Can I trust you to find your way back to the right one?"

Justin took no offense at the sarcasm. "Well, there are worse fates than searching one bawdy house after another," he joked, and at once regretted it, for Aldith had emerged in time to hear. She was too well mannered to berate a guest in her home, but the look on her expressive face left no doubt that she was not pleased at the prospect of her lover taking a tour of the town's brothels. Justin was sorry to cause her any distress, for she was not only good-hearted, but one of the most desirable women he'd ever met. "I know the house," he assured her hastily, "and we'll be able to pluck de Vitry from his soft nest and haul him off to the castle in no time at all."

Aldith's smile was stilted. "I'll wait up for you, Luke," she said pointedly.

Luke shrugged. "Lock the door after us," he instructed Aldith, grazing her cheek with a kiss too casual to give her much reassurance. "Let's go, de Quincy."

Justin bade Aldith farewell and followed Luke out into the night. Although neither man would have admitted it, they were pleased to be working together again, sharing a familiar excitement, one common to hunters everywhere. The chase was on.

Prostitution was illegal as well as immoral, much deplored by the Church but tacitly tolerated by city officials as a necessary evil. The fact that brothels were often owned by respected citizens, even churchmen, made it all the more difficult for the law to close them down. The bawdy houses of Winchester could not compare in size or scope to the more infamous brothels of London—the Southwark stews. The one chosen by Giles de Vitry was a two-storey wooden structure, gaudy even in the moonlight, for it had been painted a garish shade of red. Light gleamed through the chinks in the shutters and the door was opened at once by a painfully thin maidservant with huge hollow eyes and a fading bruise upon her cheek. As soon as they were ushered inside, a matronly woman in her forties came bustling over, ready to bid them welcome. Justin guessed correctly that this was the bawd. Her smile faltered as Luke stepped within the glow cast by a smoking rushlight.

"Master de Marston, this is a surprise," she said, her voice flat and toneless. "Surely the neighbors have not been complaining about the noise again? I can assure you that we have taken your warnings to heart. You'll find no drunkards or troublemakers here. We'll take no man's money unless he is sober, civil, and old enough to know what he's about."

Luke played the game, saying blandly, "It gratifies me to hear that, Emma. My life would be much easier if only

the other bawds were so law abiding and prudent. I was
just telling Master de Quincy here that we could rely
upon your discretion and expect your full cooperation."

Emma's eyes narrowed to the merest slits, apprehensive and suspicious. "I will do what I can," she said cautiously. "If a complaint has not brought you here, what
then? I swear by the Rood that all of my girls are free of
the pox, and I hire no wayward wives or runaway servants or—"

Luke cut her off before she could insist that her whores
were as fresh as country lasses newly fallen from grace.
As an under-sheriff, he knew better than most men the
miseries of that precarious profession. "We are seeking a
man," he said, "who arrived as curfew was being rung.
He is not overly tall, with a scar on his cheek. Tell us
where to find him and I'll not look for other laws broken
or bent."

Her relief was palpable that they'd come for a customer; men were expendable, her whores harder to re-
place. "A man with a scar . . ." She pretended to ponder
it, then nodded. "The man who took Arlette for the entire night is likely the one you want."

"Where?"

"Above-stairs. The inner chamber is Arlette's," she
said, and stepped aside hastily as they brushed past her.
The common room was almost deserted. By the hearth a
drunk nodded blearily into his wine cup, and in the
corner a ruddy, stout man held a half-dressed woman on
his lap. He gave a startled yelp as they burst in, beginning
to rise and inadvertently dumping the girl into the floor
rushes. By then they were already through, plunging into
the darkened stairwell, loosening their swords in their
scabbards. They were at the top of the stairs when they
heard a woman scream.

Luke was in the lead. Swearing, he flung himself at the
door and shoved it open. The chamber was small and

cramped, holding only a stool, a basin, and a bed. A couple was entangled in the sheets, gaping up at these intruders. But the man was dark haired and unscarred. Ignoring his sputtering protest, Luke hit the inner door with his shoulder. It gave way at once, catapulting him inside.

This room was even shabbier than the first one, almost all of its space taken up by a rumpled bed. A buxom redhead was kneeling in the middle of it, oblivious or uncaring of her nudity. "He went out the window," she cried, "without paying, curse him! And when I tried to stop him, the whoreson struck me!"

Luke's headlong rush into the room had sent him stumbling into the bed, nearly tumbling down on top of the indignant Arlette. Justin swerved around him and lunged for the window. He was not so reckless as to jump, though, lowering himself as he clung to the sill and then dropping the remaining four or five feet to the ground.

He landed on his feet like a cat. His eyes had to adjust again to the darkness, and at first he could see nothing. He thought he was in the courtyard behind the brothel, but he could not yet be sure, for clouds hid the moon. He stood very still, waiting for the shadows to reveal their secrets, and then heard the soft, ragged inhalation of breath. As he turned toward the sound, a gleam of starlight bounced off the blade of a thrusting dagger. If he'd not spun around, it might have found his heart. As it was, it slashed through the folds of his mantle with just inches to spare. The man had put the full weight of his body behind that lethal lunge and before he could recover his balance, Justin sent his fist thudding into his belly. Gasping, the attacker reeled backward, and Justin fumbled for his sword. As it cleared its scabbard, a dark form came plummeting from the overhead window, crashing into Justin's assailant and knocking him to his knees.

The quarry was momentarily stunned by the impact, giving Justin the time he needed to level his sword at that heaving chest. "You so much as blink and you're dead." As threats went, it was simple and effective; the man lay perfectly still as Justin kicked aside the dropped dagger. Luke had regained his feet, was struggling now to regain control of his breathing.

Lowering his sword until it was almost touching his captive's windpipe, Justin glanced swiftly toward the deputy. "Well done, Luke!" he said admiringly. "However did you see to land on him like that? I was half-blinded when I first went through the window!"

"I was lucky," Luke panted, coming forward to peer down at his victim. "Is this the one?"

Justin nodded. "Meet Giles de Vitry." But something about Luke's modest response did not ring true; he'd never known the deputy to shrug off praise before. As a sudden shimmer of moonlight brightened the courtyard, he studied the other man's face, and then he grinned. "Admit it, you did not plunge from that window with a hawk's unerring precision. You lost your grip and just happened to fall on him, didn't you?"

Luke regarded him impassively. "Can you prove it?" he said at last, and they both laughed. Giles de Vitry chose that moment to make an ill-considered escape attempt. He squirmed sideways, only to freeze again when the point of Justin's sword pricked the skin of his throat, drawing a thin trickle of blood.

"You're not one for listening, are you?" he said reprovingly, much to Luke's amusement.

"You sound like a tutor reprimanding an unruly student, de Quincy! If we bring him back inside, we'll have to protect him from Arlette. Let's take him into the stables for our talk." Drawing his sword, Luke prodded their prisoner to his feet. "You're in the mood for a talk, aren't you, de Vitry? Reasonable men always prefer talking to the alternative."

De Vitry gave Luke as venomous a look as Justin had ever seen. He did not protest, though, wisely allowing them to shove him across the courtyard without resistance. A wide-eyed groom was cowering in the stables, with no intention of investigating the mayhem occurring outside. When the combatants invaded his refuge, he bolted out the back, leaving them alone with several horses and a spitting calico cat. Luke found a length of rope, trussed up de Vitry, and pushed him down upon a bale of hay. Taking the groom's lantern from its wall hook, he said, "He is all yours, de Quincy."

De Vitry flinched as Justin unsheathed his dagger. Ignoring the other man's recoil, Justin applied his blade to the neck of de Vitry's tunic. The material tore easily, revealing a leather pouch suspended upon a braided cord. Its contents were a disappointment: money, no letter. Luke had found de Vitry's saddlebags, stored with his gear in the tack room, and Justin searched them next, although without expectation of success; if the missing message had been concealed in the saddlebags, de Vitry would not have left them unguarded out in the stables. When his pessimism proved well founded, he came back to the courier, stood gazing down at him thoughtfully.

"Now what?" Luke was appraising their prisoner, too, green eyes speculative enough to give de Vitry a chill. "You think he memorized the message?"

Justin considered the possibility, then shook his head. "Not likely. If the message says what I think it does, its recipient would need proof that it indeed came from John."

At the mention of John's name, de Vitry's head came up sharply. Recovering some of his confidence, he said hoarsely, "You've got my money. What else do you want from me?"

Luke glanced toward Justin. "I hate it when they insult my intelligence. You're not being robbed, hellspawn. You're under arrest . . . as you well know."

"You're the law?" De Vitry strove to sound shocked. "God's Truth, I thought you were bandits!"

"Do not stop now," Luke said encouragingly. "I am waiting with bated breath for the rest of your story, eager to hear why you chose to jump out of a window in the middle of the night, only half dressed in the bargain. Your explanation ought to be riveting."

De Vitry ran his tongue over dry lips. "I . . . I was seeking to avoid paying the whore."

Luke shook his head in disgust. "So to save yourself a half-penny, you'd leave a valuable sword behind and risk breaking your neck. I can see this will be a long night. Shall we take him back to the castle, de Quincy?"

"No," Justin said, "not yet." He'd been studying the courier, his eyes taking in the man's dishevelment as he reconstructed those frantic moments in Arlette's chamber. De Vitry had been alerted to danger, hearing them on the stairs. He'd hastily snatched up his tunic and mantle and gone out the window, forced to abandon his chausses, braies, boots, and even his sword. Doubtless he'd have come back for them later, if he'd been able to evade pursuit. "Do you know what I find most puzzling, Luke? His choices. It makes sense to grab for a dagger, especially for one so quick with a blade. He already had the money around his neck. I can see, too, why he'd pull on his tunic ere he bolted. A man running mother-naked through the streets would find that hard to explain, after all. But then he took his mantle. Does that seem as odd to you as it does to me?"

De Vitry had stiffened noticeably. Luke also saw where Justin was going with this and he smiled suddenly. "Indeed it does. Our lad here has peculiar priorities. If it were me, I'd have taken enough time to retrieve my sword, mayhap even tossed my boots out the window, too. But he's willing to go out into the night barefooted and bare-assed rather than give up a quite ordinary brown mantle. Are you that susceptible to the cold, de Vitry? Did you forget it was April, not December?"

De Vitry did not react to the deputy's mockery, his eyes focused unblinkingly upon Justin. When the younger man reached for the mantle, he seemed about to resist, then realized the futility of it and slumped back as Justin claimed his prize. Carrying it over to the lantern, he began a thorough inspection, almost at once straight-ened up with a triumphant smile.

"There is something stitched into the hood." Care-fully splitting the seams to reveal a tightly rolled sheet of parchment, he held it up toward the light.

His sudden intake of breath told Luke that it was even worse than he'd expected.

"What is it, de Quincy? Do not keep me in suspense, man!"

Justin slowly lowered the parchment. "According to this letter, a French fleet is assembling at Wissant, mak-ing ready to invade England."

That was more than Luke had bargained for, either. "May I see that?" He held out his hand and Justin passed him the letter. "Christ Jesus, John is conniving with the Count of Flanders and the French king, too! You've served the queen well this night, for certes, de Quincy."

"We both have," Justin said, reclaiming the letter to read it again, half hoping that he'd mistaken what was written in John's own hand, for who would trust such an incendiary message to a scribe. "What if this man had gotten through? We had God on our side, Luke," he said soberly, and then spun around when Giles de Vitry laughed.

"And John has the Devil," he jeered. "I was not the only messenger, you see." He stared at them, his eyes agleam with hatred and bitter triumph. "John sent another man by way of Dover. By now he ought to be well on his way to the French king."

3

WINCHESTER

April 1193

Justin awakened with a start. As the furnishings of Aldith's cottage came into familiar focus, so did his memories of the night's events. He and Luke had taken Giles de Vitry to the castle gaol and then returned to the cottage for a few hours of sleep. He'd bedded down on the settle and as soon as he stirred, he winced, for his body was stiff and sore from two days in the saddle. His movement had attracted Jezebel's attention and he hastily flung up his arm to keep the mastiff from joining him. It was not the dog who had awakened him, though. As he sat up, he heard the angry murmur of voices coming from the bed hangings.

"Justin is a man quite capable of looking after himself. Why should he need your help with his prisoner?"

"Because it will be easier to get him safely back to London if there are two of us. Common sense would tell you that, Aldith."

"Why does it have to be you? Why not send your serjeant?"

"This is too important a matter to entrust to Wat. He does well enough with cutpurses and chicken thieves, but we're going up against the Devil's own."

"I still do not see why you must be the one to accompany Justin to London. Let him deal with John. After all, he is the queen's man, not you."

"Why are you being so unreasonable about this? I

31

spend half my time on the roads of the shire, so why are you balking now? For the love of God, woman, I'm off to London, not Sodom or Gomorrah!"

"Do what you want, Luke. You always do."

"Is that what this is all about? Because I said we could take our time in making wedding plans? I did not say I was unwilling to wed you, Aldith!"

Justin had heard more than enough. Feeling too much like an eavesdropper for his own comfort, he deliberately dropped his boots into the floor rushes, then began to croon to Jezebel, trying to sound like a man who'd just awakened and hadn't heard a word of that painful, intimate argument. As he'd hoped, his stirring put a stop to the quarrel, although there was a distinct coolness between Luke and Aldith when they finally emerged from the curtained cocoon of their bed, a coolness that had not thawed by the time Luke and Justin were ready to depart.

While Justin thought Luke was crazed to risk losing Aldith, it never occurred to him to express that opinion to the deputy. Men did not offer advice of the heart; that was the province of women. He contented himself with a neutral comment once they were on the road, a casual remark that Aldith had seemed to be in an ill temper, thus opening the door a crack in case Luke wanted to talk. When Luke responded with a grunt, Justin let the subject drop, his duty done. How could he throw Luke a lifeline when he was bogged down himself, trapped and sinking fast in Claudine's quagmire?

They left Winchester in midafternoon, riding fast and hard. Three days later, the city walls of London came into view. Halting upon Old Bourn Hill, they kept a wary eye upon their prisoner while sharing a wineskin. "Shall we take him to the Tower straightaway?" Luke suggested, and gave Justin a surprised look when the younger man shook his head vehemently.

"No, not the Tower. We need a safer place to stow him, where there will be no chance that John can discover his whereabouts."

"Safer than the Tower?" Luke asked skeptically. "Unless . . . you think that John has spies in the queen's household?"

"Yes," Justin said, tersely enough to discourage Luke from probing further, at least for the moment. "We need a special kind of shepherd to watch over this particular sheep, one willing to fend off royal wolves if need be."

Luke smiled. "Jonas?"

Justin nodded. "Who else?"

The main entry into London from the west was through the massive stone gatehouse known as Newgate, which was also used as a city gaol. Luke's credentials as an under-sheriff of Hampshire gained them easy entry and no one questioned their claim that they were delivering a prisoner to Jonas. They needed to be no more explicit than that, for to the gaolers, the name Jonas could refer to only one man—the laconic, one-eyed serjeant who was the sheriff of London's mainstay and the bane of the lawless from Cripplegate to Southwark.

They were giving instructions in Jonas's name when the serjeant himself put in an appearance. If he was startled to see Luke and Justin paired up again, he hid it well; Justin suspected that he'd long ago lost his capacity for surprise. Not as tall as either Justin or Luke, he was still able to command attention by his physical presence alone. His face, weathered by the sun and wind, scarred by a killer's blade, his hair silvered and lank, he moved with the daunting confidence of a man who trusted both his instincts and his reflexes. Despite the rakish eye patch, there was no swagger in his walk, no bravado in his manner. He was matter-of-fact and deliberate in the performance of all his duties, whether it was scattering street urchins or tracking the ungodly through the city's sordid underbelly. Now, his lone black eye gleaming with a sardonic cast, he intercepted them as they returned to the guards' chamber after depositing Giles de Vitry in the underground dungeon known as the pit.

"I hear I have another prisoner," he said by way of greeting. "Careless of me to have forgotten about him. Would I be prying if I asked his name?"

"Giles de Vitry. He is to be kept under close watch until I come back for him." Justin stepped closer, pitching his voice for the serjeant's ear only. "He is Lord John's man."

Jonas nodded impassively. "I did not imagine you'd be bringing me some hapless cutpurse or poacher. With you, I can forget robbery or petty thievery and plunge right into the fun of assassination, conspiracy, and treason."

Justin grinned. "What can I say? I keep bad company. Come by the alehouse later and I'll buy you a drink, give you what answers I can."

"I'll settle for being warned if this is likely to get me hanged."

Eleanor showed but one moment of weakness, a brief hesitation before reaching for the parchment. When she raised her eyes from the incriminating letter, she had taken refuge in the role she'd been playing for decades. "I want you to return tonight after Vespers," she said coolly. "The Archbishop of Rouen must be made aware of this threat to the peace of the realm, as must the other justiciars. They may well have questions for you. Bring your friend de Marston, too."

"I will, Madame," Justin promised. He yearned to tell her how sorry he was to have given her such dire news. Her hands were clasped tightly in her lap and she'd lost color, looking so fragile and delicate that he was reminded forcefully of her advanced years. Now in the deep winter of her life, she deserved better than this, than to be caught between the conflicting claims of her own sons. But he dared not intrude into the private pain of this very public woman. It was not for him to comfort a queen.

"I will have ready a writ for de Vitry's arrest," she continued. "I daresay I can find a dungeon deep enough to hide him away from the world, where he can repent the sin of rebellion . . . or rot."

Justin, the bishop's son, murmured dutifully, " 'He that diggeth a pit shall fall into it.' " He found himself wondering what Scriptures said of a mother who must pass judgment upon her own son. It was easy enough to cast de Vitry into a sunless prison. But how would she deal with John?

As he emerged from the queen's chamber, Justin was waylaid by the Lady Claudine. It was as neatly done an ambush as he'd ever encountered. Just when the path seemed clear, she materialized at his side, slipping her arm through his. "When I was a girl," she said, "I had a pet cat. My father insisted cats were good only for catching mice, but I would not heed him and doted upon my kitten, naming him Midnight and feeding him cream and whatever delicacies I could coax from the cooks. But when he got older, he began to roam. I cried each time he disappeared, and one of my brothers fashioned a leather collar with a small bell for him. It did not keep him from wandering, but at least I could hear him coming back. I am beginning to wonder, Justin, if I need such a collar for you."

He forced a smile. "I did not have time to let you know I'd be going away. It was sudden . . ." What excuse could he give? "My father was taken ill."

Claudine's eyes widened. "Justin, you've never spoken

of your father before! I assumed he was dead. I am sorry to hear he is ailing. He will recover, will he not?"

Justin was as astonished as Claudine by his own words. What had possessed him to mention his father? He'd been doing his very best to keep those memories fettered, out of reach. How had they broken free with no warning? "He is on the mend," he said hastily. "He . . . he took a bad fall."

"I am glad it was not serious. Why did you never tell me about him, Justin? I've told you all about my family back in Aquitaine."

"We have long been estranged." At least that was no falsehood. Passing strange, that he found it so hard to lie to her. Lies seemed to rest as lightly as feathers on her own conscience. She was expressing her sympathy and as always, she sounded sincere. Mayhap she even meant it. The queen had said she was no whore, would not bed a man she did not fancy. He wanted to believe that. He needed to believe that.

Claudine smiled up at him, letting her fingers entwine in his. "I have nothing to do for the queen this afternoon."

"I do," he said, and she sighed.

"What a pity. Do you realize it has been over three weeks since we've had any time alone together?"

The memory of their last lovemaking was one he'd take to his grave, for it was then that she'd inadvertently betrayed herself. What he still did not understand was why she did John's bidding. Was it for the money? Had John seduced her into it? Eleanor believed she had been lured by the adventure of it, convinced her young kinswoman saw spying as a game, one that did no real harm. If that were so, the game had taken a lethal turn. Did Claudine realize she was involved in treason? Would she care? He wanted to believe she would. Yet there was no way to put that belief to the test. How could he tell her of John's conspiracy when he dared not trust her?

* * *

Justin and Luke gave their report that evening before an audience of luminaries: the Queen of England, the Archbishop of Rouen, and all of the justiciars save Hugh Bardolf, who was John's liege man and therefore suspect. Eleanor had already disclosed the contents of John's seditious letter, and Justin's part in the council was blessedly brief. He related how he had tracked John's courier to Winchester, after being tipped off by a source he was not at liberty to reveal, and then described how he'd discovered the letter sewn into Giles de Vitry's mantle. Luke's role was even more circumscribed: to confirm Justin's account. After answering some brusque questions, they willingly retired to the outer edges of the circle, for it was somewhat intimidating to find themselves at the very center of royal power.

Acting upon the logical assumption that John's other messenger had gotten through, they wasted no time in vain regrets, concentrating upon what must be done to thwart an invasion. Justin listened in fascination as plans were rapidly made to close the ports and call up the levies in the southern shires. It still did not seem quite real to him, that he, an unwanted foundling, should be privy to the queen's secrets.

Once they had agreed upon the defensive measures to be taken, an awkward silence settled over the chamber. Justin understood why. Staving off a French fleet was child's play compared to the challenge that now confronted them: What to do about John? How did they punish a rebel who might well be king himself one day?

Eleanor was the one to breach the wall first. "What we need to do next is to locate John," she said dispassionately. "He is no longer in London and his whereabouts are unknown. I've heard rumors that he has been garrisoning his castles at Windsor and Wallingford, so I suggest we start the search there."

There were quick murmurings of agreement. Justin marveled at her composure. He'd been given a brief glimpse of the mother earlier that day, but now only the queen was in evidence, revealing nothing of her inner disquiet as she launched this hunt for her son. Given his own conflicted feelings toward his father and Claudine, Justin found it all too easy to empathize with Eleanor's plight. Even if it was true that Richard had ever been her favorite, how could she be indifferent to the fate of her youngest-born? If John's rebellion resulted in his death, would she grieve for him as David had mourned for his defiant son, Absalom? His gaze shifting from Eleanor's court mask to Will Longsword's taut profile, Justin felt a sense of foreboding and silently cursed John for the evil he had let loose amongst them.

Once the council ended, Justin and Luke stopped at the cookshop by the river and had a hearty supper of pork-filled pie and ginger wafers, washed down with cider, before returning to Justin's cottage on Gracechurch Street. Justin was too exhausted by then to crave anything but sleep. After making up a pallet for Luke, he collapsed onto his own bed and found instant oblivion.

His awakening was a rude one, his dreamworld dispersed by a loud, insistent pounding. Lack of sleep had made him as groggy as an excess of ale did, and he fumbled for his tunic while Luke stirred reluctantly and damned their unknown caller to eternal perdition. Sliding the bolt back, Justin blinked as brilliant spring sunlight flooded the cottage and then staggered as Shadow pounced joyfully upon him, barking loudly enough to provoke another burst of cursing from Luke.

"Shadow, down!" The command was affectionately ignored and he turned his attention to the dog's escort. "Nell, I meant to reclaim him this morning, truly I did. I got in too late last night to—"

Nell waved aside his apology impatiently. "That matters for naught. Justin, you must make haste to dress, for—" She broke off, then, as Luke poked a tawny head from his blankets. "Is that you, Luke? This is indeed a stroke of good fortune!"

Luke yawned. "I am gladdened to see you again, too, Nell. But if you really want to win my heart, come back later. I try never to rise ere the sun does."

"The sun is well up in the sky," she insisted. "Even if it were not, your sleeping is over. I have need of you, Justin. Get this sluggard up and join me at the alehouse. I'll make breakfast and explain all. Do not tarry, though." Pausing at the door, she said darkly, "There has been murder done."

4

LONDON
April 1193

Nell ushered Justin and Luke into the alehouse's kitchen. "Here," she said, sliding a stale loaf of bread across the table. "Cut yourselves trenchers whilst I finish cooking the sausage."

Breakfast was the day's dubious meal, not quite respectable, for people were supposed to be able to satisfy themselves with a hearty dinner and a lighter supper. Hunger was a more powerful motivation than convention, though, and only a few stalwart souls did not break their night's fast with meat or cheese or roasted chestnuts. The aroma of frying sausage was a lure neither Luke nor Justin could resist. Justin did wonder what price he'd be paying for this tasty fare. Nell's ominous comment about *murder* was not one to be easily forgotten.

"What did you want to talk to me about, Nell?"

"Actually, it is Agnes who needs to speak with you. I told her to meet us over here after Prime."

"Who is Agnes?" Luke asked, spearing a sausage. "Another one of your mystery bedmates?"

Justin ignored the deputy's heavy-handed humor. "Agnes is Odo the barber's wife." He liked Agnes, a kindly neighbor who'd helped tend to his wounds after he'd been attacked by Gilbert the Fleming. But he could not imagine what she'd want to discuss with him so early in the morn. "What was that you were muttering about murder, Nell?"

"Whilst you were in Winchester, a young girl was found dead in St Mary Magdalene's churchyard." Nell set two tankards of ale on the table, then sat down across from them. "You may have seen the peddler who sometimes sold his wares here on Gracechurch Street. She was his daughter."

Justin had no memory of the man or the girl. "I am sorry," he said. "How does Agnes come into this? Was she kin to the lass?"

"No . . . her nephews are suspects in the killing."

Justin sat up in surprise. Putting down his knife, he said, "Why?"

Nell shrugged. "I do not know all the particulars. Agnes was too distraught to make much sense. She says neighborhood talk had them sharing her bed, so she thinks that is why suspicion has fallen upon Geoffrey and Daniel."

Luke was amused. "The both of them, eh? Was she a harlot, then?"

Nell shrugged again. "She was probably no better than she ought to be. But I doubt that she was whoring for money. She was free-spirited and a bit wild, was Melangell, and most likely smitten with Geoffrey. That lad breaks hearts every time he smiles, bless him."

"Melangell," Justin echoed. "She was Welsh?"

Nell nodded. "Half Welsh, I think. She grew up in the Marches, told me that her mother died last year and her father took the family to London in January to make a fresh start." Her brisk tones wavered and she said sadly, "Poor little bird . . ."

Justin had come to London, too, in January, fleeing his past like Melangell and her grieving family. "I am sorry," he said again, and meant it, although he still did not understand. "Why does Agnes want to talk to me about this, Nell?"

Nell hesitated, then said with a trace of defiance, "I told her you'd clear her nephews of suspicion."

"You did what?" Justin stared at her in dismay. "Nell, how could you do that? I have no authority to meddle in a murder!"

"You are the queen's man, are you not? What greater authority could you ask for than that?"

"This killing is for the London sheriffs to solve, not me. Even if I knew how I could help Agnes's nephews, I'd not have the time to spare. We've learned that Lord John is plotting with the French king to seize the throne by force."

Nell was not impressed by his revelation. The high-born were always up to no good, but what of it? No matter who sat on the throne at Westminster, she'd still be fretting about that leak in the roof and her daughter's need for new shoes. "Agnes found the time to nurse you after the Fleming ambushed you," she said pointedly. "Besides, how much time can it take? As likely as not, a talk with Jonas will clear it all up. Agnes is sure they played no part in the poor girl's death."

Justin gave her a reproachful look that was quite wasted, and then glared at Luke, who was chuckling at his predicament. "I'll talk to Agnes," he said grudgingly. "I can do no more than that."

Nell had never doubted that she'd get her way. Any man who'd go to the trouble of rescuing a stray dog from an icy river was a man with a heart too soft for his own good. "Fair enough," she agreed, sure that Agnes's tears would do the rest. "Now let me tell you something of the family ere she arrives. Agnes's younger sister, Beatrice, married above herself, snaring a husband who has become quite prosperous. Humphrey Aston is a member of the Mercer's Guild, and to judge by Beatrice's bragging, he has done right well for himself. I've met him only once, for he's not keen on breaking bread with the likes of Odo and Agnes. I thought he was full of himself, as prickly as a hedgehog, a man who'd bite off his own tongue ere he'd admit he was in the wrong. Beatrice may have more comfort in her life, but Agnes got the better husband in Odo, for he loves her wholeheartedly and I doubt that Humphrey loves anyone except himself . . . well, possibly Geoffrey. Agnes says he does dote on the lad."

"Geoffrey is the firstborn?"

"Yes. He is twenty, and by all accounts, a son any man would be proud of. The younger lad, Daniel, is the black sheep, the one who makes a botch of all that he does. But Agnes swears he is no killer—" Nell paused, head cocked to the side. "Did you hear anything?" Shadow took his attention away from the sausages long enough to give a distracted bark, and Nell pushed back from the table, went to let Agnes in.

Agnes was a plump, maternal woman in her early fifties, as basic and comforting as freshly baked bread. Her gratitude was tearful and heartfelt and embarrassing to Justin. "They are good lads," she said, stifling a sob. "I never was able to bear children of my own; the Lord God willed otherwise. Geoffrey and Daniel were the sons I could not have, and I've loved them as if they were mine. Neither one would ever hurt that child. I know that, Master de Quincy. I know it in the very depths of my soul."

Justin did not doubt her sincerity. He was not so sure, though, of her judgment. "Can you tell me about their involvement with the dead girl?" he asked gently. "What was she to them?"

Agnes wiped her eyes with a napkin. "Geoffrey has had girls chasing after him since he was fourteen or thereabouts, and I'm sure he sometimes let them catch him. Melangell was a shameless flirt and very pretty in a foreign, Welsh sort of way. But Geoffrey would not have taken their dalliance seriously. His father was about to announce his plight troth to the niece of the master of the Mercer's Guild, a great match for Geoffrey. Melangell may be a passing fancy, but no more than that."

"And what of the younger son?"

"I think it was different with Daniel," she said slowly. "I believe he was a little in love with her. Not that he'd admit it. He is not one for confiding in others. That has always been his curse, that stubborn silence of his. Take that woeful business about his apprenticeship . . ."

"What about it?" Justin asked, not because he thought it was material to the girl's death, but because he could not be sure if it was not. His recent experience in tracking down Gilbert the Fleming had taught him that clues often seemed insignificant at first glance; it was only later that the threads came together in a woven, discernible pattern.

"Geoffrey completed his apprenticeship this past year, with Master Serlo. And now that he is to wed Adela, his future seems assured, for she'll bring a goodly marriage portion. But Daniel . . . nothing ever comes easily to him. Humphrey apprenticed him to a mercer in Cheapside, a man utterly unlike Master Serlo, and it went wrong from the first."

"Why did Humphrey not apprentice his sons in his own shop?"

"That is only done when the boy cannot be placed elsewhere. Better that he learns trade secrets from another master. And an apprenticeship opens doors in the future, as it did for Geoffrey. Adela is Master Serlo's niece. But Daniel's apprenticeship ended in disgrace, when he ran off and refused to return. Humphrey was enraged, for he forfeited the bond of surety he'd put up for Daniel. They dissolved the contract and he took Daniel into his own shop, but he has not forgiven him. Daniel did not help matters by refusing to explain why

he'd run away. Later, he told me. The man was brutal to
his apprentices, beat them without reason or mercy. The
other boys endured the abuse; Daniel would not. It took
a long time ere I could get the truth out of him, and by
then, it was too late. His father was not of a mind to
listen . . ."

"How do the brothers get along?"

"Better than you'd expect. Daniel has never seemed to
blame Geoffrey for being the chosen one." Her mild blue
eyes filled with fresh tears. "I've always feared that
Daniel believed himself to be undeserving of love. I did
what I could, but it is hard to overcome a father's indifference, Master de Quincy."

That Justin well knew. He could not help sympathizing with this youth he'd not yet met, caught between
a golden brother and an unforgiving father. But his sympathy did not blind him to the fact that Daniel seemed to
have a motive for murder. If he was smitten with Melangell, he might well have rebelled when she became another one of his brother's conquests, may have tried to
claim her for himself, with tragic consequences.

Almost as if she sensed his doubts, Agnes leaned across
the table, timidly touching his hand with her own. "Daniel is no murderer, Master de Quincy. Neither he nor
Geoffrey caused that girl's death. I beg you to do what I
cannot—to prove that to the sheriff."

Justin did not see how he could prove it, either. Nell
had a lot to answer for. "Agnes . . . I can make no
promises. But I will talk to the sheriff, see what I can find
out about the crime."

Agnes smiled tremulously, with far greater confidence
than his assurance warranted. "I knew you would help
us, Master de Quincy, I knew it!" She departed soon
thereafter, with a lighter step, eager to tell her husband
that the queen's man would be making things right for
her nephews.

Justin finished the rest of his ale, then got to his feet. "I'll see if I can find Jonas," he said tersely.

Nell was unfazed by his obvious anger; he'd get over it. When Luke did not rise, too, she frowned at the deputy. "Well? Are you not going with Justin?"

"Why should I? I do not owe Agnes anything."

"No . . . but you do owe me. You know full well that you'd not have caught the Fleming without my help."

Luke scowled back at her, but her logic was unassailable. "I should have known this was not going to be a free breakfast," he said, reaching for one final mouthful of sausage. "Come on, de Quincy, let's go track Jonas down."

Justin snapped his fingers for his dog, but made no move to go. "Tell me this, Nell. Have you given any thought to how this could turn out? What happens if I discover that one of Agnes's nephews did indeed murder Melangell?"

Nell was silent for a moment. "Well," she said, "if that is true, at least the poor girl will have justice."

It took several hours to run Jonas to earth. They finally found him in an Eastcheap tavern, having a belated dinner of baked lampreys, a pottage of cabbage and onions, and a loaf of hard rye bread. When he looked up and saw Justin and Luke coming toward him, he held up a hand to ward them off.

"Ere you say a word, I'd best warn you about the day I've had so far. I was rousted out of bed before dawn to chase some young fools who filled a wine cask with stones and then set it rolling down to the bridge, waking up scores of scared citizens, sure that the clamor meant the world was coming to an end. Then I had to race over to Southwark to help catch a 'demon from Hell,' which turned out to be a peddler's runaway monkey. I got back into London in time to fish a body from the river, so bloated only the Almighty will ever know who it was. This is the first chance I've had to eat a mouthful since last night, so unless you've come to tell me that Westminster Palace is afire or Lord John's army is laying siege to the Tower, I do not want to hear it. This is one meal I mean to savor in peace."

"Savor?" Luke picked up one of the chunks of rye. "By God's Bones, Jonas, you could use these torts for paving stones. And why ever are you eating lampreys when it is not a fish day?"

Justin pulled up a stool, signaling to the serving maid for wine. "Pay him no heed, Jonas. We are bringing you no new troubles, I swear it. No royal plots, no fresh murders, not even rumors of plots or murders. We have a few questions to ask, nothing more sinister in mind. So you eat and we'll talk . . . fair enough? Luke might even be willing to pay for your dinner."

"Pace yourself with that wine, de Quincy; you're beginning to babble." Luke straddled a bench, decided the serving maid was not worth flirting with, and fed Shadow a piece of rye tort. "Is there nothing this beast will not eat? You have to hear us out, Jonas. The lad is on a mission of mercy."

Justin did not think that was funny. "What was I supposed to do?" he protested. "That woman would put any poacher to shame, so deftly does she set and spring her traps. I was caught ere I even realized my danger."

Jonas continued to dig into his lamprey pie. "Now that you're here," he said ungraciously, "you might as well unburden yourselves. Remember, though, that I'm in no mood for high treason or conspiracies involving the fate of all Christendom."

"How about a mundane murder in a churchyard? Go on, de Quincy, ask him about the peddler's daughter." Luke smiled, for that was the punch line to any number of jokes, most of them bawdy. Justin was younger and less inured to violent death. Giving the deputy a reproving glance, he said quickly:

"What can you tell us, Jonas, about the young girl found slain in St Mary Magdalene's churchyard?"

Jonas spooned the last morsel of lamprey pie into his mouth, used his sleeve for a napkin. "Why do you want to know?" he parried. "You're not likely to convince me that the peddler's lass was a spy in the pay of the queen's son."

"No . . . this has naught to do with the Queen's Grace."

"He is acting on behalf of your chief suspects," Luke said with a grin. "Nell prodded him into it, for their aunt is her neighbor."

Jonas grinned, too. "I've rarely met a female with such a God-given talent for prodding," he conceded. "But I'm not the man you ought to be talking to. Tobias is the serjeant who was called to the churchyard, not me."

That brought Justin up short. "Well, we'll certainly seek him out," he said, after a pause to consider this new development. "But we'd be grateful for anything you can tell us about the crime."

"What do you want to know?"

"How was the girl killed?"

"We think she died resisting a rape. Her body was found by a woman come to tend her husband's grave."

"How did she die . . . a stabbing? Strangulation?"

"A head wound. She either fell or was pushed against the churchyard cross. Tobias said it was dripping blood."

"What makes you think she was raped?"

"Her bodice was ripped open and her skirts pulled up, her chemise torn. But I did not say she was raped."

Justin was puzzled. Luke, who'd investigated a number of sexual crimes, was not. "No bruises or scratches on her breasts or thighs, then?"

Jonas shook his head, explaining for Justin's benefit, "That would indicate the man broke off the attack.

Most likely he panicked when he realized she was either dead or dying. Tobias said there were imprints in the ground, as if he knelt by the body, but there was no evidence of penetration. Nor were there any stains on her clothing to show he'd spilled his seed too soon. My best guess would be that he did not mean to kill her. When she balked, he sought to force himself upon her, and the next thing he knew, he had a dead woman on his hands."

"What of her nails?" Luke asked, his earlier irreverence forgotten, caught up now in professional curiosity.

"Not broken, and with no scrapings of skin under them. So the man will have no scratches to mark him out. She was a little bit of a lass, like Nell. It would have been all too easy to overpower her. And it does not seem that she had a chance to put up much of a fight."

Justin's wine suddenly tasted sour. As little as he knew about this peddler's daughter from the Welsh Marches, he was certain she had deserved better than she'd gotten. Jonas had made the pain and fear of her final moments much too real. Shoving the flagon away, he said tautly, "Can you tell me why Geoffrey and Daniel Aston are suspected in her death?"

Jonas considered and then nodded. "Why not? We know Geoffrey Aston was bedding her. Sometimes she'd sneak him into the room her family rented, sometimes he'd bring her to an inn on Wood Street. In fact, the churchyard where she died was a favorite meeting place for them. As for the younger son, he was always sniffing about her skirts. We have witnesses willing to testify that he and Melangell had a heated argument on the day she died. And then there was the piece of silk found under her body, much too costly for a peddler's daughter, but just the sort of gift she'd have gotten from a mercer's son. Not enough evidence to start building a gallows, I'll grant you. But enough to warrant further investigation."

Justin could not argue with that. What had Nell gotten

him into? He felt another surge of pity for Melangell, who'd come to London to start a new life, only to find death in a twilit churchyard. He pitied Agnes, too, for it was beginning to seem all too likely that one of her nephews was guilty of murder.

After their meeting with Jonas, Justin and Luke headed for the Tower. The queen was not in the great hall, and to Justin's relief, neither was Claudine. He did not need to seek Eleanor out, though, for Will Longsword was on hand, and he admitted glumly that their scouts had not reported back. John's whereabouts were still a mystery.

By the time Justin and Luke were on their way again, a soft April dusk was settling over the city. Justin had borrowed a lantern from one of Will's men, and they started up Tower Street. Luke was complaining that they ought to have taken their stallions; like most horsemen, he rarely walked anywhere if he could help it. But Justin's sojourn in London had taught him that horses were often an inconvenience in the city. For all that it held over twenty-five thousand people, London's walls enclosed a little more than a square mile. Justin had discovered that he could walk from the Tower to Ludgate in half an hour, whereas on horseback, that trip could take much longer, depending upon the time of day and the flow of traffic.

"Anyway," he pointed out when Luke continued to grumble, "you have to find a place to hitch the horse every time you dismount. Look at all the stops we had to make in our hunt for Jonas. If we'd been on horseback, we'd have had to . . ."

When his words ebbed away, Luke glanced curiously in his direction. "What?"

Justin was studying the street behind them. The day's crowds were thinning as the sky darkened. An occasional bobbing light was evidence of a pedestrian's lantern. A cart's wheel had broken, and the driver was cursing

loudly as he inspected the damage. The church bells of
All Hallows Barking were chiming for Vespers and a few
tardy parishioners were straggling in for the Mass. A
woman who seemed none too sober had accosted a man
passing by, and they'd begun to dicker over terms. Shadow
had halted to acknowledge another dog. The street scene
appeared perfectly normal, nothing amiss. Still, Justin
hesitated, heeding instinct rather than reason.

"What is it?" Luke was picking up now on his unease.
"You see something?"

"I guess not . . ." Justin took a final glance over his
shoulder, then shrugged. "I got a sudden prickling at the
back of my neck," he confessed. "I suppose I am overly
cautious, thanks to the Fleming. For a moment, I had this
sense of danger, the way I did in the Durngate mill."

There was no need to elaborate; Luke had been with
him when they'd cornered the Fleming over the body of
his latest victim. The deputy nodded, for he, too, had
learned to trust the inner voice that whispered of unseen
enemies, unknown perils. "Never apologize for caution,
de Quincy. Without it, no man can hope to make old
bones. Now . . . what shall we do about supper? Stop at
the cookshop or see if we can coax Nell into feeding us
again?"

"The alehouse," Justin said, adding emphatically, "Nell
owes me a meal. The more I learn about this killing, the
less hopeful I feel. Jonas makes a persuasive case for his
suspicions. So what do I tell Agnes?"

"Well, look at it this way: By implicating one nephew,
you'll be clearing the other."

"Somehow I doubt that will give Agnes much comfort," Justin said dryly. "And which nephew?"

"The younger one," Luke said without hesitation. "If
you own a cow, what need have you to steal milk? Why
would Geoffrey Aston try to rape the girl if she was
coupling with him willingly? No, if this were my case, I'd

be looking long and hard at Daniel. Even Agnes admits he was besotted with her. She rebuffs him earlier in the day, when they were heard to quarrel. Nursing a grievance, he confronts her later in the churchyard. She rejects his overtures again, and this time he goes too far. Unfortunately for Agnes, this killing is likely to be right easy to solve."

"I fear so," Justin agreed. "If only—Jesú!" For a heartbeat, he wasn't sure what had happened. There was a blurred motion, a rush of air upon his face, and then a thud. He hastily raised the lantern and his breath caught in his throat at the light's flickering revelation: a dagger still quivering in a wooden door scant inches from his head. Flattening himself against the wall, he flung the lantern into the street to avoid offering a lighted target. Luke had taken cover, too, and for several moments, there was no sound but their labored breathing. By now the street was a sea of heaving shadows, deep enough to drown an army of assassins. They forced themselves to wait, motionless, until they were sure the danger was past. Retrieving the lantern, Luke watched as Justin freed the dagger.

"It looks like you've been making enemies again, de Quincy. No man would throw away a good knife in a random attack."

When he wrenched the knife loose, Justin noticed the scrap of parchment wrapped around its blade. Holding it toward the lantern's light, he saw a single word scrawled in a bold hand. He read the message, and then gave an angry, incredulous laugh. "Would you believe this is a letter?"

Luke stared at him. "Delivered at knifepoint?"

"See for yourself." Justin held out the parchment fragment toward the deputy. "The queen has a man in John's household. This is his handiwork, warning us that John is at Windsor."

"Jesus God." Luke shook his head in disbelief. "He has an odd way of communicating his messages!"

"You do not know the half of it," Justin said, searching the darkness again for signs of the knife wielder. He knew it was useless, though. Durand was long gone. He'd delivered his warning—with a vengeance—and had no reason to linger.

Luke was looking again at the hole Durand's knife had gouged in the door. "You know," he said, "he did not miss you by much."

"No," Justin said grimly, "he did not."

5

LONDON

April 1193

Eleanor gazed down impassively at the scrap of parchment. "You are sure this came from Durand?"

Justin felt again that surge of air on his face as the blade buried itself in the door. "Very sure, Madame."

William Marshal was standing several feet away, waiting at a discreet distance until his queen had need of him. When Eleanor glanced in his direction, he moved swiftly toward her. "Madame?"

"John is at Windsor."

"I'll see to it, my lady."

To Justin's surprise, that was all. After that terse exchange, Eleanor turned away abruptly, crumpling Durand's message and letting it fall into the floor rushes at her feet. Justin hesitated, then fell in step beside William Marshal as he strode toward the door.

"What are you going to do?" he asked, surprising himself by his willingness to interrogate one of the queen's justiciars. But he was done with fumbling around in the dark; what he didn't know could get him killed.

Marshal seemed to take it for granted that he was entitled to ask such questions. "I will go to Windsor, demand that John surrender the castle to the queen and the justiciars."

"And if he refuses?"

"Then we shall lay siege to it."

Justin considered that possibility. "And once you've

54

captured the castle, what then, my lord? What will be done with Lord John?"

Marshal gave him a sidelong smile. "I would to God I knew, lad," he said, and Justin nodded slowly. How did they punish a man who was likely to inherit the very crown he was now trying to usurp?

"Are you sure you know where we're going, de Quincy?" Luke swerved to avoid a wayward goose. "And what of Agnes? Ought she not to be coming with us?"

"She was summoned to the Astons' house early this morn to tend her sister. She left word with Nell that she'd wait for us there." Justin shaded his eyes against the bright glare of noonday sun and whistled for Shadow, who was foraging in the street's center gutter. "She said their shop is on Friday Street."

"Is the sister ailing?"

Justin shrugged. "Even the most stout-hearted soul might well be undone when murder is suspected, and Beatrice seems frailer than most. Nell says she takes to her bed whenever a family crisis looms."

"And they'll be looking to you as their savior. What happens when you cannot deliver all that Nell promised?"

Justin shrugged again. "Mayhap we'll get lucky and prove the killer is not one of the nephews, after all," he said, although without much conviction; it was hard to argue with Luke's jaded insistence that in most killings, the victim's loved ones were the logical suspects.

"Well, you'll have to catch the killer without me. I thought I'd head for home on the morrow."

Justin was sorry, but not surprised. As much as he'd have liked Luke's help, he had never expected the deputy to remain much longer in London, not with duty and Aldith both pulling him back to Winchester.

Luke glanced in his direction, then away. "I was thinking I'd stop over at Windsor. If there is going to be a siege, the sheriff of Hampshire will be one of those summoned. It makes no sense to go all the way to Winchester, only to have to come back again straightaway."

Justin turned to stare at him. Luke's logic sounded forced to him, the reasoning of a man who—for whatever reason—was not that eager to go home. Was his quarreling with Aldith as serious as that? Before he could respond, Luke suddenly grabbed his arm.

"Do you see that woman in the green gown? She is about to pluck a pigeon . . . Ah, and there he is."

Justin saw nothing suspicious about the woman in question; she was young and pretty and respectably dressed, her gown of good wool, her veil of fine white linen. She was carrying several bundles, one of which slipped from her grasp as Luke's designated "pigeon" crossed her path. When he gallantly retrieved it, he was rewarded with an enchanting smile, and within moments, he was insisting that he tote the rest of her parcels for her.

Watching with a knowing grin, Luke nudged Justin with his elbow. "Now the hawk swoops down on our pigeon's money pouch," he predicted, nodding toward a burly youth in a pointed Phrygian cap, who was striding purposefully across the street, apparently oblivious of the couple in his way. The victim was mindful only of the young woman clinging to his arm and a collision seemed imminent . . . until Luke lunged forward, calling out in a loud, jovial voice sure to turn heads, "Is that you, Ivo? By God, it is!"

The victim looked puzzled as this boisterous stranger bore down upon him. The stalker veered off, was soon swallowed up in the crowds thronging the Cheapside. The woman frowned, recoiling as Luke draped a friendly arm around her shoulders. "But this is not Berta. Ivo, you sly dog!"

"I'm not Ivo! I've never laid eyes upon you . . . wait,

lass!" This last plea was addressed to the woman, who'd snatched back her parcels and was already moving hastily away. Disappointment finding expression in anger, the man glared at Luke. "You oaf, you scared her off!"

"Be glad he did," Justin interjected, "for he thwarted her partner from lifting your money pouch."

The man's hand went instinctively to the pouch. Reassured to find it still swinging safely from his belt, he glanced dubiously from Justin to Luke. After a moment to mull it over, his scowl came back. "A likely story," he scoffed. "I know women right well and that little lass was no thief. But the pair of you look like you were born for the gallows. You were the ones trying to steal my money, not her!" Backing away, he flung a threat over his shoulder about summoning the Watch and then strode off indignantly, shoving through the press of interested spectators.

Justin and Luke stared after him in astonishment, but as soon as their eyes met, they burst out laughing. "Well," Luke said, with a grin, "now you know why I was so suspicious of you from the first moment we met. You've got a cutthroat's look to you, for certes!"

"He thought we both looked like outlaws," Justin reminded him. "How did you know they'd planned a theft?"

"I saw the wench and her man signaling to each other once they picked out their quarry, the same hand signals I've seen cutpurses use back in Winchester." Luke shook his head in mock regret and gave Justin a playful shove. "Devil take me if I foil any more crimes in this accursed city of yours, de Quincy. You Londoners are an ungrateful lot!"

Justin pushed him back and they began to laugh again . . . until a voice said coldly, "Are these the men you recommended, Agnes?"

The words themselves might be neutral, but the tone

dripped disdain. Justin and Luke swung around to stare at the man regarding them with evident disapproval. He was of medium height and stocky build, with reddish hair sprinkled with grey, and eyes even greener than Luke's. Agnes was half hidden behind his broad-shouldered body; all they could see was her face, scarlet with embarrassment.

"I am Humphrey Aston." He flung the name out as a challenge. "When you did not arrive on time, we went to look for you." He left unsaid the rest of the sentence, the unspoken accusation: that they'd been engaging in tomfoolery whilst he'd been kept waiting. The message was clearly conveyed, though, in the pursed lips, the frigid eyes.

By the time he'd stopped talking, Justin had decided that Humphrey Aston was the last man in Christendom deserving of his help. But Agnes was mouthing a silent "please" and so he resisted the urge to turn and walk away. "I am Justin de Quincy," he said coolly, "and this is Luke de Marston, the under-sheriff for Hampshire."

Humphrey acknowledged the introductions with a grudging nod. "My wife's sister thinks you can help us. What I want to know is how much that help will cost."

It had never occurred to Justin to charge a fee. He started to say that, but his dislike of Aston was too strong. "That depends. What is a son worth to you?"

His attempt to rattle the older man failed; Humphrey didn't even blink. "Which one?"

Luke swore softly. "Come on, de Quincy. Why waste our time?"

Justin shook his head, feeling a sharp thrust of pity for Humphrey's sons. "You could not afford me," he said. "I am doing a favor . . . for Agnes."

Humphrey reddened, then looked balefully at Agnes, as if Justin's insolence was somehow her fault. "We'll talk at home," he said at last, turning on his heel. Justin patted Agnes consolingly on the shoulder, blocked Luke's escape, and they followed, reluctantly, but they followed.

The mercer's shop fronted onto Friday Street, with the family quarters above. Humphrey Aston's prosperity was such that he'd been able to afford a hall, set at a right angle to the shop, extending back along the property line. It was here that he led the men, bypassing his shop and entering by a side gate that opened into a crowded courtyard. His family was gathered in the hall, seated at a wooden trestle table. They'd been talking among themselves, but fell silent at the sight of Humphrey, appearing more apprehensive than relieved by the patriarch's return.

Beatrice Aston was younger than her husband, somewhere in her forties. She probably had been quite appealing in her youth, for she still retained a faded prettiness. Coiled blond hair shone beneath a gossamer veil, and her eyes were wide set and as blue as cornflowers. But any assurance she'd ever possessed had been stripped away, leaving her insecurities and anxieties painfully abraded and exposed. Although she did her best to make Luke and Justin welcome, she kept glancing toward Humphrey, as uneasy about incurring his disapproval as the timid little maidservant who served them wine and wafers.

Justin could not help sympathizing with Humphrey's cowed wife; he would have sympathized with anyone unlucky enough to live under the same roof with the domineering mercer. But his interest was much greater in the Astons' two sons.

Geoffrey was by far the handsomer of the two, with his mother's fair hair and deep blue eyes. He showed the poise expected of a firstborn son, the family favorite. He did indeed have a heartbreaking smile, as Nell had claimed, although it seemed to surface now from habit, never reaching his eyes. Justin had wondered if he'd be too smug and spoiled to realize the danger he faced; clearly that was not the case. Geoffrey was doing his very best to appear calm and optimistic, but he could not sit still for more than a few moments and his eyelids were faintly swollen. Had he shed tears for the peddler's daughter . . . or were they all for this calamity that threatened to engulf his family?

The younger son, Daniel, had inherited his father's height and build and color. He had an untidy mass of curly red hair, wary green eyes, and a square-cut face filled with freckles. Unlike his restive, edgy brother, he was unnaturally rigid, his the intensely focused stillness of an animal caught in a trap, awaiting discovery. Geoffrey's greeting had been effusive and heartfelt; Daniel's terse to the point of rudeness. Geoffrey might welcome their intercession; Daniel obviously did not.

Once the introductions were over, there was an uncomfortable silence. Justin glanced toward Luke for guidance, but the deputy was amusing himself by tossing bits of wafer to Shadow, much to Humphrey's smoldering annoyance. Justin took a deep breath and plunged in. "Suppose you tell me of the day Melangell died."

He'd been addressing Geoffrey, but it was Humphrey who answered. "We've already been over this with the sheriff's serjeants. We know nothing of this girl's death. She was most likely killed by a disgruntled customer." Seeing Justin's lack of comprehension, he said impatiently, "She peddled more than the cheap goods on her father's cart. She was a harlot, plain and simple, and I do not doubt that her whoring brought about her death."

Geoffrey's head jerked up. He seemed about to speak, but then subsided, his shoulders slumping. Daniel glanced up, too, giving them a brief, unsettling glimpse of a white-hot rage. But he also kept quiet. Melangell's defense came not from either of the young men said to have been her lovers. It was Agnes who spoke up, nervously, for she, too, was intimidated by her brother-in-law. Yet this plump, placid barber's wife had a strong sense of fair play, strong enough to give her the courage to lodge a timorous protest.

"I do not . . ." She hesitated, coughing to clear her throat. "I do not believe that Melangell was a whore. She was flighty and reckless at times, yes, but not wicked—"

"What do you know of evil?" Humphrey snapped. "What do you know about anything at all? This peddler's chit was a wanton, as any man with eyes to see could tell, strutting about in her beads and her whore's scarlet, bold as can be and shameless, exposing herself to the stares in the street and laughing at the leers and jests—"

Justin had heard enough. "Be that as it may, we've gone astray. I did not ask you about her morals or the lack of them. I need to find out how she passed her last day. Can you help me with that, Master Aston? If not, I'd suggest that you let your sons speak for themselves."

Humphrey was not accustomed to being interrupted. His mouth fell open and he stared at Justin, ignoring his wife as she reached over and placed a placating hand upon his arm. But there was fear behind his bluster, and it won out. As much as it galled him to admit it, he needed Justin's help. "I did not see the girl that day," he said curtly.

Justin glanced then toward Geoffrey. "Did you?"

Geoffrey seemed startled to find himself suddenly the center of attention, but he answered readily enough. "No, I did not." He looked from Justin to Luke, saw their skepticism, and repeated his denial. "It is true I sometimes met her in the churchyard. It was close to our shop . . ." This time his gaze flicked toward his father. "But not on that day. The last I saw of her was on Tuesday, two days ere she . . . she died." He kept his voice level, but he swallowed hard and his lashes swept down, veiling his eyes.

"And you?" Justin swung around to face Daniel. "We

know you met with her. There are witnesses willing to swear you were quarreling on Cheapside earlier in the day. Suppose you tell us what that quarrel was about."

Daniel's eyes slitted. "I do not remember."

Justin did not believe him. It was obvious that his father did not, either. "I warned you," Humphrey said ominously, "that your memory had better improve, did I not?"

Justin looked from the sullen boy to his belligerent father, then over at Geoffrey, flushed and unhappy. Beatrice daubed at the corners of her eyes with a table napkin, but she did not attempt to mediate between her husband and son. She seemed to Justin more like a bystander than a member of the family. He'd always mourned the loss of his own mother, who'd died giving him birth. For the first time, he realized that death was not the only means of losing a mother. When his gaze met Luke's, the deputy jerked his head sideways. Justin agreed wholeheartedly; they needed to get out of there.

Rising, he said, "You've given me enough for now. I will see what else I can find out about this crime and get back to you." Adding, as if in afterthought, "I would like Geoffrey and Daniel to accompany me to the churchyard where these trysts were held."

Humphrey opened his mouth to object, but both his sons jumped to their feet so hastily that they forestalled him. Their departure was swift, almost an escape, and within moments, they were standing together out in the street in front of the mercer's shop.

Geoffrey waved to a neighbor, then turned to face Justin and Luke. "We'd best start walking," he said. "My father will soon be out to watch for us. We can show you where the church is, but I'd rather not go into the churchyard. I do not want to see where she died and I am sure Daniel does not, either. I thought—hoped—your request was merely an excuse to talk with us alone."

He looked at them quizzically and Justin found himself responding to the other youth's forthrightness. "You're correct," he admitted. "I did think that we'd do better on our own."

Geoffrey nodded. "I did not kill her, Master de Quincy. My brother and I are innocent."

Geoffrey sounded sincere. Justin wanted to believe him, but he suspected that the gaols were probably filled with killers who could sound no less convincing. Glancing toward Daniel, who'd remained silent so far, he said, "What about you, Daniel? Has your memory gotten any better?"

Daniel hunched his shoulders, staring down at his feet. "I've nothing to say to you."

"You'll talk to us if we take you down to Newgate Gaol," Luke said brusquely. "Make no mistake about that, lad."

It was obvious that Luke was not impressed with the younger Aston son. Justin wasn't much taken with Daniel, either. But he wanted to be fair and it was likely the boy's surly defiance was born of fear. "We cannot help you, Daniel, unless you cooperate with us."

"Help me?" Daniel echoed, not troubling to hide his disbelief. "How stupid do you think I am?"

"That remains to be seen," Luke drawled. "Were you stupid enough to let yourself become besotted with a young Welsh whore? Were you stupid enough to kill her when she rejected you?"

Luke's provocation was calculated—and effective. Geoffrey frowned, protesting, "That is not fair."

Daniel's reaction was less controlled and more revealing. His face twitched as if he'd taken a blow. "Damn you, she was no whore!"

"Your father says she was," Justin pointed out, feeling as if he and Luke were dogs baiting a bear.

"My father . . ." Daniel choked up, spat out an unintelligible obscenity, and bolted, running as clumsily as a young colt, a boy who hadn't yet grown into his own body. They watched until he ducked into an alley off the Cheapside, none of them speaking. Geoffrey was pinioning his lower lip, showing even white teeth, his eyes conveying mute reproach. He stood his ground, though, awaiting his turn.

"Who is right?" Justin asked abruptly, "your father or brother? Was Melangell a whore?"

"No," Geoffrey said, showing a prickle of resentment, "she was not. She liked men and she took her pleasures where she found them. But she was no whore."

"Did you kill her?"

"No, I did not . . . and neither did Daniel."

"Did you love her?"

Geoffrey started to speak, stopped. "I cared about her," he said, for the first time sounding defensive. "I tried to be honest with her, told her about Adela . . . that is the girl I'm to wed. At least I was until this happened." His smile was rueful. "When we were negotiating what I'd be bringing to the marriage, not once was the suspicion of murder mentioned."

Geoffrey paused then, waiting for questions that did not come. "Is there anything else you want to ask me?" When they shook their heads, he smiled again, this time politely. "If you're done, then I'll be off. I ought to see if I can find Daniel."

"Go on," Justin agreed, adding as Geoffrey turned to go, "I do have one last question. Do you know where Melangell is buried?"

Geoffrey was taken aback. "I . . . I do not know," he stammered. "I could not attend her funeral. My father . . . well, you heard him. He'd never have stood for it . . ." His voice trailed off. He'd only gone a few feet when he stopped. "She should have been buried in Wales," he said softly, "for she loved it so . . ."

"Why," Luke asked, as they watched him go, "did you ask that?"

"I was curious," Justin said. "I wanted to know if he mourned her."

"And do you think he does?"

Justin whistled for Shadow, who was frisking happily after Geoffrey's retreating figure. "Yes," he said, "I think so."

Luke arched a brow. "And does that eliminate him as a suspect?"

"No," Justin said, somewhat regretfully, "probably not."

Luke grinned. "By God, de Quincy, there is hope for you yet. So . . . now what?"

"We go," Justin said, "to find her family."

Jonas had told them that the peddler, Godwin, rented a room on Wood Street, close by Cripplegate. As they expected, he was out selling his wares; even the death of a daughter did not lessen the need to pay rent and buy food. The landlord was loquacious, though, especially after Justin took out his money pouch, and cheerfully shared what little he knew about the peddler and his family. Godwin had been living there since their arrival in January, a decent sort who kept to himself and paid his rent on time and tried, without success, to keep Melangell from running wild.

Surprisingly, the man's eyes filled with tears at the mention of the dead girl's name. A sweet lass, he said mournfully, with bright eyes and a laugh as rich and dark as honey. She'd flirted with every man who crossed her path, wheedled scraps from the butcher to feed an army of stray cats and dogs, played childish pranks, and once climbed out of the window on a knotted blanket when

her father locked her in their room. "The whole neighborhood wept for her," he said, "God's Truth, they did. She
was good-hearted, was Melangell. You find who hurt
that little girl. Find him and make him pay."

It took the rest of the afternoon to track the peddler
down. They finally found him at Billingsgate, trying to
sell his goods to sailors as they came off the ships docked
in the basin. Godwin's rickety cart and aged, cantan-
kerous mule offered mute testimony to their owner's
hardscrabble past, as did the man himself.

According to the landlord, Godwin believed he'd lived
through about forty winters, or so Melangell had claimed;
she'd been as free with their secrets as her father was sparing. By the look of him, though, Godwin could easily
have carried another decade on his stooped shoulders
and lanky, lean frame. His hair was brown and long,
somewhat matted, his beard bushy, his eyes deep set and
dark, as opaque as marble and as unyielding.

"I do not understand," he said, speaking with the
slow, cautious deliberation of a man more comfortable
with silences. "Why do you want to talk about my girl's
death? Did that serjeant send you?"

Justin did not know how to answer him. He could not
very well admit he'd been engaged to clear the chief suspects in Melangell's murder. Yet he was reluctant to lie to
this man; if he could not share Godwin's grieving, at least
he could respect it.

Luke had no such scruples. "I am the under-sheriff,"
he said, conveniently forgetting to clarify that his authority was rooted in another shire. "I wanted to go over
what you told my serjeant."

Godwin was quiet for a moment. "That serjeant of
yours did not seem all that interested in what I had to
say."

He had to be talking about Tobias, the serjeant first

called to the scene; whatever Jonas's failings, he was nothing if not thorough and would give a peddler's daughter the same diligence due the highborn. "Well," Luke said smoothly, "another serjeant will be conducting the investigation from now on, a man named Jonas. I think you'll find him more obliging."

Godwin smiled dourly, for a lifetime's experience had taught him how improbable it was that the authorities would ever be "obliging" to the likes of him. "I told the other one that I knew who murdered my girl. You find the man who seduced her, who bedazzled her into playing the whore for him, and you'll find your killer."

"Why do you think she had a lover?"

"She was always sneaking off, refusing to tell me where she'd been, even when I took my hand to her. And after she died, I went through her belongings, found trinkets and cloth and a brass mirror. She had no money to buy such stuff, and she was no thief. He gave them to her, and then he killed her."

Godwin's voice was oddly without emotion, flattened out and stolid sounding. Justin had heard these tones before, from those who'd long ago stopped expecting life to be easy or even fair. He found himself thinking that a lack of hope was as onerous as the lack of money. But then he thought of Melangell, escaping out a window to keep her moonlit trysts in a deserted churchyard. A little less hope might have kept her alive.

The rest of the interview with Godwin was unproductive. According to him, Melangell had offered to pick up his shoes from the cordwainer, did not return. When he got back from making his rounds, he'd gone looking for her, not becoming truly fearful until darkness fell. He'd spent the night searching for her and got home at dawn to find the serjeant, Tobias, waiting to take him to identify his daughter's body.

But he claimed to know nothing of her churchyard

rendezvous and could shed no light on her last hours. When they pressed him, he became more and more taciturn, spending his words like a miser's hoarded coins. Luke had seen this act before: the rustic peasant who was too slow-witted to be worth interrogating. Even when it didn't work, it was a hard shell to crack, and he did not protest when Godwin insisted he must get back to work.

"Papa!" A child was running toward them, weaving agilely between the sailors clogging the wharf. "A ship is about to pass through the bridge! Look . . . they are taking down the mast. Can I go onto the bridge to watch?"

"If you do not get underfoot," Godwin agreed, waving her on. By then she'd noticed Luke and Justin. Sharp black eyes peered at them curiously through a ripple of wind-tossed ebony hair, for she was too young to wear a veil; Justin guessed her age to be about eleven. She had a thin little face, an equally angular body, as yet showing no softening curves, swathed in a well-mended gown that was too big for her; one of Melangell's hand-me-downs? Justin had almost forgotten there was a younger sister.

One glance was enough to tell her that these men were good prospects; a man wearing a sword was a man sure to have some money to spend. "Papa, did you show them those new hats, the ones with the wide brims? Or the brushes made with boar bristles? Or the—"

"They are not here to buy, Cati. They are looking into your sister's death."

Cati did not have her father's stoicism. Emotions chased across her face, like shadows encroaching upon sunlight. There was pain, so raw the men flinched to look upon it, followed by rage that was utterly adult in its intensity, and then the saddest response of all—suspicion.

Justin supposed it was only to be expected that Cati would mistrust those in authority. Peddlers were viewed as a necessary evil, tolerated and rousted by turns, all too often convenient scapegoats for crimes in need of quick solving. Although he did his best to reassure Cati of his goodwill, he got nowhere fast, his smiles and gentle questions met with a blank stare. If Cati had been privy to her sister's clandestine love affairs, she was not about to break faith with Melangell now. She shook her head mutely, shrugged, even lapsing into Welsh once or twice. Justin soon gave up. Luke had not even tried, for he knew that none were more tenacious in the safeguarding of their secrets than children, especially secrets that were forbidden.

Afterward, they walked slowly back home, tired and disheartened, as the day's light faded and the sky's sunset afterglow gave way to a deepening twilight haze. They'd stopped at the riverside cookshop to buy pork pies for themselves, sausage for Shadow, and by the time they reached Gracechurch Street, the city was silvered in moonlight.

Justin was more discouraged than Luke, for he was the one bound by Nell's rash promise, and it was pinching and chaffing more and more. After an entire day chasing down Melangell's elusive ghost, he was still groping for answers. He could not rule out either Geoffrey or Daniel Aston as suspects in the girl's killing. Luke had helpfully pointed out that even her father might well be a suspect, too, for he had no alibi for the time of the murder. When Justin expressed skepticism, Luke reminded him that men had killed in the defense of family honour since the dawn of time, and to that, Justin had no comeback.

"Why could it not be a stranger?" Justin argued, almost plaintively, for he was in a precarious situation and well aware of it. If one of the Aston boys were guilty, he'd fail Agnes, a woman to whom he owed much. Yet if the girl's father had slain her in a fit of misguided rage, what would become of Cati?

"It could have been, I suppose," Luke conceded, throwing him a bone. "I doubt it, though. No one heard any screams, did they? It's been my experience that when a woman is accosted by a stranger, she'll scream her head off. But if she is there to meet someone she knows, she's not as likely to realize her danger until it is too late. Even if they were quarreling and even if she was afraid, would Melangell have feared that her father or her lover had killing in mind?"

Justin winced, for the dead girl was beginning to seem real to him. He could envision her humming under her breath as she hastened to meet her lover, admiring herself in that brass mirror, teasing her little sister and coaxing the landlord into doing small favors for her. A girl who was spirited enough to defy her father, who doted on animals and "liked men," a girl who'd died too young and far from her Welsh homeland, probably buried in a pauper's grave. It occurred to him now that he wanted to catch her killer as much for Melangell as for Agnes or Cati.

"Of course," Luke theorized, "if that jackass Aston is right and she was a harlot, then the killer could have been almost anyone, for half the men in London would tumble a pretty young wench if the time and price were right."

"I do not think she was a harlot," Justin said, so firmly that Luke glanced at him in amusement.

"Can you be so sure of that? We're not talking about the Blessed Virgin Mary, after all, but a girl who . . . how did Geoffrey so delicately put it? . . . liked men."

"That does not make her a whore," Justin insisted, and even he could not have said if he was also defending his own unknown mother, defending Claudine.

"I pity you, de Quincy. Any man so trusting of women is like a sheep for the shearing. As it happens, though,"

Luke conceded, "I tend to agree with you. It does not sound as if the girl was out on the street, at least not full-time. So we're back to a closed circle. The lover? The spurned lover? The father?"

"The truth, Luke, is that I have no idea who killed her."

"Neither do I," Luke acknowledged cheerfully. "But then, I'm leaving on the morrow so it—What? What is amiss?" he asked, for Justin had come to an abrupt halt on the path, only a few feet from the cottage.

Justin answered by pointing toward the door. After being stalked by Gilbert the Fleming, he'd gotten into the habit of snagging the latchstring around a nail whenever he left the cottage. Now it dangled free, offering swaying proof that the latch had been lifted. But was the intruder still within? Bathed in moonlight, silent as a cemetery, the cottage gave away no secrets. All seemed normal. All had seemed normal, too, in Gunter's stables just before the Fleming had launched his murderous attack.

Someone else might have shrugged, assumed the string had broken free, and barged on in. But Luke was never one to mock caution; on several occasions, that niggling sixth sense had saved his life. He and Justin slid their swords from their scabbards in unison. They worked well as a team, but then they'd had some practice at it. Justin hit the door first, with Luke right behind him, entering fast to take any intruders by surprise.

The tactic worked. Claudine was certainly surprised, sitting bolt upright in bed with a startled scream. She'd lit a cresset lamp, and it gave off enough light to reveal that the shapely body in the bed was naked under the sheet. Her skin looked golden and glistening in the lamplight, her hair spilling over her bared shoulders, darker than the night itself, and Justin's breath caught in his throat.

Claudine was still clutching the sheet, her eyes wide.

But as she looked from Justin, who was slowly sheathing his sword, to Luke, who was leaning against the door, grinning widely, a smile flitted across her lips.

"Oh, my," she said, and began to laugh.

6

LONDON

April 1193

Reluctantly taking his eyes from the laughing Claudine, Luke glanced toward Justin, who had yet to move or speak. "There's a sight to strike any man dumb," the deputy joked, although he sensed there was more at play here than sexual tension. "It looks like I'll be bedding down tonight in Gunter's smithy. You'll not be getting rid of me without paying a price, though, de Quincy. I'm going nowhere unless I'm introduced to this vision in your bed."

Justin grudgingly complied and Luke sauntered over to the bed to kiss Claudine's hand, much to her amusement. "Lady Claudine, you have given me a memory sure to warm up the coldest winter nights. I thank you for that. Sadly enough, it is a debt I can only repay by leaving. I shall take myself off to the smithy and try to figure out what you can possibly see in de Quincy."

"Passing strange, for that is the same thing I've often wondered about Aldith and you," Justin said, with a smile as strained as his humor. As soon as the door closed behind Luke, he shoved the latch into place. "What are you doing here, Claudine?"

She'd begun to pet Shadow, who was wriggling happily under her caresses. Her eyebrows arched, both at the question and the tone. "If you need to ask that, Justin, it has definitely been too long since we've lain together!"

Justin hastily sought to recover lost ground. "I meant

73

how did you get here. Surely you did not come on your own? The streets are not safe for a woman after dark, especially one who looks like you." There was no need to feign concern over her safety; he discovered now that his anxiety was quite genuine.

She was mollified by the ring of sincerity in his voice. "I asked a friend to bring me; you remember Nicholas de Mydden?"

"The coxcomb with straw-color hair?" He saw her eyes crinkle at the corners and knew she thought him to be jealous. Not that he was, he assured himself. How could he be jealous of a woman he meant to walk away from? That would make no sense. She had propped herself up on one elbow, watching him through the sweep of those improbably long lashes. Jesú, but she was beautiful. If Bathsheba had been even half as lovely, no wonder King David had been smitten at first sight of her in that rooftop bath.

His treacherous imagination immediately conjured up an image of Claudine in her bath, soft and wet and slippery with soap, a wayward mermaid, eyes filled with moonlight and that midnight hair flowing free, trailing over her breasts into the water like silken seaweed. But he'd not shared a bath with Claudine, knew that he never would. Theirs had been a love affair of stolen moments and no talk of tomorrows; even before he'd learned that she was John's spy, he'd known there could be but one ending for them. And now it was done. She was the most desirable woman he'd ever bedded, and the most deceitful. No matter how much he wanted her, he could not trust her. Even more troubling, he could not trust himself when he was with her. It had to end.

"Claudine, we need to talk."

"Yes, we certainly do," she agreed. "But first can you find us something to drink? I've been waiting for over an hour and I am parched."

Justin had a half-full wineskin on the table. When he found a cup, she stopped him from searching further, saying, "No, do not bother. We can share it." He did not think that was a good idea, but there was no tactful way to refuse. He carried it to the bed and she slid over to make room for him. Against his better judgment, he sat beside her and held out the cup. She drank deeply, smiling at him over the rim. "Now . . . you first. What did you want to talk about?"

Justin sought to keep his gaze on her face; it was no easy feat, as her sheet had slipped. "About us."

"Me, too." She leaned over to hand him the cup, and her movement sent the sheet into free-fall, sliding down to her waist. She made no attempt to cover herself. "I love it when you look at me like that," she murmured, "as if you could never get enough of me."

Justin's breath had stopped again. His brain made a last-ditch attempt to remind him of his resolve, but common sense could not begin to compete with that tempting red mouth, wild black mane, and slim, smooth body. He didn't bother to set the cup down, just tossed it into the floor rushes, and reached for her. She laughed, wrapping her arms tightly around his neck as he jerked away the sheet.

The lovemaking that followed was unlike anything Justin had experienced before. There was more than lust in their eager, out-of-control coupling. He'd brought anger into the bed, too, a stifled rage that found expression now in the urgency of his demands. He was not gentle, not tender, afire with his need for release, for redemption, for oblivion. Claudine was soon caught up in his incendiary passion, burning with the same frenzied fever, and for a brief time, there were no secrets between them, no betrayals, nothing but sweat and scratches and muffled cries and pleasure so intense it was almost akin to pain.

When it was over, Justin was exhausted, drenched in perspiration, and shaken, both by the reckless abandon of their lovemaking and that it had happened at all. This was not what he'd wanted; at least he no longer wanted it now that his body's desperate hunger had been slaked. He was in no mood to appreciate the irony of his plight, too troubled by this alarming evidence of the power Claudine still wielded over him. In her own way, she was no less dangerous than John.

Claudine's breathing was still uneven, her lashes fanning her cheeks, the hint of a smile hovering in the corners of her mouth. Her hair cascaded over the pillow, over them both, not quite hiding the faint shadows on her skin . . . bruises in the making? He frowned at this physical proof of his own rash behavior, his fingers twitching with the urge to touch those shadows, caress them away. "I am sorry if I hurt you," he said, awkwardly. "I did not mean to be so rough . . ."

Her lashes flew upward, dark eyes glowing. "Darling, you should be bragging, not apologizing! Mind you, the other times we made love were quite satisfying, but this . . . At the risk of puffing up your male pride beyond bearing, this was truly remarkable. Anyway," she added, with a mischief-making grin, "I'm the one who ought to be apologizing, not you. Take a look at your back . . . I clawed you well and proper, my poor love."

"It does not matter."

"You might change your mind in the morning, especially when you splash cold water on that back. And I'm sure you do not have any useful balms or salves lying around, do you? Well, I'll bring something over the next time I come." Twirling a long strand of hair around her finger, she used it to tickle his chest. "Even with the queen sending you all over creation on one mysterious errand after another, are you not sorry now that you did not steal some time for us?"

"What do you think?" he said evasively. "I know I've been away a lot lately, but it was none of my doing."

He was wondering if that sounded as lame to her as it did to him when she asked, "Where did you go? Were you trying to track down John for the queen?" Justin sat up so abruptly that she glanced over at him in surprise. He avoided her eyes, lest she see how that innocuous question had rattled him. Was it truly innocent . . . mere curiosity? Or was she still spying on John's behalf?

Getting out of bed, he started to collect his clothes. They were scattered all over the cottage, for when he'd stripped, his only concern had been speed. Claudine sat up, watching in puzzlement as he pulled his tunic on. "Why are you getting dressed, Justin? Do you need to fetch something . . . wine or ale?"

"No . . . I am going to take you home."

She smiled, settling back against the pillow. "That is sweet, love, but unnecessary. I got the queen's permission to stay the night. Not that I told her I'd be with you, of course. I doubt that she'd be perturbed, though, if she knew the truth. The queen is a very worldly woman, after all, with enough scandals in her own past to . . . Justin? Why are you still dressing?"

"I think," he said, "that you will want to go back to the Tower after you hear what I have to tell you."

Her quizzical smile faded. "And what is that?"

"I think we ought to put an end to these trysts."

Her lashes flickered, but other than that, she did not react. "Why?" she asked, and he realized he had no idea what she was thinking, proof—if he needed it—that he'd been bedding a stranger for these past few months, making love to a woman he'd never truly known.

"We have no future together," he said, striving to sound matter-of-fact. "You made that plain from the first. The longer we see each other on the sly, the more likely one of us will be hurt . . . or we'll be discovered. I do not share your certainty that the queen would not object to my bedding one of her ladies in waiting, a kinswoman. I could lose my post in her household and you could be sent back to Aquitaine in disgrace. The risk is just too great, Claudine."

"You would not have said that a quarter hour ago," she reminded him dryly. "You'd not want to eat a meal without salt, would you? Then why would you want a life without risk? Have you not learned by now, Justin, that risk is an aphrodisiac?"

"Not when there is so much at stake," he said stubbornly, and saw her eyes narrow slightly. Her scrutiny made him uneasy, for she was too clever by half. What if she guessed the truth? When she finally spoke, her words took him totally by surprise.

"Who is she?"

He blinked. "What?"

"I am not a fool, Justin, so do not treat me like one!" Her anger was sudden, disconcerting. "Do not try to make me believe you've tired of me, not after that wild way you made love to me tonight. And do not talk of risk and disgrace and discovery, for you knew of all that from the outset of our affair. Nothing has changed . . . or has it? I can think of only one reason why you're so conscience stricken. You've gotten involved with another woman, haven't you?"

He hesitated, then grabbed the lifeline she had unwittingly thrown him. "Yes."

"I knew something was amiss," she cried, bitterly triumphant. "I could sense the change in you, should have realized . . . Well, the truth is out now, and it is time for some plain speaking. I'll not pretend I like it any, but I know men; the body part that is usually in command is not your brain. So you strayed. That is not a sin beyond forgiving. But I do not share my lover, not now, not ever. I'll need your promise that you'll not see this woman again."

"I cannot promise that, Claudine," he said softly, and saw her confidence crack, saw the disbelief and shock etched across her face. Had she ever been rejected before?

"Are you saying you're choosing her over me?" She sounded so incredulous—and suddenly so vulnerable—that he had to struggle with the urge to take his words back, to take her into his arms again. But he stayed where he was, let his silence speak for him.

Claudine stared at him, patches of hot color beginning to burn along her cheekbones. "You bastard," she said at last, a double-edged insult that besmirched both his paternity and character. "Get out!" Then she seemed to remember that the cottage was his, for she added, "I want to dress and I'll not do it in front of you."

Justin was not about to point out the illogic of that demand. He headed for the door, escaped with relief out into the cool April night. He'd done what he must. So why did he not feel better about it? He'd not expected her to take it so badly. Was it her heart that he'd bruised—or her pride?

When she finally emerged from the cottage, she was fully clad, hair hidden away under a silken wimple and veil, appearing immaculate and elegant—as long as one didn't look too closely. She strode past him as if he didn't exist, and he had to hasten to catch up with her. "I'll take you home now."

"The Devil you will!" she snapped, continuing on up the path toward the smithy.

"Be reasonable, Claudine. I'm not going to let you wander about the streets all by yourself!"

"You have nothing to say about it!"

By now they'd reached the smithy. When Justin sought to open the door for Claudine, she brushed by him and then slammed it in his face. When he jerked it open again and followed her, he discovered they now had an audience. Gunter and Luke looked up, startled, from a game of draughts, while the farrier's young helper, Ellis, nearly dropped a hammer on his foot, so intent was he upon ogling Claudine.

"For God's sake, Claudine," Justin began, uncomfortably aware of the other men, "you cannot go off on your own merely to spite me. It is too dangerous!"

"I will do as I damned well please," Claudine insisted hotly, but then her gaze fell upon Luke, lingered. Ignoring Justin, she walked over to the deputy and smiled. "Luke, was it not? Well, Luke, how would you like to escort me home to the Tower?"

Luke looked at Justin, then at Claudine. "My lady, it would be an honour," he said, at his most courtly, and Justin wanted to hit him.

"It is settled, then." Claudine swept on out of the smithy, without so much as a backward glance. Luke got hastily to his feet and hurried after her. At the door, he paused. Glancing back at Justin, he shrugged, then disappeared out into the night.

After their departure, the silence was smothering, at least to Justin. The taciturn Gunter mercifully refrained from comment, and Ellis was too shy to say anything, although Justin knew he'd waste no time in spreading the story the length and breadth of Gracechurch Street. Justin considered his options, none of which he found appealing, tossed a terse "Goodnight" in Gunter's direction, and plunged through the doorway.

The street outside was quiet, for Gracechurch's denizens were either ensconced before their own hearths or over at Nell's alehouse. Luke and Claudine were almost out of sight already, turning the corner onto Cheapside. Justin stood, irresolute, for several moments, then found himself drawn toward the light spilling from the ale-house's open door.

The alehouse was only half full. A game of hasard was in progress, people drifting over to watch the dice being thrown, making desultory side bets and cheering the players on. A prostitute was hovering nearby, hoping for some action of her own. Nell discouraged solicitation in the alehouse, on pragmatic rather than moral grounds; too often it led to brawling. But this was a neighborhood woman, a hard-pressed widow with three children to feed, and so Nell turned a blind eye to her nocturnal hunting. After serving another ale to the priest from St Benet's Church and pausing briefly to banter with several of her regular customers, Nell picked up a flagon and two cups, then headed toward the corner table Justin had staked out for himself and Shadow.

"Here," she said, "have a drink on me. So . . . what happened?"

For a dismayed moment, Justin thought she'd already heard about his quarrel with Claudine. But even Nell's sources were not that good and he relaxed somewhat with her next question. "Well?" she prodded. "You met the Astons today, did you not? What did you think of them?"

Far from resenting her interrogation, Justin welcomed it; as long as he was talking about the Astons, he need not think about Claudine. "Geoffrey strikes me as a lad with some practice in pleasing people. He is obviously the family pride and joy, unlike his brother, who seems cast as the family scapegoat. An odd thing about roles; people tend to live up to them."

Nell nodded emphatically. "Exactly," she agreed. "Geoffrey can seem a bit glib, saying just what is expected of him. Affability is his shield, his way of surviving in that hellish household. Whereas poor Daniel never learned any survival skills, either lashing out or retreating, like a turtle into its shell." She poured for herself and Justin from the flagon, then grinned. "And what was your opinion of Master Humphrey Aston?"

Justin responded with a pithy, colorful phrase that would not pass muster in polite company, and Nell laughed outright. "He is, isn't he?" she agreed. "If you seek to understand the sons, you need look no further than the father. I suppose the man must have a stray virtue or two, but his vices are so much more noticeable . . . and not even grand vices, but the low, petty sort."

"Which vices are those?" Justin asked, more to keep the conversation going than for any other reason. By his reckoning, it should take Luke and Claudine about a quarter hour to get to the Tower. Then another quarter hour for Luke to get back. His eyes flicked toward the candle notched to help the alehouse patrons keep track of the time until closing. "Which vices?" he asked again, and Nell gave him a curious look.

"Were you not listening? I said he was a bully and a miser, and pompous in the bargain. But by far his most damning sin is the way he wields his love like a club."

That caught Justin's attention. "What do you mean?"

"From what Agnes says, he has ever favored Geoffrey over Daniel. Unequal love like that is a burden, both to the one loved and the one not loved. Imagine what it was like for Daniel growing up, knowing that he could never measure up to his brother no matter how hard he tried. Is it surprising that he soon stopped trying?"

"No," Justin conceded, "I suppose not." And oddly enough, he suddenly found himself thinking of John, for he, too, had grown to manhood in the smothering shadow of a better-loved brother.

Nell was studying him pensively, for neither his preoccupation nor his bleak mood had escaped her notice. She'd been intrigued from the first by his eyes, a clear grey that darkened to slate when he was angry and was shot through with silver whenever he laughed. Now they put her in mind of a December sky, a color without warmth or cheer or even hope. Reaching out, she surprised him by brushing a lock of black hair off his forehead, a gesture that was almost maternal. "Do you want to talk about whatever is troubling you? I can keep a secret when need be, Justin, better than most people realize."

Justin was half tempted to take her up on her offer, but somehow it seemed a betrayal of Claudine to talk about her to another woman. Why he should care about keeping faith with a woman who'd played him for such a fool was a question he could not answer, one he could only ignore. "Some troubles need to ripen like cheeses ere they can be brought out into the open," he said, as lightly as he could, and instead, he told her about the rest of his day, about the scene in the Aston household and then the meeting down on the quay with the father and sister of Melangell. He'd begun to think of her by name now, always as Melangell, not just as *the murdered girl* or *the peddler's daughter*. Nell listened intently, asked sensible questions, and for a time, he forgot to glance over at that notched candle, forgot to wonder why Luke had not yet returned. Nell agreed with him that there was more to Melangell's death than met the eye. It was not likely to have been a random killing, she declared, unconsciously echoing Luke's verdict. He must search for a motive, find out who had reason to want her dead. And he must also seek out the little sister again, for if Melangell had a secret worth killing over, Cati would be the one to know. Sisters share, she insisted, and Justin nodded somberly, seeing again Cati's slanting black eyes, too knowing and guarded for a child of eleven. She would not be easy to win over, this wary Welsh wood-sprite. She was not like Melangell.

He stayed at the alehouse until the curfew bells echoed

across the city and Nell announced she was closing, ignoring the pleas from patrons for one more round of drinks. Collecting Shadow, he crossed the street, circled around the smithy, and headed across the pasture toward the cottage. Light shone through chinks in the shutters and he remembered that he'd not extinguished the lamp in his rush to catch up with Claudine. That would have been poor payment for Gunter's kindness, if he'd burned down the blacksmith's cottage by his carelessness. Reaching for the latchstring, he opened the door and then stopped abruptly, for Luke was sitting at the table with a flagon.

"I bought some wine on my way home," the deputy said. "There is enough for us to have one last drink . . . if you've a mind to?"

After a moment, Justin shrugged. "Why not?" Glancing once at the rumpled bed and tangled sheets and then away, he joined the other man at the table, watched as Luke poured the remaining wine into two cracked cups.

"Where were you?" Luke asked, with a casualness that was almost convincing. "Over at the alehouse?"

"Yes." Justin paused. "Did you see Claudine back safely?"

Luke nodded, and a silence fell between them, as charged as the stillness before a breaking summer storm. "I did not make up the pallet," Luke said, "for I was not sure if you'd want me to sleep here tonight."

"Is there a reason why I should not?" Justin asked, very evenly, and their eyes met for the first time.

"No," Luke said, "no reason." He took a deep swallow of the wine, then set the cup down with a thud. "Hellfire, de Quincy, that is one beautiful woman. Of course I agreed to escort her home. But a friend once told me that he was not one for poaching in another man's woods, and neither am I."

Those words were Justin's own, his assurance to Luke

that he'd recognized Aldith was not fair game, already spoken for. He almost asked Luke if Claudine had offered him anything more than a walk home, then decided he didn't truly want to know. "Death to all poachers, then," he said with a crooked smile and he and Luke clinked their cups ceremoniously.

Luke was quiet for a moment, green eyes probing. "I do not know what you did, but you'll have no easy time making your peace with her. She is right wroth with you, man."

Justin drank, saying nothing, and Luke reached again for his own cup. "You can get her back, though," he said, "for when we reached the Tower, there were tear tracks on her cheeks."

Justin looked away, but not in time. The other man was staring. "My God, you've got it bad," he said. "Then why did you let her leave like that . . . and with me!"

"I do not want to talk about it, Luke."

"Why not?"

"Probably for the same reason that you do not want to talk about what has gone wrong between you and Aldith," Justin said, and Luke grimaced, then grinned reluctantly.

"That sound you hear," he said, "is a trumpet signaling retreat."

They finished the wine in silence and then retired for the night, Luke on his pallet by the hearth, Justin in the bed that still bore the imprint of Claudine's body, the scent of her perfume. He did not sleep well that night.

Windsor Castle rose up on a chalk ridge a hundred feet above the River Thames. Just twenty miles from London, it had been chosen for its strategic significance by John's great-great-grandfather, William the Bastard. The motte was flanked by two large baileys, crowned by a stone shell keep known as the Great Tower. Standing on the battlements, John gazed down upon the small village nestling in the shadow of Windsor's walls.

Daylight was fast fading but he could still see the parish church, the cemetery, the open market square, the wattle and daub houses. The narrow streets were empty of villagers. New Windsor resembled a plague town, for the inhabitants had fled, some to the deep woods south and west of the castle, others trying to reach the hamlet of Bray or the nunnery at Bromhall. Ordinarily in time of danger, villagers would have sought refuge in the castle, but Windsor Castle was no sanctuary. It was a target.

A few forlorn dogs still roamed the streets, abandoned by their panicked masters, and pigs would soon be foraging in the untended gardens, until they ended up on spits over soldiers' campfires. John paid no heed to the deserted village and the stray animals, keeping his gaze upon the road that stretched toward London. The dust clouds were growing thicker, kicked up by hundreds of horses and marching men.

"My lord?" He turned to find that Durand de Curzon had joined him at the wall embrasure. Together they watched the approaching army. The banners were visible now, the royal lions of the English king, his absent brother, hopefully rotting in an Austrian dungeon. John leaned his elbows upon the merlon, hearing again his mother's cool, clipped tones as she warned that she'd do whatever she must to protect Richard's throne.

"My lord?" Durand repeated, somewhat impatiently this time.

"What?"

"They are going to demand that you surrender the castle to the queen. Will you?"

Until that moment, John hadn't been sure himself what he would do. "No," he said. "I will not."

7

LONDON

April 1193

Luke left the next morning, after coaxing Nell into making him a hearty breakfast of fried bread and sausages. Justin saw him off with an exchange of affable insults and hoped that the other man would not tarry too long at the Windsor siege. If Aldith grew tired of waiting, there would be no lack of men eager to take Luke's place in her bed. After the deputy's departure, he found himself reluctant to return to the cottage, where the scent of Claudine's perfume still lingered. Nell insisted upon serving him another helping, waiting with rare patience for him to eat his fill before she broached the subject of Melangell's murder.

"Must you seek out the queen today?"

"I might stop by the Tower later, check to see if she has need of me. This morn I thought I'd see for myself where Melangell died and then pay another visit to her family."

Nell's blue eyes brightened. "Take me with you," she urged. "I'll get Ellis to open the alehouse whilst I'm gone. I can sniff out untruths faster than a pig can unearth acorns. Did I not prove that when we fooled the Fleming's whore?"

She was anticipating an argument, but Justin did not offer any objections. Nell's verve would keep his own dark mood at bay, and if her presence vexed the irascible Humphrey Aston, so much the better. Cutting up his

trencher, he fed the gravy-soaked bread to Shadow, and
then rose to his feet. "What of Lucy?"

Lucy was Nell's five-year-old daughter, the one pure
legacy left by Nell's late husband, an amiable dreamer
who'd died in a drunken accident. "I'll ask Agnes to look
after her," Nell declared, jerking off her apron before
Justin could change his mind. Solving a murder was infinitely more satisfying, after all, than tending to the demands of querulous alehouse patrons.

The parish church of St Mary Magdalene was just off the
Cheapside, on Milk Street, so conveniently close to the
Aston family's shop that it was easy to see why Geoffrey
and Melangell had chosen it for their trysts. Church-
yards were popular places for dalliances, for any number
of secular activities frowned upon by the Church. People
played camp-ball and quoits; children darted between
the wooden crosses in games of hoodman blind and hunt-
the-fox; goods were bartered; prostitutes occasionally
lured men into the shadows to sin; it was not unheard of
to find goats and sheep placidly cropping the grass over
the graves. And on an April evening less than a week ago,
Melangell had gone to her death in this deceptively tran-
quil setting.

The churchyard was still and deserted. The morbidly
curious had already flocked to the site to gawk at the
bloodstains; the more squeamish would keep away until
the spectre of violent death had faded from memory. Not
all of the graves were marked; some had wooden crosses,
a few had flat gravestones, and others lay hidden under a
blanket of new spring grass. Several earthen mounds
were still visible, evidence of recent burials. They'd be
the last for some time to come, for a churchyard polluted
by bloodshed could not be used again until it was recon-
secrated, the spiritual stain purged with holy water and

Holy Scriptures. Melangell's murder would cause grief to a few, inconvenience to many.

Entering the churchyard, Justin nearly stumbled over a little mound of earth. It resembled a grave, but why had it been dug on the very edge of the cemetery? Nell saw him frown, and answered his unspoken question. "A babe who dies unbaptised cannot be buried in consecrated ground. Some priests will allow them to be laid to rest as close as possible to the cemetery's hallowed soil. Others are less merciful, and it is not unknown to refuse burial to a woman who died in childbirth if the babe was still within her womb."

Justin said nothing, gazing down at that small pitiful grave. Had his mother been shriven ere she died? Was she buried in holy ground? He had no way of knowing, for it was not likely his father would ever tell him. He did not even know her name. With an effort, he shrugged off his own ghosts and looked about for Melangell's.

Jonas had said she'd died by the cross, and as he drew near, he could see the dried blood darkening the greyish-white stone. The grass was trampled and torn by the base and it was all too easy to envision a girl's body crumpled in the dirt. With Nell watching him intently, as if he were an alchemist working his unholy magic, he studied the death scene in silence. She'd either fallen or been pushed, and had struck her head against one of the cross's outstretched arms. Panicked, the assailant had fled, leaving her dead or dying in the twilight dusk. Had he meant to kill her? Had this been a rape gone awry as Jonas suspected? If so, that would make Daniel a more likely suspect than Geoffrey.

Nell picked up on his thoughts. "Poor Agnes," she said softly.

Justin was turning away when something caught his eye. Bending down, he retrieved a rock from a thicket of nearby bushes. It was about the size of a man's fist, looked as if it had broken off from a grave slab. Holding it up toward the sun, he ran his fingers over the reddish-brown stain, and Nell blurted out:

"That looks like blood! Do you think it is Melangell's?"

Justin did. Melangell had died on Friday night, just five days ago, five days without rain. If the blood was not Melangell's, whose was it? And if it was hers? Suddenly her death did not seem so accidental, after all. Squeezing the rock into his money pouch, he said, "We're done here. Let's go on to Friday Street, see if we can find some answers there."

They found the Aston household in disarray. Beatrice was abed, not receiving visitors; the little maidservant mumbled that her mistress was "unwell." Daniel and Geoffrey were at work in the mercer's shop, the former helping another apprentice to sort through piles of newly imported silks and linens, the latter going over the accounts. But Humphrey Aston was nowhere in evidence, and all in the shop—journeymen, apprentices, even customers—seemed easier for his absence.

"My father had to go to the Mercer's Guild. But he ought to be back soon," Geoffrey said, with a glint of hidden humor. "I am sure you'd not want to miss seeing him."

"Indeed not," Justin agreed gravely. "Suppose I talk with you and your brother whilst we await his return?"

Daniel flung down an armful of silks, with such vehemence that they slid from the counter, fluttering into the floor rushes. "I do not have to talk to you," he said combatively. "You're not the sheriff or even one of his men!"

"He is the queen's man, you foolish boy," Nell said irritably. Daniel had already wheeled; the door banged as he retreated into the storeroom.

"His nerves are on the raw," Geoffrey said, stating the

obvious with an apologetic half-smile. "He was fond of Melangell."

"How fond?"

The tone of Justin's voice took Geoffrey's smile away. "He . . . he may have fancied her. Is that so surprising? She was very pretty, after all."

Justin gestured for Geoffrey to join him and they moved toward the doorway, out of eavesdropping range. "And you were not jealous?"

Geoffrey looked startled. "No, of course not."

"Why not?" Justin was deliberately abrasive. "Because you knew she loved you and you alone? Or because you did not consider your brother to be a rival worth worrying about?"

Geoffrey flushed slightly; he'd had little experience in deflecting hostility. "Both, I suppose," he admitted. "Daniel is pitifully awkward with girls, so tongue-tied that they either laugh at him or avoid him altogether."

"Which did Melangell do?"

"Neither—she befriended him. Melangell was ever one for taking in strays."

Justin changed the subject abruptly, hoping to throw Geoffrey off stride. "What of the silk cloth found under her body? Did you give it to her?"

"No, I did not. I'd given her presents in the past, when I could. But we do not sell that sort of silk weave, a patterned twill."

Justin did not expect Geoffrey to fall into so obvious a trap, but he still had to ask. "I take it you've seen the silk in question, then?"

Geoffrey nodded. "The serjeant . . . Tobias, I think he was called . . . showed it to us."

Justin hoped that Tobias had thought to show it to the others who worked in the Aston shop; he wasn't very impressed so far with the serjeant's investigation. "Can anyone account for your whereabouts that night?"

Geoffrey smiled faintly. "Besides me, you mean? No, I regret not. I'd gone on an errand on my mother's behest, in search of henbane and bryony root and black poppy, for she was in need of a sleeping potion. But when I got to the apothecary's, he had already closed up for the night."

Justin sighed, sure that Beatrice Aston would verify Geoffrey's story, and sure, too, that her confirmation was meaningless; what mother would not lie to save her son? "That is all for now," he said, and then, suddenly, "Do you think your brother killed her?"

Geoffrey was not flustered by the unexpected question. "No," he said emphatically, "I do not."

Justin studied him for a long moment. They were of an age and could have been mirror images of each other, both tall and lean, although Justin's hair was dark and Geoffrey's was flaxen. "Would you tell me if you did suspect him?" he asked, and was not surprised when Geoffrey immediately shook his head.

"No," he said, "I would not," and Justin felt a faint flicker of respect. He'd grown up without a father and had felt the loss keenly. Geoffrey's father had been there since his first day of life, ever present and omnipotent, and Justin would not have traded places with him for half the riches in Christendom.

"Geoffrey!" The voice was a female one, unfamiliar to Justin. He turned to see a young woman coming up the street toward them. She was tall and willowy, and although she was modestly veiled and wimpled, her skin was so fair and her eyes so blue that Justin was sure her hidden hair color was blond. She was accompanied by a male servant, heavily laden with packages and bundles, so deferential that Justin knew at once this must be Adela, Geoffrey's prospective bride.

Geoffrey confirmed his guess even before the introductions were made, glancing toward Justin in mute entreaty. Justin understood what he was asking: to say nothing of Melangell's murder. Did Adela know suspicion had fallen upon her betrothed? Surely her uncle did by now. No wonder Geoffrey was uneasy, for the plight troth had not yet been finalized; Adela could still disavow him, put an end to the marriage plans if the scandal grew any worse. And it was obvious that Geoffrey wanted this marriage to take place, for there was an edginess underlying the affection in his greeting. Adela was a marital prize, niece to the master of the Mercer's Guild, and Humphrey Aston's choice of a bride for his son. With so much at stake, Justin was not surprised that Geoffrey should be nervous, and he obliged by identifying himself as a "friend of Geoffrey's, eager to meet his bride-to-be."

Geoffrey shot him a grateful look before giving Adela a circumspect kiss on the cheek. The talk was banal, mostly of Adela's shopping purchases in the Cheapside market, offering Justin an opportunity to appraise Geoffrey's future wife. She was undeniably elegant, but somewhat aloof, putting him in mind of a swan, regal and unapproachable, as unlike the earthy, wanton peddler's daughter as chalk and cheese. Would this pampered, bloodless child of privilege stand by Geoffrey if he fell under serious suspicion? Or would she shrink from the scandal, from a man less than perfect? If he were asked to wager on it, Justin would have put his money on the latter likelihood. And yet . . . those pale blue eyes were guarded, not vacant, and one of her well-tended, soft hands was resting possessively on Geoffrey's arm. Mayhap he had been too quick to judge, to assume that propriety was her ruling passion.

"Geoffrey, I would like you to escort me home." Adela seemed to take his compliance for granted, for she then bade Justin a polite farewell and signaled for her servant to follow. Justin watched them move off down the street, wondering how much—if anything—Adela knew about

Melangell. And then he stepped back into the shop, where Nell was chatting easily with the journeymen, and went in search of Daniel.

He found the boy in the storeroom, sitting on a barrel surrounded by items of luxury, for while mercers dealt primarily in silks and costly textiles, they also sold toys, hats and caps, belts, and spices. Daniel's face was blotched with color, his eyes bloodshot and puffy. He glared defiantly at Justin, square chin jutting out, freckled fists clenching on his knees. "Are you still here? I'm getting bone-weary of running into you every time I turn around!"

Justin slammed the door shut behind him, then leaned back against it, arms folded across his chest, saying nothing. It didn't take long. Daniel was soon squirming under his cold-eyed appraisal. "What are you staring at?" he demanded. "Why will you not leave me be?"

"If I do, lad, you're sure to hang," Justin said brutally, and saw Daniel quiver under the impact of his words. "I do not know if you killed the girl. I do know you're the one likely to answer for it, and on the gallows. So if you can clear yourself, now is the time to speak up . . . ere it is too late."

Daniel's ruddy color had ebbed away. "I did nothing wrong," he said hoarsely. "I did not kill her!"

"I need more than your denial, Daniel. I need answers. Where were you on the night of Melangell's death?"

"I was down by the wharves."

"Alone?"

Daniel nodded. "I . . . I filched a flagon of my father's wine, and went off to drink it where I'd not be seen."

Justin didn't know whether to laugh or to swear. "Of all nights, you and your brother would pick that one to shun the company of others."

Daniel blinked. "Geoffrey cannot prove where he was, either?"

"You did not know that? Did you not talk to him about the killing?"

"No," Daniel said, so simply that Justin believed him. On reflection, it was not as odd as it first appeared. The Astons were not a confiding family, more like separate, lonely islands in a sea churned up by Humphrey's bile.

"What did you and Melangell quarrel about, Daniel, on the day of her death?"

Daniel looked at him bleakly, finally mumbling, "I told you I do not remember."

"Do not be a fool, Daniel," Justin warned, but he was too late. The door, having opened a crack, now slammed shut again. Daniel's face was stony, green eyes staring stubbornly off into space, looking anywhere but at Justin's face.

Justin soon saw further discussion was futile. "Never have I seen someone so eager to get himself hanged," he said impatiently, and left Daniel to the solitude of the storeroom and his own troubled thoughts.

As soon as Justin stepped back into the shop, he felt the change in atmosphere. One glance pinpointed the source of tension: Humphrey Aston had returned. He was blocking the open doorway, shutting out the light, and judging from his stance and his scowl, he was not pleased with what had been occurring in his absence. The apprentices were visibly wilting under the heat he was giving off, the journeymen had suddenly found urgent tasks to perform, and even the few customers seemed uncomfortable. Only Nell appeared unfazed by Humphrey's ire. She was regarding him with the same detached distaste she showed whenever her Lucy brought snails and toads inside for her inspection and identification.

Humphrey was startled by the sight of Justin. "Why did no one tell me you were here?" he asked irritably. "Well? What do you have to report? Have you found out who killed that peddler's wench?"

"No."

Humphrey waited for Justin to continue, and drew a shallow, aggrieved breath when he realized that terse response was all he was going to get. He may have been a bully, but he was no fool, and he'd grudgingly concluded that Justin was not easily intimidated. Swallowing his anger, he said dismissively, "I'd hoped you'd have made more progress by now." As his eyes roamed the shop, taking inventory of his realm, he noticed then two conspicuous absences. "Where are my sons?"

When it became apparent to Justin that no one else was going to answer, he said, "Geoffrey left to escort Adela home."

"Adela was here?" It was the first time Justin had seen Humphrey show pleasure and it was a moment before he realized that teeth-baring grimace was indeed a smile. "Well, that was what he should have done," the mercer said, so indulgently that Justin understood exactly why Geoffrey was so anxious to wed Adela. Humphrey's satisfaction was short-lived, though. Remembering that he had another son still unaccounted for, he demanded to know where Daniel was.

Again, it was left to Justin to respond. Deciding that it was better to reveal Daniel's whereabouts than to have Humphrey conclude he had sneaked off as soon as his father's back was turned, he said, "He is working in the storeroom," and hoped that the boy would have the wit to appear busy as soon as he heard that familiar heavy tread. Catching Nell's eye, he headed then for the door.

Once they were out in the street, Nell said indignantly, "You should have heard the way he was browbeating those poor souls! What a pity he was not the one murdered instead of little Melangell."

"Murder is probably not the best way to cull the wheat from the chaff," Justin said, with mordant humor.

"Did your conversation with the apprentices and journey-men yield anything of interest?"

"They all loathe Humphrey, of course. But the sons do not seem to be following in the father's footsteps, for Humphrey's hirelings bear them no ill will. I get the sense that they find Geoffrey more likable, but Daniel has earned their respect—on a few rash occasions, he actually dared to stand up to his father. You can well imagine what his courage cost him in bruises and welts. Humphrey will not abide the slightest opposition to his will, and has a temper that kindles faster than sun-dried straw. But they say he fawns over Adela as if she were the Blessed Virgin Mary, so eager is he for an alliance with Master Serlo, the girl's uncle."

"I saw that, too," Justin agreed. "I'd even wager he hungers for the prestige of such a union as much as the marriage portion she'd bring to his son. What of Melangell? Did the other apprentices know about her dalliance with Geoffrey?"

"Indeed, they did. It had to be one of the worst-kept secrets in all of London. The other lads were quite envious of Geoffrey's 'good fortune,' for they thought Melangell looked like a 'right ripe piece,' a judgment they delivered with much smirking and rolling of eyes." Nell did some eye-rolling now of her own, for she had little patience with youthful male braggadocio. "What of you? Did you have any luck with the sons?"

"Well, I got Geoffrey to admit the dalliance was more serious than he'd have us think, at least on Melangell's part. When I asked if she loved him, he conceded as much. And Daniel unbent long enough to insist he was innocent."

"Do you believe him?"

"I'd like to," Justin hedged. "Nothing would make me happier than to be able to clear Agnes's nephews. Like

Geoffrey's protestations, Daniel's denial sounded sincere. Alas, the world is filled with people who can lie as easily as they draw breath," he said, thinking of his father, thinking of Claudine. "Nor is it helpful that neither brother can prove where he was whilst Melangell was being attacked."

"So," Nell prompted, "what does your gut tell you?"

"That I'm hungry again," Justin joked, and grinned when Nell shoved him. "You wanted a serious answer, did you? Well, I think Daniel Aston has something to hide," he said, his fingers straying toward his money pouch, feeling for the outlines of that bloodstained rock.

Despite Nell's protests, Justin escorted her back to the alehouse, left her scolding Ellis for broken crockery while Lucy played in the kitchen with Shadow, and set out in search of Tobias. He found the serjeant at the London gaol, where he had just delivered a prisoner. Jonas was on the scene, too, and gave Justin an ironic smile when he ever so casually invited the two of them to share a meal, well aware that Justin hoped for his help in extracting information from Tobias. Both men accepted the offer, though, and led Justin to a tavern on Fleet Street, not far from the river where he'd rescued Shadow from drowning.

Justin waited until they'd been served heaping helpings of mutton stew before he broached the subject of Tobias's investigation. He was treading with some care, lest Tobias take offense, not yet knowing if the other man would view his involvement as meddling, his suggestions as interference. He soon saw, however, that he had no reason to worry, for Tobias was a far different breed of peacekeeper than Jonas.

He was younger than Justin had expected, only about thirty, and better dressed, too, his tunic spotlessly clean, his hair combed onto his forehead in the newly fashionable fringe. He was also extremely friendly; far from resenting Justin's interest in his case, he seemed to welcome it. Puzzled at first, Justin did not understand until Tobias leaned across the table to confide how pleased he was to be able to work with the queen's man.

So that was it! Tobias was ambitious, hoping to curry favor with one who might mention his cooperation to the sheriff or even the queen herself. Tobias had begun to talk about the capture of Gilbert the Fleming, so effusive in his praise that Justin was at a loss for words and Jonas faked a cough to camouflage a gleeful cackle. When the serjeant finally paused for breath, Justin seized his chance, politely asking if he could discuss with Tobias some of the more murky aspects of Melangell's murder.

The other man beamed. "By all means! My guess is that the mercer's youngest son will turn out to be the culprit. Although it could have been one of the girl's other lovers. From what I hear, she was a wanton, as willing to bed a man as look at him. Such killings are hard to solve, for women like that naturally know more than their share of knaves and felons."

"You said you suspect the younger Aston son. Not the elder son, then?"

"Well, Daniel's motive makes more sense. Also, Master Serlo of the Mercer's Guild gave the older lad a right favorable recommendation, says he is of good character and a responsible worker. Whereas the younger boy has a history of stirring up trouble, running away from his apprenticeship the way he did . . ." Tobias paused to swallow a mouthful of stew. "He seems the obvious suspect and it has been my experience, Master de Quincy, that the man who looks most guilty usually is."

Especially when he had no one of importance to speak up for him, like Master Serlo. Justin dared not look at Jonas, whose face was impassive, but whose one black eye was agleam. "What about the silk found under

Melangell's body? Have you been able to find out who sells it?"

"Well . . . no, I saw no need. If she was killed by Daniel Aston, what does it matter who sold it?"

It was quiet for a time after that, as the serjeants devoted their attention to their meal and Justin sipped his wine, trying to figure out how best to bring Jonas on board this leaking boat. He finally decided upon blatant and shameless flattery and smiled across the table at Tobias.

"I want you to know how much I appreciate your cooperation. I'll be sure to tell Roger Fitz Alan that the next time I see him."

At the mention of the sheriff, Tobias set down his spoon, his food forgotten. "I'm happy to help," he said expansively. "If there is anything else I can do, anything at all—"

"As it happens, there is." Justin reached for the flagon and topped off Tobias's wine cup. "I know you have more than your share of felons to chase down. It must be hard to find time for a killing like this. But I would like to solve this crime quickly, if we can. In all honesty, Tobias, my duties for the Queen's Grace do not allow me much time away from the court. It occurred to me that mayhap Jonas might assist you in your investigation, do what he can to expedite matters so we can bring this sad case to a speedy resolution."

Tobias looked over at Jonas, back at Justin. "It is fine with me, if Jonas here is willing . . . ?"

"I'd be overjoyed," Jonas said, wincing slightly when Justin then kicked his ankle under the table. The rest of the dinner passed without incident, and by the time Tobias was ready to depart, he was reveling in his newfound friendship with Justin, slapping him on the back in familiar farewell. The other two men watched him go and Jonas, finding that his wine cup was empty, reached over to claim Justin's. "You owe me," he said.

"What else could I do, Jonas? You heard the man. He does not care who killed Melangell—a peddler's daughter and part Welsh in the bargain? We'll never get to the truth with Tobias hot on the trail, and you well know it. Melangell deserves better than that, and so does Daniel Aston. If he is going to hang, I need to know he is truly guilty, not just a convenient solution to an inconvenient crime."

"I have to admit that Tobias could not find water if he fell into the river," Jonas conceded. "All right, I'll see what I can learn about this scrap of silk. That seems to be the only clue we have."

"Not necessarily." Justin took out his money pouch, laid it on the table. "I know you were never called to the scene of the killing, but you must have seen her body afterward. How else could you have been so specific with Luke, telling him that there was no blood under her nails or bruises on her thighs?"

"Yes, I saw the body. What do you want to know?"

"Tobias concluded that she struck her head on the cross, and there is indeed blood on it. But I need to know what her injury looked like. Could she have hit her head on the cross, fallen, and then been struck again as she lay helpless on the ground? Was the wound deep enough for there to have been a second blow?"

"I'd say so." Jonas frowned as he sought to call that particular grim memory to mind. "It was a nasty wound, a lot of blood and bone fragments. She could easily have been hit again. What put you onto that?"

Justin opened the money pouch, shook out a few coins to pay for the meal, then extracted the rock. Jonas reached over, weighed its heft in the palm of his hand. Even in the dim light of the tavern, the dried blood smears were easily visible. Jonas's inspection was thorough and un-hurried, his face giving away nothing of his thoughts. Justin waited as long as he could, finally blurted out im-patiently, "Well? What do you think?"

"I think," Jonas said, "that if you're right, this changes everything."

The Tower of London's great keep rose up against the hazy dusk sky, over ninety feet high, a formidable citadel as well as royal palace. Justin had passed through the Land Gate countless times before, but never had he felt such a sense of unease, as if he were venturing into enemy territory. And a right dangerous enemy it was, too, a slip of a lass who would not weigh much over one hundred pounds soaking wet, armed with those deadly female weapons, dimples and come-hither dark eyes. Mocking himself didn't help, though. He was still loath to face Claudine.

But she was not present in the hall, and he began to hope he could avoid an encounter that would be awk-ward at best, painful at worst. As was his custom, he sought out Peter of Blois, Eleanor's secretary-chancellor, who would then inform the queen of his arrival. If she had need of him, he would be admitted to her presence; if not, he was free to return to Gracechurch Street and his other world. He was expecting a dismissal, but to his sur-prise, Peter beckoned him forward to enter the great chamber.

There he received another surprise, for Eleanor was alone. His private audiences with her were rare occur-rences, usually the result of some new mischief-making by her son. As he came forward to kneel before her, Justin remembered his earlier assumption, that all moth-ers would lie to save their sons. He dared make no such facile assumptions about Eleanor and John. He could as easily understand the inscrutable feline mind of a female lion on the sun-baked plains of distant Africa. How often did a lioness swat a troublesome half-grown cub when he misbehaved? When did she finally turn upon him in a fanged fury, drive him from the pride?

Even after reaching her biblical three-score years and ten, Eleanor was still a compelling woman, the high, hollowed cheekbones and enigmatic hazel eyes attesting to the great beauty she'd once been, to the younger self who'd left a trail of broken hearts and broken rules from Aquitaine to England and triumphed over her enemies by outliving them all. On this Wednesday in mid-April, though, she looked very tired to Justin, showing more of the physical frailties of age; the hand extended for his kiss held the faintest of tremors and was hot to the touch.

"Madame . . . are you well?" That was as far as he dared go. At times there was an odd intimacy between them, but he never forgot, not for a moment, that she was England's queen and he was a bishop's by-blow, plucked from obscurity by the vagaries of fate and her royal whim.

She caught the echoes of concern in his voice, and smiled. "There is nothing wrong that a good night's sleep would not cure, lad. You'd think I would have learned by now how to banish worries and cares from the bedchamber."

"Not even Merlin could do that, Madame," Justin said, with feeling, for his memories of last night's broken sleep were still vivid. "May I get you wine?"

She nodded. "Pour for yourself, too." Taking a gilded cup from him, she sipped some of the spiced red wine with pleasure, for it came from the vineyards of her native Aquitaine, the homeland she'd loved more deeply than any man. "The news is not good, Justin," she said after some moments of silence. "The French king has invaded Normandy. He has seized Gisors and Neaufles and I learned today that he is now laying siege to Rouen itself."

Justin set his own wine cup down, untouched. If John's ally succeeded in taking Normandy, that would go far toward bolstering John's claim to the English throne. "I am indeed sorry to hear that, Madame."

She seemed lost in her own thoughts, gazing down into her wine cup pensively. "Stay close to London," she said at last. "I may need to send you to Normandy."

"Of course, Madame," Justin said, startled, for he'd never been out of England. He wondered what she had in mind, most likely a message she'd not want to risk falling into unfriendly hands. He was enormously touched that she had such faith in his abilities, and could only pray he'd not let her down. He was watching Eleanor attentively, waiting for an indication that he'd been dismissed, when the door opened and Claudine entered the chamber.

"I have the oil of roses for your headache, Madame," she said, holding up a small glass bottle. She halted as her gaze fell upon Justin, and although she managed an expression of supreme indifference, she betrayed herself by the sudden surge of color into her cheeks.

Justin got hastily to his feet, saying as politely as he could, "Lady Claudine." She acknowledged the greeting with a curt nod of her head, the sort of grudging recognition accorded those of inferior rank and importance.

"Would you like me to rub it into your temples now, Madame?" she asked, approaching the queen with a solicitous smile.

Eleanor gave her a bland smile in return, "No, dearest, not until after Master de Quincy and I are done."

"Oh . . . of course," Claudine said, as if she'd forgotten Justin's presence altogether. "I will await your summons." For Eleanor, there was another smile and a graceful curtsy. For Justin, enough ice to freeze him through to the very bone.

Once the door closed behind Claudine, Eleanor sat back in her chair, regarding Justin intently. "Well?"

Justin found himself shifting uncomfortably under those unsettling amber-colored eyes. "Madame?"

He was stalling and they both knew it. Eleanor's brows came together in an imperious frown. "Do not play games with me, Justin. I am much better at them than you. What has happened between you and Claudine?"

"We . . . we quarreled," he said reluctantly and she shook her head impatiently.

"That is obvious to anyone not blind and deaf! It is also obvious that she considers herself to have been wronged. Why?"

"I led her to think I was seeing another woman." Justin bit his lip, searching for a way to make her understand. "I lied to her about the other woman so she'd not suspect the truth, that we know she has been acting as John's spy. I had to take the risk, Madame. I could not keep bedding a woman I dared not trust."

"Ah, Justin . . . I'd forgotten how young you still are," she said, with gentle mockery. "It is true I did not want Claudine to realize she'd been found out. But I did not mean you must continue with a liaison you find painful. Fortunately, lovers can be shed much more easily than husbands or wives."

"Fortunate, indeed," Justin agreed wryly, although he'd found nothing remotely easy about casting off Claudine. Eleanor was holding out her hand and he took that as his signal to depart. Bending over to kiss those jeweled fingers, he bade her farewell. But there was one question he still needed to ask. "Madame . . . what is happening at Windsor?"

"The castle is under siege," she said, very evenly.

8

LONDON

April 1193

When Justin received an early summons from the queen the next morning, he assumed he'd soon be Normandy-bound. But there had been a change of plans. Eleanor now wanted him to depart at once for St Albans and its great Benedictine abbey. Justin did not know what was in the letter he bore, nor did he ask; queens were not ones for confiding. He'd expected to be back on Friday, for St Albans was less than thirty miles from London, a day's journey as long as the weather was good. Abbot Warren was not at the abbey, though, and Justin had to track him down on one of the monastery's Hertfordshire manors. He then had to wait for the abbot's response, and so he did not return to London until Sunday evening as Compline was being rung.

He went at once to the Tower, where he delivered the abbot's letter to Eleanor and was snubbed again by Claudine. With Eleanor's admonition to be ready to depart for Normandy at a moment's notice ringing in his ears, he rode back to Gracechurch Street, retrieved his dog from Nell, and fell into bed. His dreams that night were fragmented and disjointed, filled with foreboding. Durand stalked his sleep and the French king set Rouen afire, and there was a confusing confrontation with an unknown, overbearing bishop who bore an uncanny resemblance to his father. The most troubling of the dreams came just before dawn; in it, he returned to the cottage and found Claudine in his bed—with John.

The next morning, the sky was marbled with clouds and there was an occasional distant rumble of thunder; rain was on the way. Bypassing breakfast, Justin headed out early, wanting to catch Godwin before the peddler set off on his rounds. Arriving at the Wood Street dwelling, he was welcomed cheerfully by the garrulous landlord, who told him that Godwin had sent Cati to bargain with the chandler for a few tallow candles and was himself down the street in the stables; his elderly mule was faring poorly.

That was bad news for Godwin; the loss of his mule might well mean the loss of his precarious livelihood. He was hovering helplessly by the suffering animal, so haggard and gaunt that he looked ill himself, acknowledging Justin's greeting with a preoccupied grunt.

"What do you think ails him?" Justin asked. "Colic?"

Godwin shrugged. "His belly is very tender," he said, and though the words were uttered without emotion, Justin sighed, for that sounded like an inflammation of the bowels. Even colic could be a death sentence for the ancient animal. Justin had learned a fair amount about horses when he'd acquired a lamed stallion for a pittance, then patiently nursed Copper back to health, and he suggested what remedies he could think of: a hot bran poultice, linseed oil. Yet he doubted if anything shy of a miracle would save the old mule, and he could tell that Godwin shared his pessimism.

"Why are you here?" Godwin straightened up so slowly that it was obvious he'd been keeping vigil all night in the stables. "I suppose it is too much to hope that my girl's killer has been found."

"No . . . not yet. I wanted to ask you a few more questions—"

"I've nothing to say to you."

Those were the very words Justin had gotten from Daniel Aston. It was frustrating that suspects and victims alike were so unwilling to cooperate with authorities. Justin decided to see if he could shame Godwin into being more forthcoming, and he said sharply:

"If I am willing to labor from dawn to dark to bring your daughter's killer to justice, surely you can spare a few moments of your time to talk to me!"

Anger did not come easily to Godwin; it needed a more combustible fuel than despair. He gazed blankly at Justin, as if struggling to summon up enough energy for indignation, and then said flatly, "Why should I trust the lot of you to find my girl's killer when you cannot even find her pilgrim cross?"

"Pilgrim cross? What are you talking about?"

"I'm not surprised you know nothing about it." Godwin shook his head wearily. "One of the sheriff's men probably stole it from my poor girl's body. What crime can be lower than stealing from the dead?"

"Tell me about this pilgrim cross," Justin insisted, but Godwin merely shrugged again and turned back to his mule, his suspicion of authority as strong as chain-mail armor and even harder to penetrate.

Justin had no intention of giving up, though. What he could not learn from the peddler, mayhap he could learn from Cati. With Shadow in tow, he began moving slowly along Wood Street toward the Cheapside, keeping a close watch upon people passing by. He soon caught sight of Cati, moving at a brisk trot up the street, swinging a small sack from side to side.

Recognition was mutual. She came to a sudden stop, shoulders hunched, dark eyes regarding him warily, a woodland creature sniffing out snares. Justin wondered if Melangell had been as out of place in this city setting as

Cati was. Barefoot and barelegged, tousled black hair hiding half her face, she looked like an imp out of Welsh legend, at once ageless and heartrendingly young. "I know you," she said. "You were asking questions about Melangell."

"I am Justin. Can I talk with you, Cati?"

She gave him a sidelong glance, then shrugged. "I have to get home."

"Suppose we talk and walk, then," he suggested. It would not be easy to get past her defenses; this was a rose surrounded by thorns. But as he'd hoped, she shared her sister's fondness for God's creatures and was eyeing Shadow with interest. The young dog responded to her overture with his endearingly awkward brand of galumphing enthusiasm, thumping his tail madly as he slurped at her face with a wet tongue.

Squatting in the dusty street, Cati wrapped her arms around Shadow's neck. "Is this your dog?"

"He is now," Justin said and told her how he had rescued the dog after two young louts had thrown him into the River Fleet. By the time he was through, Cati was looking at him with far greater friendliness.

"That was a very good deed," she said approvingly, "and just what Melangell would have done, too."

When she artlessly introduced her sister's name into the conversation, Justin felt a prickle of guilt; this was almost too easy. Reminding himself that he was manipulating this child in a good cause, he asked casually, "So Melangell liked dogs?"

And that opened the floodgates. Cati informed him that Melangell had lavished love on an odd assortment of pets over the years: cats and dogs and a baby hedgehog, but never birds, for she could not abide to see one caged, robbed of its freedom to fly. She'd even made a pet of Job, their crotchety old mule, and yes, that name was Melangell's doing. "She always said that names matter, and had to be picked with care. Our mama's name was Olwen, which comes from an ancient Welsh legend, about a giant's daughter who was wooed and won by a brave youth, Culhwch, with some help from King Arthur and his knights. It was said clovers grew wherever Olwen walked." She grinned suddenly. "The Olwen in the tale, not my mama. Though Melangell always claimed Mama smelled sweeter than clover, and she did, too."

"When did your mother die, Cati?"

"Last Martinmas. She cut her hand on a rusty nail and the cut festered. After we buried her, Papa took it into his head for us to leave the Marches and go to London. We'd make a new start, he said, free of memories and ghosts." The child looked at Justin solemnly. "We'd have been better off with the ghosts."

"Yes, lass, probably so . . ." Justin felt a sudden, sharp ache for this lost little girl and her beleaguered father. With an effort, he remembered the task at hand. "After your mother died, did Melangell look after you, Cati?"

"I am nigh on eleven, do not need looking after! I can tend to myself," Cati insisted, with a toss of her head. Then a faint smile curved her lips. "Melangell was always after me to braid my hair," she admitted. "She'd brush it out for me . . ."

Those black eyes seemed suspiciously bright and Justin hastily plunged into the conversational waters, giving her time to banish any brimming tears, sure that Cati would not want to cry in front of him. "I think I would have liked your sister," he said, getting a jerky nod of the head and a sniff in response. "It is plain that she had a good heart and a sense of humor, too . . . Job was an inspired name for a mule. What else can you tell me about her? Did she have a temper?"

"Not like me. I get angry too quick for my own good. But Melangell was always laughing, and could never stay serious for long, even when Papa punished her for running off to meet Geoffrey." Cati swooped down suddenly and buried her face in Shadow's soft ruff. Justin watched in silence; so she knew the name of her sister's lover. How much more did she know?

"Did she love Geoffrey, Cati?" he asked quietly, and she raised her head, then nodded, almost imperceptibly.

"She was so pretty, was Melangell. She had her heart set on a red gown, the shade of strawberries. Papa did not approve, saying that was too bright and garish a color, not respectable, but she kept coaxing him until he agreed. He bought it for her two days ere she . . . she died. We buried her in it."

Justin did not know what to say. What possible comfort could he offer this grieving child? "Cati, I very much want to catch your sister's killer. Will you help me do that?"

"How?"

"Tell me about this pilgrim cross of hers."

"It was a St Davydd's cross, had belonged to Mama. When she was a little lass, she'd fallen ill and her father made a pilgrimage to St Davydd's shrine, prayed for her recovery. St Davydd heeded his prayers and Mama wore his cross on a chain around her neck until she died. Papa gave it to Melangell on her fifteenth birthday last month and—What? Why do you look at me so oddly?"

"Your sister was only fifteen?"

She nodded, puzzled. "She was born in God's Year 1178, during the coldest spring anyone could remember. Why?"

"I did not realize she was so young."

"Fifteen is not so young," she objected. "In Wales, a lad is a man at fourteen and a lass old enough to wed. But you asked about the St Davydd's cross. Shall I show you what it looked like?" When he nodded, she borrowed his dagger and drew in the dirt, sketching a distinctive figure that resembled a cross with feet. "It was lead," she said, "and well-worn, blessed with my mama's prayers. How will knowing this help?"

"I am not sure yet, Cati. Why does your father think it was stolen by the sheriff's men? Could it not have been taken by the man who killed her?"

"I suppose . . ." she mumbled, no longer meeting his eyes, and he sensed that there was more to the story of this pilgrim cross than she was willing to tell him. He did not push her, though; that was not the way to gain Cati's confidence.

"I thank you for your help," he said. "I promise you I will do all in my power to see that someone pays for Melangell's death."

She studied him intently and then handed him back his dagger, hilt first. *"Odid addewid a ddel,"* she said. "That is a saying of my mama's people: Rare is the promise that is kept. Keep this one, Englishman. Find who killed my sister . . ." The rest of her sentence was lost. She gulped, shuddered, and flung her arms around Shadow one last time. Then she whirled and fled up the street, bare legs flashing and black hair streaming out behind her, racing her grief and her crumbling control. Justin watched until she was out of sight, but she never looked back.

Justin then set out to find Jonas. The trail led from Newgate Gaol to the Fishmonger's Guild Hall, where the mayor and aldermen had passed judgment upon a man accused of selling putrid mackerel and herrings. The guilty fishmonger had been sentenced to the pillory and so Justin headed for Cornhill Street.

There he finally found the elusive serjeant, overseeing the fishmonger's punishment. The man's head and wrists had been forced through holes in the wooden pillory frame, and a crowd was already gathering to savor his public humiliation. Justin caught Jonas's eye, waiting until the serjeant could come over to join him.

"They are about to burn the rotting fish around him," Jonas warned, "so we might want to get upwind. Since I'm done here, I'll let you buy me a drink." Telling his men to keep the bystanders at bay and disperse them if they began flinging anything more lethal than insults and jeers, Jonas followed Justin across the road to a nearby alehouse.

Over a flagon of ale, Jonas related what he'd found out since he and Justin had last spoken. "I traced the silk," he said, holding up his hand to dampen Justin's enthusiasm. "Wait till you hear me out ere you start to celebrate. It took some doing, but I was able to determine that it was part of a shipment of cloth brought over by a Flemish mercer, who'd arrived in London from Ypres the same day as the killing."

"Well done, Jonas! Could he tell you who bought that piece of silk?"

"He might . . . if ever I can ask him. It seems he left London on Monday last, supposedly on his way to see customers in Stamford and Cambridge. At least that is what he told the master of the ship he'd sailed on. He will eventually come back to London, but as to when, your guess is as good as mine."

Crestfallen, Justin slumped back in his seat. "Damnation! Why does it always have to be so hard?"

"It is the nature of the beast. Murders are either solved straightaway, due to the stupidity of the culprits, or it takes a lot of labor and luck. But do not abandon hope yet, lad. You and I know the Flemish mercer has disappeared in a cloud of dust. The Astons do not."

Justin liked the sound of that. "Have you been devious again, Jonas?"

"Well . . . I did pay an unscheduled visit to the Astons when they got back from Mass yesterday, and in the course of the conversation, I may have led them to believe that the Flemish mercer has been tracked down and within a few days I ought to have the answers I need to solve the killing."

"That is more than devious, it is downright dishonest," Justin said and grinned. "How did they react when you threw the bait out?"

"The old man was blustering and ranting from the moment I came in the door; is he always such a jackass? The older son was nervous but eager to please, the younger lad sullen, the mother fluttering about like a trapped moth. None of them swooned or screamed when I told them about the Fleming, but murder suspects rarely do, I'm sorry to say. If one of them is guilty, though, there is always a chance that he'll panic, do something foolish. We'll just have to wait and see."

"Mayhap not," Justin said, and told Jonas about the missing St Davydd's cross.

"So . . ." Jonas said thoughtfully, "we may have two arrows in our quiver. Suppose we pay another visit to the Astons tonight and see if we can find this pilgrim pledge. Would you know it if you saw it?"

Justin nodded. "The cross has an uncommon shape. The Welsh are nothing if not imaginative. Do you truly expect to find it there?"

Jonas shrugged. "Who knows? We might get very lucky. Even if we find nothing, our search is sure to unnerve the Astons even further, so what do we have to lose?"

"Why wait until tonight? Why not go over there now?"

"Because I heard Mistress Aston say that Master Serlo and his niece were expected to dine with them tonight."

That seemed needlessly cruel to Justin. But he raised no objections, for Jonas was not a man to be second-guessed. And it was difficult to argue for mercy when he thought of that bloodied rock. What mercy had Melangell been shown?

* * *

The threatened rainstorm had arrived in midafternoon, drenching the city and dropping the temperature. The sky was still smothered in clouds as Justin and Jonas started out for the Astons' that evening, the streets muddy enough to mire several carts along Cheapside. They detoured onto Milk Street to pay a brief visit to St Mary Magdalene's. The churchyard was deep in shadow and the rain had washed away Melangell's blood. Justin showed Jonas where he'd found the rock, and they agreed the killer had been unlucky, for April was usually a wet month; a soaking rain the day after the murder would have obliterated those telltale reddish stains.

Jonas was surprised, too, to learn Melangell's age. "Mind you," he said, "I've run into my share of fifteen-year-old harlots. But it does make it less likely that she was London's own Whore of Babylon, as Humphrey Aston would have us believe."

"My thinking, too," Justin agreed, and they left the churchyard behind, continued on toward their looming confrontation with the Astons.

A servant peered at them nervously, mumbling that Master Aston would not be available until the meal was done. Jonas pushed past him into the hall, with Justin a few steps behind. The Astons and their guests looked up from their interrupted meal in varying degrees of dismay, shock, and indignation. Humphrey was so enraged that he seemed at risk for an apoplectic seizure; his face was beet-red and sweat beaded his brow and upper lip as he excoriated them for their intrusion. Beatrice looked mortified by the uproar, Geoffrey and Daniel alarmed, the servants flustered. Master Serlo, a no-nonsense, take-charge type in his late thirties, frowned at the interlopers over his roast capon, but significantly did not add his voice to Humphrey's tirade; clearly this was a man who

knew when to fish and when to cut bait. Adela, richly
dressed in sapphire-colored silk, showed herself to be
more committed to the Astons than her uncle as she
groped for Geoffrey's hand.

"How dare you interrupt our meal?" Humphrey flung
his napkin to the floor as if it were a gauntlet, and pushed
away from the table. "We've already told you all we
know about that wretched girl's death. I'll be damned ere
I let you inconvenience or embarrass my family and
friends in my own home. My sons will answer no questions tonight. You'll have to come back on the morrow."

Justin was not surprised that Jonas seemed utterly unperturbed by this diatribe; the serjeant had faced down
men far more formidable than Humphrey Aston. "We
are not here to ask questions," he said composedly. "So
there is no reason why your supper need be ruined.
Whilst you eat, we'll conduct our search."

Humphrey made a strangled sound, much like a
squawk, and Beatrice began to sob. Geoffrey was on his
feet now, too. "What are you looking for?" he asked,
sounding bewildered, and Jonas smiled at him, so indulgently that Justin had a sudden vision of a wolf wagging
its tail.

"I cannot very well tell you, now can I, lad?" Beckoning to his men, who'd been hovering in the doorway, he
declared, "We'll take the hall. You start with the kitchen
and buttery."

"Can they do this?" Daniel turned, not to his father,
but to Master Serlo for enlightenment. "Do they have
the right?"

Thus appealed to, Master Serlo nodded tersely. "I
think it best if Adela and I depart," he said, and it was his
defection that seemed to take the heart out of Humphrey
Aston. Standing helplessly midst the wreckage of his perfect evening, he could only watch in disbelief as his
guests prepared to flee and Jonas's men to dismantle his

home. Adela was obviously a reluctant fugitive, but her murmured protests went unheeded as her uncle ushered her toward the door. Geoffrey trailed after them uncertainly, Beatrice was being fanned by a wide-eyed serving maid, and Daniel sank down upon the closest coffer, for once appearing more confused than defiant. Even the family dog was intimidated, retreating under the table to give an occasional tentative bark. Jonas was already turning toward the cupboard. Feeling like one of the Vandals who'd sacked Rome, Justin joined him.

What followed was an uncomfortable experience for all but Jonas. Humphrey fumed in silence, Beatrice moaned at the sight of strangers rooting through her belongings, the servants gaped, and the Aston sons fidgeted uneasily as Justin and Jonas searched the cupboard and then the coffers. When they finally closed the last coffer lid, an unspoken sigh of relief seemed to ripple across the hall. The reprieve was short-lived, for Jonas then announced, "We'll search the bedchambers now."

"No!" Humphrey sounded as if he were choking on his own tongue. Jonas paid him no mind, telling the sons to lead the way. Humphrey hesitated, then hastened after them as they headed back toward his shop.

The shop was closed for the night and dark, but there was an extinguished cresset lamp on a table, and after several fumbling tries, Geoffrey managed to light the wick with a candle taken from the hall. A narrow spiral stairwell in the corner led up to the family quarters: a bedchamber for Humphrey and his wife, a much smaller one shared by their sons, and up under the eaves of the roof, a tiny garret for the apprentices. The boys crept down the stairs in baffled response to Humphrey's summons, and when he ordered them to occupy themselves elsewhere for an hour, they hurriedly unlatched the door and escaped out into the street.

Humphrey swore at the sight meeting his eyes: neighbors and passersby clustered outside his shop, drawn by the commotion. For a man whose fear of scandal and disgrace was primal, this was a waking nightmare, and in his frustration, he lashed out at any available targets, first warning the curious away from his shop, then cursing at Daniel when the youth stumbled against the table and almost tipped over the lamp, and finally turning upon the absent Agnes, berating her bitterly for having brought Justin into their lives.

Daniel flushed scarlet, but Justin and Jonas ignored the harangue, heading for the stairwell. They started in Humphrey's bedchamber, a spacious room dominated by a large curtained bed, soon concluded a cursory search, and moved into the chamber shared by the Aston sons. This room was much tidier than Justin would have expected; apparently Humphrey's exacting standards carried over into every corner of his offspring's lives. There were two pallets, both carefully made up, several coffers, chamber pots and washing lavers, but nothing to reveal the personalities of the occupants. As Jonas set about searching the bedding, Justin opened the first coffer chest. It smelled pleasantly like newmown hay, for the contents had been sprinkled with sweet woodruff to disguise the more pungent odor of the herbs used to deter moths. The clothes were winter woolens, neatly folded, and the St Davydd's cross was hidden under the second garment, a moss green mantle.

Justin sat back on his heels, staring down at that small lead cross. He hadn't really expected to find it in the Aston household. After a startled moment to reflect what this meant, he said, "Jonas, over here," and their hunt moved into its next phase.

The Aston men were waiting below in the shop. "It took you long enough," Humphrey grumbled. "Now can we stop this tomfoolery and—What do you have there?"

Justin held up the green cloak. "Whose is this?"

"Mine." Daniel started to reach instinctively for the garment. "That is my winter mantle. Why?"

"He has not worn it since March." Geoffrey moved swiftly to his brother's side. "So if a witness saw someone at the churchyard in a green mantle, it could not have been Daniel. You need not take our word for it. Look at the wool, how heavy it is—"

"The mantle does not matter. It is what we found under it," Justin said and extended his hand toward the light, palm up.

Daniel's gasp was clearly audible to them all. He stared at Melangell's missing cross as if stupefied, the blood draining from his face. "I . . . I do not know how that got there . . . I swear I do not!"

"We're going to have to talk about that at the city gaol, lad," Jonas said, and Daniel started to shake. His eyes were darting about the shop and when he took a backward step, Jonas tensed, for he knew the danger signs well. But it was not Daniel who acted, it was his brother.

"Run, Daniel!" Geoffrey spun toward the table, knocking the cresset lamp onto the floor and plunging the shop into blackness. "Run!"

Chaos resulted. Jonas dived for Daniel, but he was no longer there. Justin grabbed for the boy, too, collided with Geoffrey instead. Daniel had the advantage, for he knew the layout of the shop even in the dark, and he reached the door first. As he flung it open, a glimmer of twilight illuminated the room and Jonas lunged toward the light. Again, Geoffrey got in the way, collapsing in a heap by the door with Jonas on top of him, swearing hotly. By the time he untangled himself, Daniel was gone. Shouting for his men, Jonas barreled through the door and out into the street. "Where?" he demanded. "Where did he go?" A few of the spectators shuffled their feet and averted their eyes, not wanting to deliver up a neighbor's son to the law. Most had no such qualms and a dozen fingers pointed up Friday Street. Jonas took off, with Justin at his heels and the serjeant's men strung out behind them.

Daniel was already nearing Cheapside, but when he slipped in the mud and almost fell, his pursuers gained ground. The cloud-choked sky had brought on an early dusk, but there was still enough light to make out their quarry. By now the Hue and Cry had been raised, and as men heard the English *Out* and the French *Haro*, they hurried from homes and alehouses to join in the chase. With so many eyes upon him, Daniel dared not duck into an alley, unable to seek a hiding place until he could put more distance between himself and the mob. He'd been running full-out and his chest was heaving, his eyes burning with unshed tears. By the time he reached the site of the fish market, he was at the end of his tether, his pumping legs leaden, his lungs starved for air, and his staggering pace made capture seem not only inevitable but imminent. Then he suddenly swerved to the left, into the churchyard of St Paul's Cathedral, and Jonas began to curse, long and loud.

Daniel's lead had now shrunk to a few precarious yards. Sprinting past Paul's Cross, he hit the Si Quis door with his shoulder, catapulted into the nave of the church. Vespers had already ended, but there were still parishioners present, and they gaped in amazement at this sudden invasion of God's House by shouting, swearing men. Stumbling through the doorway in the pulpitum screen, Daniel sank to his knees before the High Altar, sobbing for breath.

"Get a priest," he begged one of the startled women. By now Jonas had reached him. Shrinking back against the Altar, he stared up at the serjeant in desperate defiance. "You cannot take me," he panted. "I claim the right of sanctuary!"

9

LONDON

April 1193

Robbed of their prey, the mob crowded into the nave of the cathedral, jostling and muttering and cursing. Daniel scrambled to his feet and darted behind the High Altar, but his fears were needless. Jonas would never have allowed him to be dragged out by force, for men who violated sanctuary were sure to incur the wrath of the Holy Church. The sacristan was already on the scene, indignantly swatting at the intruders whenever one came within range. When the dean also arrived, demanding that these impious malcontents be gone straightaway or risk eternal damnation, Jonas yielded to the inevitable and ordered his men to disperse the crowd.

"There will be no violence done here," he assured the priests brusquely. "We are withdrawing." Turning, he skewered Daniel with a cold stare. "I'll have men posted outside, so if you try to bolt, you'll not get far."

Daniel raised his chin. "I am staying right here," he said, with feeble bravado that few found convincing, Jonas least of all.

"Not for long, boy," the serjeant shot back, "not for long."

Justin gave Daniel one last, probing look, then hastened to catch up with Jonas. Recognizing the other man's frustration for what it was—the disappointment of a thwarted hunter—he gave Jonas time to recover his emotional equilibrium, and then ventured a bit of wry humor. "Well . . . at least we'll know where to find him now."

The corner of Jonas's mouth twitched. "I suppose it could have been worse," he conceded. "If he'd gotten to St Martin le Grand, he could have lived out the rest of his days in sanctuary. At St Paul's, he gets forty days and then he's mine."

"Are you so sure now that he's guilty?"

"I do not get paid to cook the fish, too, just to catch them." Jonas spent the next few minutes giving instructions to his men, for it would be no easy task to keep watch over St Paul's; the cathedral precincts covered more than twelve acres. Striding back to Justin, he said, "Come on."

Justin obligingly fell in step beside him. "Where now?"

"To put the fear of God into Geoffrey Aston."

They did not have to go far. They soon saw Geoffrey and Humphrey hastening up Cheapside, following the path of the mob. They were both flushed and appeared to have been quarreling. Geoffrey quickened his stride at the sight of Jonas. "Where is Daniel? Did he get away?"

"No."

"You arrested him?"

"No."

Geoffrey looked bewildered and then horrified. "He . . . he is not dead?"

"No . . . he is in sanctuary at St Paul's."

That was an option neither Aston had anticipated and there was a moment of shocked silence, until Geoffrey blurted out, "Thank God, he is safe, then!"

Justin thought that was highly debatable, and Jonas said curtly, "You'd do better to worry about your own skin."

"Me? What did I do?" Geoffrey protested, sounding scared.

Jonas glared at him. "Your brother would not have escaped if you had not knocked over that lamp!"

"That was an accident!" Humphrey shoved in front of his son, telling Geoffrey to say nothing more. "The lad stumbled and fell against the table. It was a mishap, not deliberately done, and you cannot prove otherwise!"

Jonas had never intended to arrest Geoffrey, but he was not about to tell the Astons that. "You may be surprised by what I can prove," he said ominously and pushed past them.

Justin followed, and they moved on. Neither man was pleased with this unexpected outcome. To Jonas's way of thinking, sanctuary was not a satisfactory solution to murder. And to Justin, the case seemed even murkier now than ever. All he knew for certain was that he would be returning to Gracechurch Street that night with news sure to break a good woman's heart.

It rained again after midnight, and light, intermittent showers were still falling the next morning. The sky was grey, the air clammy and cool, and Justin's mood dampened by the memory of Agnes's tears. Dropping off Shadow at Gunter's smithy—he wasn't up to facing Nell's interrogation—he saddled Copper and headed for the Tower.

There he found the queen's household in turmoil. The Great Hall was overflowing into the stairwell, servants were buzzing about like bees at an overturned hive, the noise level was high enough to hurt sensitive ears, and Eleanor was nowhere in sight. Edging into the maelstrom, Justin began searching for a familiar face. Will Longsword and William Marshal were both at the Windsor siege, and he had no luck in tracking down Peter of Blois, the queen's chancellor. There was a sudden stir as Walter de Coutances swept through the crowd, but Justin was not about to intercept the Archbishop of Rouen and watched in frustration as the cleric was ushered into Eleanor's great chamber. The opening door gave him a glimpse of the queen, deep in discussion with a tall stately man clad in a bishop's vestments. Then the door closed, cutting off his view.

Eventually he found someone he could interrogate: Nicholas de Mydden, one of the queen's household knights. Nicholas had never been a favorite of his. The other man was too self-satisfied, too cocksure—and too familiar with Claudine. But Nicholas always knew what was going on. Justin did not even need to ask. "Have you heard?" Nicholas said as soon as he approached. "Hubert Walter is here!"

The name was vaguely familiar, and after a moment Justin was able to prod his memory into recalling that Hubert Walter was the Bishop of Salisbury, thus sparing himself the embarrassment of having to confess his ignorance to Nicholas, who was a master at the art of courteous condescension. He still didn't understand why Hubert Walter's arrival should have caused such a commotion, though, and he murmured a noncommittal "Indeed," hoping his lack of response would provoke Nicholas into revealing more.

It worked. Nicholas blinked in disappointment. "That might not be soul-stirring news to you, de Quincy, but I assure you the queen was overjoyed to get her first message from her son!"

Justin forgot about salvaging his pride. "He brought word from King Richard? How?"

Nicholas smiled complacently. "You do know that Bishop Hubert was on crusade with the king? He was in Sicily when he learned that King Richard had been captured on his way home from the Holy Land. He at once set out for Austria, where he somehow persuaded the emperor to allow him to see Richard."

"That is wonderful news! The king is well . . . he has

not sickened in captivity?" Justin asked anxiously, for he knew that must be Eleanor's greatest fear. The Duke of Austria and the Holy Roman Emperor had dared to seize a crusader-king, to defy the Church's stricture against harming those who'd gone on crusade. Would such men have qualms about maltreating their royal captive? Was Richard worth more to them alive . . . or dead?

"The bishop assured the queen that King Richard is in good health. He is being held at Trifels in Bavaria now, and is hopeful of buying his freedom. God Willing, he may soon be back on English soil!"

"God Willing," Justin echoed, no less fervently, for he would have moved heaven and earth to restore to the queen her lost son. He began to bombard Nicholas with eager questions, but it soon became apparent that the knight had no other information to impart. Whatever else Bishop Hubert had brought back from Bavaria was being shared with the queen, behind closed doors.

It was obvious that Eleanor would have no need of him today. As soon as he could politely disengage himself, he threaded his way across the hall and moved into the stairwell, where he promptly collided with Claudine.

He reached out to steady her as she stumbled. They were so close he could see the light from the overhead wall sconce reflected in her eyes and his every breath was scented with her perfume. They'd shared their first kiss in this stairwell, and in the shadowed stillness lurked memories that were better forgotten.

"Justin," she said softly, and her voice was like a caress in the dark. She tilted her face up toward his, lips parting. "You are in my way."

He almost welcomed the flash of claws, for that was safer than the purr. "Claudine, why must it be all or nothing? If not lovers, enemies? I do not want to be your enemy."

"Well," she said, "I do not want to be your friend."

She'd meant to sound mocking, sounded bitter, instead. Justin could think of nothing to say that would not be false or betraying. He stepped aside and she gave him a look he couldn't interpret, then brushed past him and continued on up the stairs.

Justin found Daniel in the parish church of St Gregory, adjoining the cathedral. Daniel was seated cross-legged on a prayer cushion, Geoffrey kneeling by his side. Their faces were intent, their voices low; Justin would have loved to eavesdrop on that confidential conversation. As he moved around the rood screen, both youths sprang to their feet. "This is still sanctuary," Daniel cried. "The priests said I can even go out into the churchyard and you cannot touch me!"

"I am not here to violate sanctuary. I want to talk with you, nothing more."

Daniel did not appear thrilled by that prospect. But for once, he had nowhere to retreat. Geoffrey glanced from one to the other, then cleared his throat. "I have to get back to the shop ere Papa misses me," he said. "I'll stop by again after Vespers." He fell silent then, gnawing his lower lip uneasily; this was the first time Justin had seen him as tongue-tied as his brother. "Here," he said finally, thrusting a small sack toward Daniel. "I brought you a pork pie from the cookshop, and a few wafers. I'll bring more tonight . . ."

"You need not worry that he'll starve, Geoffrey," Justin said. "The Church feeds all sanctuary seekers."

Geoffrey shrugged, seemed on the verge of saying more, then turned and hurried from the chancel. They listened as his footsteps receded up the nave until a slamming door told them that he'd done what Daniel could not—rejoined the world. Noticing a pile of blankets and several hemp sacks on the floor, Justin asked, "Did Geoffrey bring you those, too?"

"No . . . my aunt Agnes."

Justin did not ask if Humphrey or Beatrice had been there; why salt the boy's wounds? "Here," he said, "I brought you something, too," and unhooked a wineskin from his belt. "Wine could not possibly make your thinking any more muddled than it already is."

Daniel took the wineskin and drank deeply. "My thinking is not so muddled," he protested. "I'm not in gaol, am I?"

"Not yet." Justin retrieved the wineskin and took a swallow. "Your right of sanctuary lasts only forty days, Daniel. Then you must either stand trial if you're indicted or confess your guilt and abjure the realm, never to return. I'd not find either of those choices appealing . . . do you?"

Daniel twitched his shoulders, saying nothing, and Justin yearned to shake him until his teeth rattled and some sense returned. "How old are you?" he asked, and Daniel was surprised into giving a civil answer.

"I'll be seventeen two days after Michaelmas. Why?"

"That is too young to die, Daniel. Once before, I urged you to speak up whilst you still could. I do not want to have to make that same speech at the foot of the gallows."

"I did not kill her!" Daniel clenched his fists belligerently, but his chin quivered. "I could never have hurt her, never . . ." His voice had thickened and when Justin passed him the wineskin again, he reached for it gratefully, taking several long swigs. Justin watched him in speculative silence. The boy was hot-tempered and impulsive, for certes. He might well have killed in anger, striking out unthinkingly. Could he have killed in cold-blooded calculation? Could he have picked up that rock and brought it down upon the head of the girl lying helpless at his feet? Justin suspected that Luke would likely scoff at his sentimentality, but he did not think Daniel was capable of a crime like that.

"I want to help you, lad, if you'll let me," he said, and Daniel put down the wineskin, regarding him with suspicion and the first flickerings of hope.

"Why?"

"I do not think you killed her," Justin said, and Daniel stifled a sound that might have been a sob.

"I did not, I swear it!"

"Then help me prove it. Give me some answers, honest ones. It was plain enough that you recognized Melangell's pilgrim cross. How did it get in your coffer? Did you steal it?" Daniel shook his head in vehement denial, and Justin moved closer. "Did she give it to you, then? If so, why? And what were you quarreling about on the day she died?"

Daniel looked at him mutely, his eyes brimming. "I cannot tell you," he said haltingly. "I cannot . . ."

His earlier denials had been defiant. This one was despairing. Justin still wanted to shake the boy. But he wanted to save him, too, if he could, for he was heeding instinct now, not logic, the inner voice whispering that Daniel was not Melangell's killer.

"The serjeant Tobias sees this crime as a very simple one. Melangell was a whore and you murdered her in a fit of jealous rage. That is what he'll argue to get a jury to indict you. And as it stands now, he'll likely get the indictment." As Justin spoke, Daniel slumped down against the wall, wrapping his arms around his drawn-up knees. His face was hidden by that mop of unruly red hair, but his body's posture bespoke defeat. He did not relent, though, and Justin feared he'd take his foolhardy silence to the grave.

"But nothing is as simple as it seems," he said. "Melangell was no whore and I do not think you're a killer. Keep your secrets, Daniel. With or without your help, I shall find out the truth."

No sooner were the words out of his mouth than

Justin winced, for that promise sounded bombastic and overly dramatic in his own ears. Thank the Lord God Luke was not here to hear him spouting such nonsense, or Jesú forfend, Jonas. Leaving the wineskin to give Daniel some fleeting, dubious comfort, he turned to go. He was already at the rood screen when he heard Daniel speak. The words were slurred and the boy's voice was so low he could not be sure he'd heard correctly. But it sounded as if Daniel Aston was thanking him.

Justin waited until early evening, when Godwin would be back from his rounds. He'd waited too long, though, for his arrival interrupted the supper being served by the landlord's wife to her family and lodgers. Algar, the landlord, welcomed Justin with enthusiasm, and the other tenants showed more interest in gawking at Justin than in eating the thick pottage of onions and cabbage being ladled out into their bowls, proof that murder could be highly entertaining—for those not related to the victim. Godwin was clearly uncomfortable with his new notoriety; the lessons of a lifetime had taught him the value of protective coloring, the danger inherent in calling undue attention to himself. Deciding that it was better to take Godwin away from his supper than to blurt out his news in front of this eager audience, Justin asked if they could talk in private. Algar looked dismayed at being cheated of such choice gossip, but he grudgingly agreed that they could meet in the kitchen.

Godwin got slowly to his feet. He seemed to be favoring his left leg, but he brushed off Justin's query and limped toward the kitchen. Justin followed, and within moments, so did Cati, who'd tarried long enough to stuff a chunk of rye bread into her sleeve; she'd had too much experience with hunger ever to leave a meal uneaten. Godwin leaned back against a barrel in which river eels swam, studying Justin with hollowed dark eyes. "Why are you here?"

Justin was not surprised that neither Jonas nor Tobias had sought out Godwin; keeping the peddler informed would be a low priority. "Your daughter's pilgrim cross has been found . . . hidden away in a coffer belonging to Daniel Aston."

Daniel's name clearly meant nothing to Godwin. Just as clearly, it did to Cati, whose mouth dropped open. The peddler frowned. "Did this man kill my girl?"

"He says not, and I am inclined to believe him. But I'll not lie to you. He is the prime suspect at present and did not help his cause any when he fled into sanctuary at St Paul's."

Godwin seemed overwhelmed by the news. "Who is he? My daughter's lover?" He looked even more baffled when Justin shook his head. "What was he to Melangell, then? Why do you think him innocent?"

"They were friends," Cati said in a small voice. "She liked Daniel well . . ."

"He is young and scared," Justin said, "and unfortunately for him, he has all the makings of a right fine scapegoat. I cannot swear to you that he is innocent, but I am not yet convinced that he is guilty."

"I do not think he'd hurt Melangell," Cati interjected, but she sounded more shaken than certain. She'd not expected the killer to be someone she knew, someone she'd trusted. It seemed doubly cruel to Justin that the churchyard killing should take from her both her sister and the last of her innocence.

Godwin shifted against the barrel, trying to take some of the weight off his leg. "Then the only evidence they have against this boy is the St Davydd's cross? That is a weak scaffolding to build a gallows on."

"I agree," Justin said, surprised that the other man seemed willing to give Daniel the benefit of the doubt.

After a moment to reflect, though, he decided it wasn't so surprising, after all. The peddler's suspicions of authority would make it easy to believe in conspiracies and miscarriages of justice, especially when the poor and downtrodden were the fish swept up into the legal nets. But his speculation about Godwin had not blinded him to Cati's discomfort whenever the St Davydd's cross was mentioned. More and more he was convinced she knew something of significance about that pilgrim pledge. There was no point in asking her in front of her father; he'd have to find a way to speak to her alone. Yet even if he could break through her defenses and get her to reveal her secret, would it be enough to clear Daniel?

"I will continue to investigate," he promised them. Neither Godwin nor Cati appeared to take much comfort from a stranger's assurance. Godwin grunted, then asked when he could recover the St Davydd's cross, and looked skeptical when Justin explained that it was evidence and must be held until Daniel either stood trial or abjured the realm. "I'll not keep you from your supper," Justin said, turning to go, and then remembering. "Godwin, how is your mule faring?"

"Dead," Godwin said tersely, and it seemed to Justin that he'd managed to compress an entire lifetime's misfortunes into that one laconic answer.

Justin kept his word, and in the days that followed he continued to probe the circumstances of Melangell's death. He talked again to Daniel, and while the boy was no longer sullen or even suspicious, he still refused to give Justin the answers he needed. Another visit to the Aston household was equally unproductive. Beatrice had taken to her bed and Humphrey seemed to think that if he ignored his son's plight, it would somehow resolve itself, for he adamantly refused to discuss Daniel with his neighbors and customers and even his family. This last bit of information had come from Geoffrey, whose composure was shredding like cabbage in the wake of Daniel's flight into sanctuary. Justin had grown up with the foundling's forlorn yearning for family, and he envied the Aston brothers, bonded both by blood and choice. Geoffrey was insistent in his protestations of Daniel's innocence, but unfortunately he could offer Justin nothing beside his testament of trust.

Ranging further afield, Justin questioned the shop-keepers and residents of Milk Street, all who lived or worked in the vicinity of St Mary Magdalene's. The wheelwright and his son confirmed what they'd told To-bias, that they'd seen Daniel and Melangell arguing hotly on the day of her death. Geoffrey's churchyard trysts with Melangell were known throughout the neighbor-hood, but related with a wink and a nudge, for few ob-jected to the sowing of wild oats in the spring. The elderly widow who cooked for the parish priest thought she'd heard raised voices coming from the churchyard, but she was so suggestible and eager to please that Justin could not be sure if this was a true memory or one culled from her imagination. But no one claimed to have heard any screams and no one reported seeing anything out of the ordinary that night. If there were witnesses able to shed any light upon Melangell's death, Justin could not find them.

He had no better luck unearthing alternative theories of the killing. The scant evidence argued against a stranger's guilt, suggested someone Melangell had known. If not Daniel, who? Why was he refusing to reveal why he'd been quarreling with Melangell? If he was not guilty, then who was he trying to protect? Geoffrey seemed the logical candidate. But Geoffrey had no motive for mur-dering Melangell. A dalliance with a peddler's daughter was too common an occurrence to jeopardize his marital prospects. In a world in which blood and class were paramount, a girl who was lowborn and dirt-poor and part Welsh and judged—fairly or not—to be a wanton could not hope to compete with a rival like Adela. The only way the marriage could have been put at risk would have been if he'd fallen madly in love with Melangell, so besotted and bedazzled that he was willing to defy his father and jettison his bright future for a precarious life on the road. And since there was no evidence whatsoever that Geoffrey had lost either his heart or his senses, that eliminated Humphrey, too, as a suspect. As much as Justin disliked him, he could not see the mercer murdering for the sport of it. As long as Melangell was no threat to the marital alliance with Master Serlo's niece, Humphrey would not care that his son was bedding her.

So who killed Melangell? Despite Luke's cynical suggestion, Justin could not cast Godwin in the role of avenger. The man was too beaten down by his losses, by life itself. Harshly put, the honour of a peddler's daughter was not worth killing over, not in their world. Justin could as easily envision Adela skulking into the churchyard and bloodying those pampered hands in an utterly unnecessary murder. No, he could come up with no other satisfactory suspects. If it was true that all roads led to Rome, all suspicions seemed to lead back to Daniel Aston. So why did it feel so wrong?

Eleanor was a creature of the night, an anomaly in an age in which people rose at first light and usually bedded down at dark. But she could afford to follow her inclinations; queens were indifferent to the cost of candles and lamp oil. She was not tyrannical by nature, though, and rarely insisted that her attendants remain awake to keep her company. To a woman whose seventy years had been lived out on center stage, these quiet nocturnal hours offered her the most precious of all luxuries: solitude. Now she paced the confines of her great chamber, oblivious of the sleeping forms on pallets near her bed, occasionally depositing an absentminded pat upon the silken head of her favorite greyhound. At last she heard the sound she'd been awaiting, a light, discreet knock. Opening the door, she said softly, "Thank you, Gerard, for fetching him. Have him enter."

Justin looked as if he'd been roused from his bed; his black hair was tousled and his eyes were sleep-shadowed. Even half awake, his manners had not deserted him, and he hastily knelt, kissing her hand. He asked no questions, nor did he show any resentment at being summoned in the middle of the night; those who served the queen were never off-duty.

"Take care," she cautioned, "lest you awaken my ladies. Get that lamp and follow me into the chapel."

Justin did as bade, although when he passed Claudine's pallet, his step slowed. Her dark hair was loosely braided in a night plait, trailing over the edge of the bed; a bared shoulder showed above the sheet, a hand clenched into a small fist, as if her dreams were troubled. Eleanor was watching from the door, her expression both indulgent and ironic. Flushing slightly, Justin hastened to join her.

Lights still burned on the High Altar and the air was scented with incense. There were no seats, of course, for worshippers were expected to kneel upon prayer cushions, but there was a small wooden bench under one of the windows and Eleanor headed toward it, beckoning Justin to follow. He hesitated, for it seemed presumptuous to sit side by side with his queen, but Eleanor gestured impatiently and he quickly complied.

Neither spoke for several moments. Justin was trying not to stare at the queen, for this was the first time he'd seen her without a veil or wimple. Her hair was coiled at the nape of her neck, shone silver in the moonlight. He found himself wondering what color it had been in her youth. He wondered, too, why she'd sent for him at such an hour, but he was in no hurry to find out; a midnight summons was by its very nature ominous.

"I suppose you know by now of Hubert Walter's return to England."

Justin nodded. "I do, Madame. I was greatly gladdened to hear that the king may soon be able to ransom himself."

Eleanor exhaled a breath, soft as a sigh. "I know that is the talk at court. I fear such optimism may be premature at best, ill founded at worst. Richard's subjects must believe that he will soon be free, back amongst us. We have no guarantees, though, that it will come to pass. The emperor, weasel that he is, is still equivocating, still refusing to commit himself, one way or another. He has indicated he'd be willing to release my son—for a high enough ransom. But he has yet to grant Richard an audience, and I have been warned that he continues to heed the agents of the French king. I need not tell you, Justin, that Philip would barter his very soul for a chance to do Richard harm."

As would John, Justin thought grimly. "I am honoured, Madame, by your confidences. I will never betray them."

Her smile was warmer than usual, almost fond. "I know that, Justin. I do not give my trust lightly or easily, but you have earned it. You did me a great service when you brought me that letter revealing my son's plight, and then again when you cleared my other son of complicity in the killing. And we might not have been able to thwart a French invasion if you'd not intercepted John's man at Winchester, giving us the time we needed to safeguard our ports. You have risked your life for me more than once. I need you now to put it at risk again."

Justin instinctively squared his shoulders. "What would you have me do, Madame?"

"You must find a way to get into Windsor Castle and deliver two secret messages, one to my son and one to Durand."

Justin said nothing, but his face revealed the extent of his dismay. Eleanor leaned over, rested a hand on his arm. "You have proven yourself to be courageous and resourceful in the past. I know it will not be easy, nor will it be safe. I know, too, that you will not fail me."

Justin thought that would make a fine epitaph. Never had he balked at doing the queen's bidding, but he'd sooner leap into a pit full of snakes than take his chances with John and Durand. What could he say, though? He could not tell the queen that John put no value on other men's lives. Even if she knew it, it could never be said. Nor could he confide that Durand bore him such a lethal grudge. Loyalty made that first admission impossible, pride the second. He found his mouth had gone dry, and he yearned suddenly for a swig from the wineskin he'd left with Daniel. "Are these messages to be written, Madame, or verbal?"

"I cannot put them in writing, lest they fall into the wrong hands. But first I would tell you why this is so important. Under the circumstances, you are entitled to know. Hubert Walter told me that if we hope to buy my son's freedom, we must raise the sum of one hundred thousand marks."

Justin gasped, for that was a vast amount, indeed. It was well known that King Richard had emptied the Exchequer to pay for his crusade; how could the queen hope to come up with so much money? And yet he did not doubt that she would; to save her favorite son, she would pawn the realm to the Devil himself if need be.

"I see you appreciate the magnitude of our task," Eleanor said dryly. "We have estimated that it will take a quarter year's income from every man of property. To raise such levies, we must have peace throughout the

kingdom. Therefore, we must come to terms with my
son John, and as soon as possible. As long as he holds
out at Windsor, the country remains in turmoil. But if we
take Windsor by force, we must deal with him as a rebel
and few of the justiciars have the stomach for that."

Justin marveled that she could sound so matter-of-fact
and dispassionate; this rebel was still of her flesh, born of
her womb. "So you hope to persuade Lord John to surrender of his own will?"

"Yes," she said. "We have offered a truce, contingent
upon the surrender of his castles into my keeping, to be
returned to him if Richard is not freed. He spurned the
offer even though his position at Windsor grows more
precarious by the day. I fear he has the bit between his
teeth and means to make this as difficult as possible for
all of us. I want you to sweeten the brew, Justin, to give
him my secret assurances that he need not yield up his
castles at Nottingham and Tickhill, that we will be con-
tent with the surrender of Windsor, Wallingford, and the
Peak."

"Why 'secret assurances,' Madame? Why not just deliver the new terms under a flag of truce?"

She smiled faintly, without any humor whatsoever. "My
son is of a suspicious nature, Justin. He thrives upon conspiracies and intrigues as naturally as other men breathe. If
he believes that I am acting without the knowledge of the
justiciars, he will see opportunity there for sowing dissen-
sion. John has never been able to resist fishing in troubled
waters."

Justin thought that was an accurate appraisal of John's
character, if remarkably unsentimental coming from the
man's mother. And John might well take the bait. "What
am I to tell Durand, my lady?"

"Tell him that he is to do all in his power to persuade
John to accept my offer. He must convince John that it is

in his best interest to agree to a truce, to end this outright rebellion."

Justin was not sanguine about Durand's prospects; to talk John into doing something he was not inclined to do, Merlin would be needed. But Eleanor had not asked for his opinion. He started to speak, then saw that she was not done. "Madame?" he prompted gently. "Is there more?"

"Yes . . . there is more. If John will not surrender and the castle falls, tell Durand that he is to keep close to my son at all times. He will understand."

Justin was not sure that he did. "But surely none would harm Lord John, Madame? Rebel or not, he is still a king's son, your son."

"Have you ever been in a siege, Justin?"

"No, my lady, I have not."

"When a castle falls, there is utter confusion and chaos. Midst the smoke and fighting and looting, who is to say if a man dies by mischance or murder?"

"But King Richard has no son of his own. Many see Lord John as his heir. It would be like . . . like killing a future king, my lady!"

"Exactly," she said, and Justin was quiet for a moment, embarrassed by the innocence of his protest. If there were men who'd kill for a pittance or a whore's smile, why would there not be men to kill for a crown? Men who wanted to see Richard's nephew Arthur succeed him, others who wanted anyone but the king's brother. John must have more enemies than Rome had priests, Justin thought bleakly. As for himself, he had only two—and they'd be awaiting him at Windsor Castle.

10

WINDSOR CASTLE

April 1193

Windsor Castle looked at first glance as if it could hold out until Judgment Day. It was as vast as it was formidable: a stone shell keep, two large baileys, more than a dozen rectangular towers, and walls faced with heath stone encompassing more than thirteen acres. A closer inspection revealed the vulnerabilities of the riverside fortress: chunks gouged out of the walls by the powerful mangonels of the besieging army, ploughed-up earth and pits in the baileys where the heavy stones had come crashing down, burned-out shells of wooden buildings ignited by flaming arrows. Plumes of smoke billowed up into the sky and the air was laden with so much dust that the castle seemed to shimmer in a haze of heat and soot. Cinders swirled on the wind, glowing embers drifting down like a hellish rain, imperiling defenders and attackers alike. Justin reined in, mesmerized by this compelling, horrific scene. All that was lacking was the acrid odor of brimstone.

The closest villages—Windlesora and New Windsor— were deserted, their unlucky inhabitants long since fled. But the army encampment was like a town of sorts, for it was crowded with soldiers, peddlers, and the inevitable prostitutes. A siege could be as tedious as it was dangerous, for it could drag on for weeks, even months; sometimes only the threat of starvation would induce a trapped garrison to surrender. Windsor's siege had not lasted long enough to dishearten the attackers and there was a mood of expectancy in the camp.

It was soon evident that an assault was in the works, for well out of arrow range, carpenters were busy erecting a belfry. Justin stopped to watch, never having seen one before. The tower would be huge when completed, several storeys high, tall enough to top the castle walls. Loitering soldiers were more than happy to show off their battle lore, answering Justin's curious questions readily. The belfry was wheeled, they told him, moved along by men inside using iron bars or else by oxen, whose traces were run through pulleys attached to stakes, so that as they pulled away from the castle, the belfry moved toward it. Once the wall was reached, a drawbridge was lowered onto it from the top storey of the belfry and the assault was on. When Justin asked how they kept the defenders from setting fire to the belfry, they explained that hides soaked in vinegar or urine would be nailed to the outsides of the structure, but when he asked if that worked, they laughed and said the poor souls inside hoped so, by God. Justin thought it would have been very interesting to see a belfry in action. Not here, though, not now, not if he could help it.

The large siege engines known as mangonels were in operation, catapulting heavy rocks against the castle walls. There was a loud thud as a load hit its target, sending dust and rubble flying. The soldiers manning the mangonel cheered and immediately set about winching the beam down to reload. Within moments, a mangonel from within the castle returned fire, and rocks rained into the army encampment. Men scattered, and Justin had some difficulty in calming his stallion. Dismounting, he led Copper deeper into the camp and began his search for William Marshal and Will Longsword.

He eventually found them supervising the construction of a battering ram. It looked to Justin's eye to be a

tree trunk, one of the largest he'd ever seen, being fitted
with an iron cap. Nearby a wheeled, wooden, shedlike
structure was almost completed; when done, the battering ram would be suspended inside it on chains, swung
back and forth until it gained enough momentum to
smash into the castle gatehouse door. If John did not surrender soon, that choice would be taken away from him.

"What are you doing here, lad?" Will's smile was
quizzical, but welcoming, too, confirming Justin's hunch
that he had a friend at court in John's half-brother. "I assume you're not here to fight since you're not wearing
your hauberk?"

"No . . . not to fight," Justin agreed, not wanting to
admit that he did not own a hauberk; chain-mail armor
was a luxury he'd never been able to afford. "If I may
speak with you in private, my lords . . . ?"

William Marshal had given Justin a greeting that was
civil but preoccupied. At that, though, he turned to study
the younger man and then nodded, for both he and Will
knew that if the voice was Justin's, the words were those
of their queen. Moving away from the battering ram, he
gestured for Justin to follow. "Well?" he said, sounding
somewhat wary. "What are the queen's wishes?"

"I face a daunting task, my lords, one that I cannot
hope to accomplish without your aid." Justin was choosing his words with care. He'd been given permission to
confide in these men, but only partially. "The queen has
a spy amongst Lord John's men." Neither man showed
any surprise, a commentary both upon the royal court
and the woman who reigned in her son's stead. "I must
get a message to him from the Queen's Grace. Can you
help me do that?"

Marshal smiled thinly. "Why not ask me to do something easy, lad . . . like teaching you how to walk on
water?"

"Well . . . since the castle ditches are dry, that would

not be of much use," Justin said wryly. "I know what I ask, but this matters greatly to the queen. She wants to end this siege quickly . . . and peacefully, my lords."

"So do we all," Will asserted. "I'm sure we can find a way to get you inside once we put our minds to it."

Marshal did not look nearly as confident of that. "It is your neck," he said succinctly. "Come by my tent tonight and we'll talk."

Justin thanked them both and was turning away when Will called him back. "You might want to stop by the surgeon's tent," he suggested. "Your friend is there . . . the under-sheriff from Hampshire."

Will had decided he ought to show Justin how to find the surgeon's tent, and as they walked through the camp, he explained how Luke had injured himself. ". . . Cut whilst trying to keep two fools from killing each other over a whore's favors. I do not think he was badly hurt, for he was more interested in throttling the culprit than in getting the wound tended to!"

Will laughed, but as they approached the tent, his step slowed. "I offered to take you for a reason of my own," he admitted. "I need to know more about the queen's message to this spy of hers. Does this mean what I think . . . that she is trying to convince John to surrender?"

Justin's hesitation was brief. Deciding that Will was entitled to know—he was one of the few who genuinely cared about John's safety—he nodded, and had his decision validated by the look of relief that crossed the other man's face. Will smiled, clapped him on the shoulder, pointed, and left him to continue on his own.

He heard Luke's voice even before he ducked under the tent flap, sounding more irate than aggrieved. Justin assumed the unseen object of his wrath was the surgeon, and as he entered, he found that was indeed the case.

Luke was objecting so vociferously that he was drowning out the surgeon's side of the argument, and Justin's entrance went unnoticed. He watched, amused, for several moments, and when Luke finally paused for breath, he said to the surgeon, "It sounds as if he needs a gag as well as a bandage."

Luke swung around with a startled oath. "Christ on the Cross!"

The surgeon took advantage of the interruption to explain that honey and salt were very effective in cleansing a wound, and Luke grudgingly agreed to submit to the treatment, albeit with poor grace. As soon as his arm was wrapped in linen, he made a hasty escape, muttering to Justin as they exited the tent, "Jesú, but I loathe leeches! Once they get hold of a man, he might as well send for the priest and pick out his plot. So . . . why are you here? Was life getting too tame for you back in London?"

"I began to worry that you'd get yourself into trouble if I were not around to watch over you . . . and of course you did."

Luke looked down ruefully at his bandaged arm. "If I had it to do over, I'd have let those louts slice each other up like sausage. Seriously, de Quincy, what has brought you to Windsor? Surely the queen does not need you to spy on John . . . it is not as if he is going anywhere!"

"The queen has bidden me to get two secret messages into the castle . . . one to John, one to a knight in his household."

"Is that all? You do not have to set off on your own for Austria to free the king?" Luke laughed, but stopped abruptly when he looked more closely at Justin's profile. "You are not serious?"

"Yes," Justin said, "I am."

"The queen's spy . . . would that be the same friendly fellow who communicates with you by throwing daggers at your head?"

"The very one."

Luke whistled softly. After a brief silence, he said, "Ere you left London, did you see a lawyer about making a will?"

Justin was in no mood to appreciate Luke's gallows humor. He made an effort to respond in kind, though, was starting to quip that he'd even picked out a tombstone, when he glanced over, saw that the deputy was not joking. Luke had been in deadly earnest.

William Marshal's tent was sparsely furnished. He was a soldier first, a courtier second, and had only scorn for those who went off to war with all the comforts of home. The meal he offered up to Will, Justin, and Luke was plain fare, too, salted herring and round loaves of bread marked with God's Cross and spiced wafers. The wine was excellent, though, and was poured freely as the evening advanced and the men sought in vain to resolve Justin's dilemma.

"At the start of the siege, they made a few sallies out of a postern door to harry our men, but they've not ventured out in more than a week. Even if they try another foray, there'd be no way to sneak in through the postern. It is too well guarded." Will paused to drink, then looked over at Justin with a regretful shrug. "That road leads nowhere, lad."

So had all of the other proposals bandied around that night. Justin had been shy about offering suggestions of his own, for he had no battle experience to draw upon. But reticence was a luxury he could no longer afford. "My lords . . . I do not know if this would work, but if there was an exchange of wounded and dead, mayhap I could be one of them . . . ?" He read their silence as rejection and said, "I suppose that was a daft idea . . ."

"No, lad, actually it was a good one." Marshall smiled approvingly at Justin. "But for it to work, we'd have to take one of their baileys first. Right now we have no bodies to barter—all their dead and wounded are still within the castle. I know, though, of a siege where a similar ruse was played, with great success . . ."

Memories were soon flowing as generously as the wine. William Marshal had passed most of his life in the saddle, sword in hand. He'd saved Queen Eleanor from an ambush by rebellious barons when not much older than Justin, had gained renown both in the brutal mêlées of the tourney and in the skirmishing and sieges of the Great Rebellion, the internecine civil war between Henry II and his sons. He'd gone on crusade to honour a promise to Eleanor's dying son, where his exploits almost rivaled the tales told of Eleanor's most celebrated son, the Lionheart. He'd known war in all its guises, and as the oil lamp sputtered and the hours ebbed away, he exercised a soldier's bittersweet prerogative, talking of bygone battles and slain comrades, sharing those stories that had been swapped around army campfires since time immemorial.

He told them of his sojourn in the Holy Land and the constant turmoil in the Marches, and then he and Will began to trade legendary tales of sieges gone wrong. They told Luke and Justin of entire garrisons put to the sword when they refused to surrender, of treacherous guards bribed to let the enemy into their besieged cities, and accounts of suffering so great they had passed into myth. The Siege of Antioch, where the starving defenders were reduced to eating mice, thistles, dead horses, and, finally, corpses. The Siege of Xerigordon, where thirst became so extreme that the desperate men drank the blood of horses and their own urine.

There was an undeniably macabre fascination in such grisly stories. Justin found his attention wandering, though, for it was difficult to concentrate upon past sieges when the present one was looming so large in his thoughts. How in God's Name was he going to keep faith with the queen? Clearly he was on his own, and that was not a comforting realization. He was taken by surprise, then, when William Marshal suddenly said briskly, "Well, back to the matter at hand. How do we get young de Quincy into the castle, preferably alive?"

"I guess that rules out sending him over the walls with one of the mangonels," Luke said with a grin. "I'll own up that I know more about chasing down outlaws and felons than battlefield stratagems. But it has been my experience that even the most diligent guards can be distracted. I remember an incident a few years ago in Winchester, when two whores got into a cat-fight at the St Giles Fair, shrieking and pulling hair and ripping clothes off and drawing quite a crowd, as you'd expect. And whilst they put on that highly entertaining performance, their accomplices were filching money pouches and robbing untended booths and stalls. Now I suppose it would take more than a couple of brawling harlots, but surely we can come up with something equally dramatic?"

"That would be the easy part," Marshal pointed out. "Getting him over the wall is the trick."

Justin had been sprawled out on the floor of the tent, nursing the last of his wine. At that, he sat up. "Can it be done, my lord?"

Marshal regarded him pensively. "Yes," he said at last. "But you'd be taking a great risk."

Justin already knew that. "How do we do it?"

"We wait till dark, preferably on an overcast night. We decide what section of the wall seems most vulnerable. The upper bailey has far too many towers, but there are stretches of the lower bailey where a man might approach undetected. A scaling ladder could get you over the wall, provided that no sharp-eyed guard happened by at the wrong time. We could improve the odds for you by feigning an attack upon the gatehouse. Night assaults are rare and would be sure to cause considerable confusion. Midst all that chaos, you might possibly get away with it, but you'd need a lot of luck."

Will cleared his throat. "One of our scouts reported to me that the guards do not regularly patrol the north side of the lower bailey. Whether they are short-handed or think the approach is too steep or are just lazy, I cannot say, but my man claims it is not as well guarded as other sections of the wall." He glanced toward William Marshal, then away. "I did not mention it until now," he said, sounding both defensive and defiant, "because I hoped it would not come to an outright assault."

An awkward silence followed. Will was clearly embarrassed and the other men were sympathetic to his predicament. Civil wars were cruel by their very nature, rending families and setting brother against brother, father against son. Justin finished the last of his wine, remembering something Will had once said, that John had grown to manhood with his three elder brothers in rebellion against their father. In rebelling against his brother now, was he merely following in their footsteps? Was Richard reaping what he had sown? Thinking suddenly of his own father, thinking, too, of Humphrey Aston and his sons, he found himself wondering why some families were like poorly defended castles, offering meagre protection against a hostile world. The queen's army might be able to take Windsor Castle by force if it came to that, but her own family was far more vulnerable to attack.

Setting down his wine cup, Justin thanked Will for that belated revelation. He did not fault the other man for wanting to protect John. Will was a good and decent man, capable of being loyal to the Crown and loyal, too, to his brother. And John? Where did his loyalties lie? Even more troubling to Justin was the ambiguous issue of Durand's loyalties. Was Eleanor's trust justified? Could a wolf ever be truly tamed? He had no answers to those questions, not yet. They would be found only within the walls of Windsor Castle.

The next few nights were disappointing, for the sky was cloudless, spangled with stars. Justin passed the time watching the assault preparations go forward. The belfry was almost completed, and work had begun on a bore. The battering ram was already done, sheltered behind a hastily erected stockade fence. The day of reckoning was not far off.

Until then, though, the siege continued, the mangonels pounding away at the castle walls, bowmen watching for flesh-and-blood targets, the castle defenders shouting defiance from the battlements. One man was particularly irksome, for after a mangonel had launched a load of rocks toward the castle, he would lean over the embrasure and ostentatiously dust off the wall. The bowmen spent much of their time trying to puncture his bravado, but to no avail. Both sides resorted to fire arrows, winding tow saturated with pitch around the shafts, and the castle soldiers made effective use of a ballista, a large crossbowlike weapon that fired bolts as well as arrows. Justin saw a bolt strike one of the cooks in the stomach; he died in agony.

It was an incongruous mixture, monotony relieved only by sudden spurts of violence, and Justin marveled that there was not more brawling in the camp. But William Marshal demanded that his commanders keep their men on a tight rein, and so far there had been only one killing. A soldier had been stabbed when he found a man rifling through his bedroll. Marshal promptly hanged the culprit from one of the mangonels and that seemed to have a salutary effect upon others tempted toward thievery or feuding.

On the third night, the moon was haloed, and the men knew that was a reliable sign of coming rain. It arrived

the following afternoon, a drenching storm. Looking up
at the cloud canopy over their heads, Marshal nodded in
satisfaction. "Tonight," he told Justin, "you'll go in."

It was agreed that Justin would attempt to scale the
wall in the third hour past midnight. Once Marshal
thought he'd had enough time to get onto the battlements, he'd launch his diversion, a loud, noisy raid upon
the gatehouse. The timing had to be almost perfect. Too
soon and Justin would find the walls swarming with
alarmed, sleepy men; too late and he risked attracting the
attention of the sentries. Following a somber supper with
Will and William Marshal, Justin retired to Luke's tent
to get some sleep.

After tossing and turning and dozing uneasily for hours,
Justin gave up and quietly exited the tent. The air was
chilly, the sky swathed in clouds, and light, patchy fog
had drifted in, giving the sleeping camp an eerie, ghostly
appearance. The weather could not have been better for
his purposes, but he was too tired and too edgy to take
pleasure in it. Moving between blanketed bodies, he sat
down beside a smoldering campfire and stirred the dying
flames back to life.

The camp was still but not silent. Sounds carried on
the damp night air: snoring, the crackling of the flames,
the jangling of harness and bit as a scout rode in, the low-
voiced queries of sentries, somewhere in the distance a
barking dog. Gazing into the fire, Justin started when a
hand touched his shoulder, then moved over to make
room for Luke.

"I could not sleep either," the deputy confided. "The
waiting is always the worst. What do you think Purga-
tory is like . . . flames and serpents and suffering? I see it
as a place where people just sit . . . and wait."

Luke's commentary had drawn groggy curses from
men sleeping around the fire, and they rose, began to
walk. "God must truly love you, de Quincy," Luke ob-

served. "Not only did you get your clouds, but fog, too! With luck like that, remind me never to shoot dice with you."

"A pity we do not have a trumpet," Justin said, smiling at Luke's puzzlement over that apparent non sequitur. "I was remembering that Joshua took down the walls of Jericho with a few blasts from his trumpets. That surely sounds better than fooling around in the dark with scaling ladders!"

"I do not know about that. I've had a lot of fun over the years fooling around in the dark," Luke said with a grin, "although never on a ladder! We'd best head back toward the tent, for Marshal ought to be sending a man to fetch us soon. If you need to write a letter, de Quincy, I can get parchment and pen and ink from one of the priests."

"You're bound and determined to make sure I do not die without a will, aren't you?" Justin laughed softly. "I've already taken care of it, and in truth, Luke, it was a humbling experience to realize how little I had to bestow! I told Nell that I wanted Gunter to have my stallion. He saved my life, after all."

"What about me? Hellfire, de Quincy, you did not leave me that mangy dog of yours?"

Justin grinned. "No, he goes to Lucy . . . and Nell had a few choice words about that bequest!"

"I daresay she did, and none of them bear repeating," Luke joked. "When I suggested the parchment, I was not thinking about a will. I thought you might want to leave a letter for Claudine."

Justin's smile splintered. "No."

"Are you sure? Whether you'll admit it or not, you're besotted with the woman—"

"Let it be, Luke!"

"Why? Think about Claudine. If you die in this lunatic quest, it might comfort her to have a letter—"

"She'll have John to comfort her!"

Luke stared at him, but the only light came from a campfire some yards away. "Are you saying what I think you are? Claudine is John's woman?"

Justin's revelation had been involuntary. But it was out in the open now and there was no going back. "She is John's spy," he said tiredly. "That I know for a certainty. The other is conjecture."

"Jesus God . . ." Luke was rarely at a loss for words, but this was definitely one of those times. "I do not know what to say," he confessed. "Aldith would say it serves me right for meddling. I am sorry, de Quincy, truly I am."

Justin shrugged. "Now that you mention Aldith, I might as well say what is on my mind, too. Why are you here at Windsor, Luke, when you ought to be back in Winchester with Aldith?"

"That is none of your concern!"

"But Claudine was *your* concern?"

Luke swore. "I did not go home because I knew we'd quarrel again. Aldith does not understand why I am loath to set the date for our wedding."

"Neither do I. You told me you wanted to marry her as soon as the banns could be posted."

"I do want to marry her!"

There was a raw sincerity beneath the anger in Luke's voice. Justin believed him. "So why then . . ." he began and then drew a sharp breath, suddenly comprehending. "Is it the sheriff?"

Luke nodded. "He does not think Aldith is a fit wife for his under-sheriff. He has enlisted the Bishop of Winchester to show me the folly of such a union. They cared not that I was bedding her, but they were horrified to learn I meant to marry her and they have made it very clear that this marriage could cost me dearly."

Justin wondered why he hadn't seen it sooner. Aldith was not gentry like Luke, but a poor potter's daughter with a dubious past, for she'd lived openly as another man's mistress before taking up with Luke. In their world, people were supposed to know their place; it was only to be expected that the sheriff's wife would shrink from having to socialize with Aldith. "What are you going to do, Luke?"

"Damned if I know. I suppose I can hope that the sheriff falls out of favor with the queen and gets replaced. Or I might get lucky and catch him in some wrongdoing," Luke said, only half joking. "The whoreson is as greedy as he is sanctimonious and one of these days I might find him with his hand in the honey pot."

"I think you ought to tell Aldith what is really going on."

"Are you daft? How do I tell her that she is unworthy to be my wife?"

"Is it better for her to think you love her not?"

Luke cursed again, helplessly, and then they both swung around as footsteps sounded behind them. Justin's pulse speeded up as he recognized one of William Marshal's men. "My lord Marshal says it is time."

With Will's "Godspeed" echoing in their ears, Luke and Justin began a cautious, circuitous approach toward the north side of the castle's lower bailey. It was slow going, for they dared not use a lantern. It had occurred to them both that they might become disoriented in the darkness and they were relieved to see a wooden palisade up ahead. The western wall of the lower bailey was the only section that had not been replaced by stone, and it served as a useful landmark, assuring them that they had not gone astray.

The fog was thickening, for they were closer to the river, and the ground was rising. Despite the damp chill, they were soon soaked in sweat, biting back oaths as they struggled to find secure footing on the muddied slope.

They now discovered that they had a new peril to cope with. Luke was startled when Justin suddenly grabbed his arm, pointing downward. The deputy flinched, for he'd been about to step upon a caltrop. This was a particularly nasty device for disabling horses, a ball with iron spikes, set so that one was always protruding upward. The slope was strewn with these insidious snares and they began to feel as if they were treading water, so slowly were they advancing. How much time did they have left until Marshal launched his attack?

At last, though, the stone wall of the bailey loomed up out of the fog. They paused to catch their breath and to share a moment of labored triumph. They could detect no movement on the walls. With a brief, heartfelt prayer that Will's scout had been right, Justin gestured and they crept forward. Luke had been carrying the scaling ladder. It was made of wood, hinged to fold in two, with spikes at the end to pierce the earth and hold it steady. It would not reach all the way, and Justin had a hemp ladder to get him to the top of the wall, fitted with hooks to grip the embrasure. It had all seemed possible, even plausible, in the security of Marshal's tent. Out here in this fog-shrouded landscape, his nerves as tautly drawn as that hemp rope, Justin found himself agreeing with Luke's assessment—a lunatic quest.

"Are you ready?" Luke whispered. When Justin nodded, he seemed to want to say more, finally settling for "Do not fall off the ladder."

"If I do, I'm likely to land on you." The fog was swirling around the castle battlements; gazing upward, Justin thought it looked as if Windsor were crowned in clouds. He loosened the sword in his scabbard, slung the hemp ladder over his shoulder, and began to climb. When he was about to run out of rungs, he braced himself with his left arm, aiming for the embrasure above his head. The hooks caught on his third try, but the sound of iron scraping stone seemed loud enough to reverberate throughout the entire castle. Justin waited, scarcely breathing as he watched for faces to appear at the embrasure. After an eternity or two, he tugged on the ladder and when it held, he slowly and laboriously ascended the remaining feet. Once he was close enough, he reached out, pulling himself up and into the embrasure.

Panting, he leaned against the merlon, his hand gripping the hilt of his sword. But no footsteps echoed on the wall walkway, no shouts of alarm disturbed the silence blanketing the bailey. Pulling up the hemp ladder, Justin dropped it down to Luke. The deputy raised his hand in a farewell gesture, then set about retrieving the scaling ladder. Justin had tucked a wet cloth into his belt and he used it now to scrub off the mud he'd smeared on his face for camouflage. Deciding to get down into the bailey where he hoped he'd feel less conspicuous, he made his way along the battlement toward the wooden stairway that gave access to the ramparts.

He could see sentries across the bailey, others at the gatehouse. Based upon his extensive experience with past sieges, William Marshal had estimated the Windsor garrison to be about thirty or forty knights and less than a hundred men-at-arms. Those were numbers large enough to give Justin a certain degree of anonymity, for how could so many men know each and every one of their cohorts? But that confidence received a sharp jolt when he reached the bottom of the stairs and found himself accosted by a scowling man with a crossbow slung over his shoulder.

"Where do you think you're going?" he demanded. "Who told you to leave your post?"

Justin considered claiming the need to "take a piss," but decided instead to sow as much confusion as he could. He knew John had a number of Welsh mercenaries among his men, and his years in Chester had given him a smattering of Welsh. So he responded with a blank look, a shrug, and *"Dydw i ddim yn deall."*

The crossbowman didn't understand, either. Glaring at Justin, he muttered something about "accursed foreigners" and then called to a man standing in the doorway of the great hall. "Sir Thomas! Will you tell this dolt to get back—"

The rest of his words were drowned out by the commotion erupting at the gatehouse. The crossbowman whirled toward the sound, Justin forgotten. As guards up on the walls began to shout, the sleeping castle came abruptly back to life. Groggy men were stumbling out of the great hall, the stables, wherever they'd been bedding down, fumbling for their weapons. No one seemed to know what was happening, but all were alarmed. Justin stood on the stairs for a moment, savoring the turmoil, and then faded back into the shadows.

It took some time for the panic stirred up by Marshal's feint to subside. The garrison had hastened up onto the battlements, making ready to repel the invaders, crossbowmen firing blindly into the fog. By then Marshal's men were withdrawing, but the ripples continued to radiate outward, until the entire castle was in a state of confusion and chaos.

Justin was jubilant. The ease with which he'd infiltrated the castle was energizing and he decided to take advantage of the pandemonium to check out the garrison's provisions. If John would not surrender, it would be very useful for Marshal to know how much food they had left. No one challenged him and he had no difficulty in finding the larders. They would normally have been guarded against theft, but now their sentinels were up on the walls. Blankets were spread out on the floor, and a lantern still burned feebly. Picking it up, he prowled among sacks of corn and oatmeal and beans. There were huge vats filled with salted pork and mutton and herring, large cheeses, and hand mills and churns. The buttery nearby held enormous casks of wine and cider, jars of honey and vinegar. All in all, enough food and wine to hold out for weeks to come.

Keeping the lantern, Justin ventured back out into the bailey. Men were clambering up and down the stairs and ladders, leaning over the embrasures to yell defiance at the enemy camp. Others were trudging toward the great hall, too agitated to sleep. Justin mingled with them, trailed into the hall, too. So far no one had paid him any heed and emboldened, he roamed the aisles, searching for Durand. Instead, he found John. The queen's son strode into the hall, shouting a name that meant nothing to Justin. He hastily ducked behind a pillar as John passed, almost close enough to touch, and then retreated toward the nearest door.

Out in the bailey again, he decided to take direct action and began to stop soldiers, asking the whereabouts of Sir Durand de Curzon. He got mainly shrugs and shakes of the head, but eventually someone pointed toward a tower in the south wall. Justin quickened his step, and had almost reached the tower when Durand appeared in the doorway. His visage was grim, fatigue smudged under his eyes and in the taut corners of his mouth. Preoccupied with his own thoughts, which were apparently none too pleasant, he walked by Justin without even a glance, heading across the bailey toward the great hall.

Catching up with him, Justin said softly, "John can wait. The queen cannot."

Durand came to an immediate halt, then spun around to confront Justin, who obligingly raised the lantern so that it illuminated his face. "Christ Jesus!" Durand blurted out, staring at Justin as if he doubted the evidence of his own senses. "What are you doing here?"

It was the first time Justin had seen the other man off

balance. "I wanted to return your dagger," he snapped.
"Use your head, man. Why do you think?"

Durand cursed under his breath. "We cannot talk out
here," he said tautly. "Come with me."

Retracing Durand's steps, they returned to the tower.
The ground-floor chamber was empty but Durand continued on into the stairwell and Justin followed him to an
upper chamber that was surprisingly spacious and well
lighted, with an iron candlestick on the trestle table and
several rushlights burning in wall sconces. A flagon and
cups were set out on the table and the first thing Dur-
and did was to pour himself wine. He did not offer Justin
any, instead said testily, "How in hellfire did you get into
the castle undetected? Was that little set-to at the gatehouse your doing?"

"Does it matter?"

"No . . . I suppose not." Durand leaned back against
the table, regarding Justin reflectively. "Why are you
here?"

"The queen wants you to do all in your power to convince Lord John that he ought to surrender."

Durand's mouth twisted. "Did she have any suggestions as to how I'm to accomplish that miraculous feat?
If I had my way, we'd have come to terms a fortnight
ago. Why fight a war we cannot win? It makes no sense.
Yet try arguing that to John!"

"Why would he want to hold out? Does he expect help
from Philip? Surely he knows by now that the French invasion was thwarted?"

Durand shrugged. "He knows. Let me tell you about
John. He is as far from a fool as a man can be. Most of
the time, he is too clever for his own good. But where his
brother is concerned, that intelligence does him no good
whatsoever, for the mere mention of Richard's name is
enough to send emotion flooding into his brain, drowning out the voice of reason."

"Is he that jealous of Richard?"

Durand snorted. "Did Cain love Abel? How else explain why we are holed up here at Windsor instead of conspiring against Richard from the safety of the French court?"

"The queen knows it will not be easy. But she is relying upon you to save John from himself—and from others who might prefer that he not survive this siege. She said that if the castle is assaulted and taken, you must see to John's safety."

That was a daunting charge, but Durand merely nodded. "Tell my lady queen that I will serve her as long as I have breath in my body." Taking a deep swallow of wine, he looked at Justin with a quizzical, faintly mocking smile. "That raises an interesting point. How do you expect to get word back to the queen? If you think I'm going to help you escape, you'd best think again. I'll risk my skin for no man, least of all you."

"Now why does that not surprise me?" Justin said, with a sardonic smile of his own. "But to allay your concerns, I expect to get out through a postern gate—at John's command."

Durand's eyes narrowed. "Now why should John do that?"

"I bear two messages, one of which is for him."

Durand's hand jerked and wine splashed over the rim of his cup. "You keep me out of it, by God! If there is even a hint that we are connected, John will hang us both from the battlements . . . if we are lucky. He trusts me now—or as much as he ever trusts any man—and I'll not have your blundering stirring up suspicions or doubts."

"It is such a pleasure working with you, Durand. Do you suppose you can compromise yourself long enough to tell me where I am most likely to find John alone?"

"Well, there is always his bedchamber, although you're not likely to find him alone there."

Justin was startled. "He brought a concubine with him into the castle, knowing it could be under siege?"

"Why not? Sieges can drag out for months. Would you truly expect him to live like a monk for so long . . . John, who cannot go more than a night without a woman in his bed?"

Durand's smile was so malicious that Justin knew they were both thinking of Claudine. "Tell me where I can find John," he said, with enough quiet menace to make it a threat. "Tell me now."

"Are your nerves always on the raw like this? That does not bode well for your chances of getting out of Windsor alive, does it? But your safety is none of my concern. As for John, you can find him here sometimes, and often after dark, on the battlements. He will spend hours up there, gazing out into the night and brooding—"

Durand cut himself off abruptly. By then, Justin heard it, too: footsteps in the stairwell. They could not be found here together and his eyes swept the room, seeking a hiding place. The only possibility was the corner privy chamber. The footsteps were louder now, approaching the door. Durand would have to delay the intruder while he hid. Justin was starting to turn toward the other man when he caught movement from the corner of his eye. Instinctively he recoiled, but it was too late. The candlestick in Durand's fist thudded into his temple and he went down into the floor rushes as the door swung open.

11

WINDSOR CASTLE

April 1193

Justin awoke to total recall, pain, and utter blackness.
For a shattering moment, he feared he'd been blinded by
the blow. It was almost with relief that he realized he was
being held in one of the castle's dungeons, as dark as the
bottom of a well. His head was throbbing and when he
moved, he had to fight back a wave of queasiness. This
was the second time in two months that he'd suffered a
head injury and by now he was all too familiar with the
symptoms. He tried to find out if he was bleeding, but
discovered instead that his right wrist was manacled to a
ring welded into the floor. Testing its strength merely set
his head to spinning. Pillowing it awkwardly upon his
free arm, he lay very still, waiting for the dizziness to
pass, and eventually he slept.

When he awakened again, the pain had begun to re-
cede and his thoughts were no longer clouded. That was
a dubious blessing, though, for he was now able to focus
upon his plight with unsparing clarity. The solitude was
soon fraying his nerves and he found it particularly troubling to have no sense of time's passing. He had no way
of knowing how long it had been since Durand swung
that candlestick. Hours? A day? It was disorienting and
somehow made his isolation all the more complete. It
was as if the world had gone on without him. Would his
disappearance stir up even a ripple at the royal court, on

Gracechurch Street? Would there be any to mourn him, to remember?

His self-pity was fleeting, submerged in a rising tide of rage. He was not going to die alone and forgotten down here in the dark. He owed Durand a blood debt and he'd not go to his grave with it unpaid. That he swore grimly upon the surety of his soul.

His embittered musings were interrupted by a sudden scraping noise, shockingly loud in the muffled silence of the cell. He struggled to sit up as a trapdoor was opened overhead and a ladder lowered into the gloom. A man was soon clambering down, a sack dangling from his belt, a lantern swinging precariously each time he switched holds upon the rungs. Even that feeble light seemed unnaturally bright to Justin, who had to avert his eyes.

"Here," the man said brusquely, shaking out the contents of the sack onto the floor at Justin's feet: a loaf of bread and a chunk of cheese and a battered wineskin. "I was told to feed you . . . although it seems a shame to waste good food on a man who's soon to die."

Justin ignored the uncharitable aside. The guard's grumbling only echoed what he already knew; spies were hanged. "Tell Lord John that Justin de Quincy must talk with him. Say it's urgent and in his interest to hear me out."

"I'll do that straightaway," the man vowed, and then laughed derisively. "Why should my lord John spare time for the likes of you?" he sneered and began his clumsy ascent back up the ladder.

The loss of that faltering lantern light affected Justin much more than he could have anticipated; it was as if the sun had been blotted out, plunging him back into an eternal night. His headache was almost gone; clearly Durand had done far less damage than Gilbert the Fleming. He had no appetite, but he forced himself to eat some of the bread and cheese. The liquid in the wineskin was warm and had a stale aftertaste. He thought it might be ale; all he could say for a certainty was that it was wet. His thirst was overpowering, though, and it was difficult to ration himself to just a few swallows. He did not know how long it had to last.

Surely John would not send him to his death without interrogating him first? John's scruples might be ailing, but he had a curiosity healthy enough to put any cat to shame. How could he not want answers as much as he did vengeance? But what if John did not know he was languishing in this dungeon? Would Durand have told him? If not, that guard's pitiless prediction was likely to come true . . . all too soon.

Justin was dozing fitfully when the trapdoor opened again. A tall figure descended the ladder, less awkwardly than the guard, and even before his lantern's flame revealed his identity, Justin knew it was Durand. The knight raised the lantern high, letting its light linger upon Justin's pallor and dishevelment. Justin's fury needed no illumination; the other man could feel it throbbing between them in the dark, giving off enough heat to scorch the very air they both breathed. A smile quirked the corner of Durand's mouth. "So," he drawled, "how is your poor, addled head? I daresay it is still pounding like a drum, no?"

Justin's fist clenched on the chain, but the anchor held. Squinting up into the glare of Durand's lantern, he called the knight every vile name he'd ever heard, with so much venom that even the most commonplace of profanities became a blistering indictment. Durand heard him out, affecting an amused indifference belied by the tautness of his body's stance, the glitter in those narrowed, appraising eyes.

"You're not taking this well, are you?" he gibed. "All

this righteous indignation seems a bit overdone to me, for I did warn you that I'd not put myself at risk. With John about to walk in and find us chatting together, cozy as can be, I did what I could to deflect suspicion away from myself, and offer no apologies for it, by God!"

"Your memory is as flawed as your honour! I was there, too, or did that slip your mind? You struck me down before the door opened, so how could you possibly have known it was John? Second-sight?"

"I recognized his footsteps," Durand said blandly, and in that moment, Justin understood fully what men meant when they spoke of a "murderous rage."

"What a liar you are! You saw your chance and took it and you'll never convince me otherwise, not in this life or the next!"

"I do not have to convince you of anything, de Quincy. I told you what happened and if you choose not to believe me, that is up to you. If I were in your place— and irons—I'd be more concerned about making my peace with the Almighty. You were caught spying, after all, and spies . . ." He paused, heaving a mock sigh. "Alas, they are hanged."

"You'd better hope that I am not."

"And why is that?"

"Because I am not about to die alone, Durand. If I hang, you'll hang with me, and that is a promise."

Durand seemed taken aback. "I do not think you'd do that," he said at last and Justin smiled coldly.

"Think again."

Durand said nothing, but his free hand had dropped to the hilt of his dagger. Justin's throat tightened. He still managed a scornful laugh, though, when the other man took a step toward him. "Go ahead," he jeered, "use your knife. That is one way to silence me. Of course you'd have to explain to John why you'd come down to the dungeons to murder a man known to be in the queen's service. But I'm sure you could think of some plausible explanation. We both know how trusting John is, how slow he is to suspect treachery . . . do we not?"

Now it was Durand's turn to indulge in profanity. He spat out a string of vitriolic oaths, of which "misbegotten son of a poxed whore" was the mildest. But he did not draw his dagger from its sheath.

Justin did his best to appear bored by the invective. "If you are done ranting, let's talk about what I want you to do."

"If you think I'll help you escape, you're in for a great disappointment!"

"I'd sooner take my chances with a pack of starving wolves, for they'd be easier to trust. All you need do is convince John to see me . . . and soon. Lest you forget, I bring him an urgent message from his lady mother. If I cannot deliver it, we'll both have failed our queen."

Durand's eyes glinted in the candlelight. He seemed about to speak, instead spun on his heel and stalked back to the ladder. He paused, a boot on the first rung when Justin said his name.

"Just remember this, Durand. Either I do my talking to John . . . or on the gallows. The choice is yours."

"Rot in Hell," Durand snarled, and rapidly climbed the ladder. Within moments, the trapdoor slammed and Justin was alone again in darkness. He sagged back against the wall, his breathing as uneven and shallow as his hopes of reprieve. Did Durand truly care whether he failed the queen or not? Had he convinced Durand that their fates were inextricably entwined? If he died in this hellhole or on the gallows, would Eleanor notify his father?

The trapdoor was flung open with a thud. A ladder was lowered through the opening and two men were soon climbing down. Justin sat up in alarm. Why two of

them? Had Durand decided to pay men to do his killing
for him? They moved toward him, fanning out to approach from each side, and the man with the lantern said
gruffly, "You've caused enough trouble already. Do not
make this any harder than it need be."

Justin yanked at the manacle in vain, knowing resistance was futile, planning to resist, anyway. Then he saw
what was in the guard's other hand: a key. At least he'd
not be dying in this accursed black pit, forgotten by all
but God. Even the gallows seemed preferable to that.
The key made a rasping sound in the lock, as lyrical to
his ears as harp music. When he tried to rise, though, he
discovered that his muscles were cramped and stiff and
he stumbled after his captors, as unsteady on his legs as a
newborn foal.

"Where are you taking me?"

"To the gallows, I expect," the second man said indif-
ferently. "But Lord John wants to see you first."

Justin gazed upward, marveling at the beauty of the
sunset-colored clouds meandering lazily above the castle
like fleecy, celestial sheep—if sheep were ever purple and
pink. He laughed suddenly and his guards eyed him
warily. He couldn't explain to them how good it felt to
be able to see the sky again, to draw clean, untainted air
into his lungs after breathing in the fumes filling that
rancid, fetid tomb. It was astonishing to see dusk was
just falling, for that meant his captivity had been mea-
sured in hours, not days. It was true what he'd once
heard, that time stopped with the slamming of a dungeon's door.

John's bedchamber was in one of the timber buildings
within the protective stone circle of the shell keep. He
was seated at a trestle table set for two, about to eat as
Justin was ushered in. Shoving him forward, the guard

asked deferentially, "Do you want us to truss him up, my lord?"

John put down his wine cup. "No," he said. "That will not be necessary . . . will it, Master de Quincy? I am assuming my lady mother sent you as a spy, not an assassin?"

Even accustomed as he was to John's slash-and-parry brand of sarcasm, this took Justin's breath away, for that was an exceedingly bitter joke for a man to make about his mother. John was watching him dispassionately. They were only five years apart in age, but worlds apart in the lives they'd led. John was the dark one in a fair family, lacking his celebrated elder brother's height and flash and golden coloring. But he did not lack for ambition or intelligence, and Justin's past encounters had convinced him that the queen's youngest son was a formidable foe, indeed, far more dangerous than a Durand de Curzon or a Gilbert the Fleming. John had his mother's compelling hazel eyes, green-flecked and slanting and utterly inscrutable. A cat at a mousehole, Justin thought, wanting to play with its prey before making the kill. "I am neither, my lord," he said swiftly, "not spy nor assassin. That was not my mission."

"No?" John arched a brow. "And what was this mysterious mission, then?" He gestured for a waiting youth to ladle food onto his trencher, and the succulent aroma of roasted chicken awakened in Justin a sudden and ravenous hunger, for he'd eaten only a bit of cheese and bread in more than a day and night. He looked away hastily, but not in time; John saw. "Hungry, are you?"

"No, my lord," Justin said stoutly, and John grinned. "You lied much more convincingly when you swore to me that you knew nothing about that bloodstained letter."

There was no longer any need for secrecy and Justin made no denials. "If I had not lied, my lord, I would have betrayed your mother, the queen. Surely you would want those in your service to be loyal to you first and foremost?"

"Indeed," John agreed, so readily that Justin tensed, anticipating the pounce. Instead John turned again to his servant. "Set a place for Master de Quincy. He looks like a man in need of a meal."

Justin was astounded. One of John's most intriguing— and unsettling—attributes was his unpredictability. It made him interesting company . . . provided he was not also one's gaoler. Whatever John's motivations, though, Justin was not going to stand on false pride. "Thank you, my lord," he said, taking the seat indicated and watching appreciatively as a roasted chicken leg was placed upon his trencher.

"Not at all," John said amiably. "The least I can do is to offer a condemned man one last meal."

Justin thought that was a dubious joke . . . if indeed it was one. Talking with John was like taking a stroll through a quagmire; the slightest misstep could lead to disaster. Before he could respond, though, the door opened and a woman entered the bedchamber. She gave Justin an incurious glance, then leaned over to kiss John, taking a seat beside him. Justin's wine cup halted, halfway to his mouth. He had seen women more beautiful. He'd rarely seen a woman whose appeal was so blatantly carnal, though. What man could look upon those smoky grey eyes, pouting red mouth, bright flaxen hair, and lush, voluptuous body and not think of mortal sins? He didn't realize he was staring so obviously until John commented, "I do not mind sharing my meal with you, de Quincy, but my generosity has its limits."

Justin acknowledged his guilt with a quick smile and an apology to John's concubine for his bad manners. Her own manners were in need of mending, for she ignored him utterly, devoting all of her attention to her chicken.

When Justin glanced back at John, he saw amusement in the other man's eyes. Unlike Durand, John was not hostile. He seemed curious, almost friendly, as if welcoming a distraction midst the monotony of the siege. The Prince of Darkness. Justin wondered suddenly if John knew about Claudine's private jest. He suspected that John would have been flattered, not offended. He must not let down his guard with this man. John could as easily doom him with a smile as with a curse.

John was gnawing on a chicken leg, watching Justin all the while. "Are you ready now," he said, "to tell me why my mother sent you to spy on me? What guilty secrets did she hope that you'd unearth at Windsor?"

"I was not sent here to spy upon you, my lord."

"Durand says he found you ransacking my tower chamber. What were you doing, then, if not spying?"

"That never happened. I was not searching your chamber."

"You are saying that Durand lied?"

Justin's mouth was dry and he paused to take a swallow of wine and draw a bracing breath now that the moment was at hand. "Do you speak English, my lord?"

John shook his head in bafflement. "No, I do not . . . why?"

"As English is unknown to you, so is the truth an alien tongue to Durand."

John laughed. "I'll not quarrel with that. But Durand does nothing without a reason. So why would he lie to me about your spying?"

"So you'd hang me."

John considered that for a moment and then grinned again. "Ah, I am remembering now . . . the two of you got into a brawl over the Lady Claudine a few weeks back. I'd already left the hall, was sorry I missed it. So he still bears you a grudge, does he? Well, I suppose it would be ungallant to suggest Claudine's charms are not worth dying for, so let's say you're speaking the truth. If you are not here to spy, why, then?"

"The queen hoped that I could convince you to surrender the castle."

"Did she, now?" John's affability had vanished; his face was a mask, impossible to read. "And how were you to do that?"

"She wanted me to tell you that she is willing to offer you more generous terms. If you agree to yield up Windsor, Wallingford, and the Peak, she will see to it that you keep control of your castles at Nottingham and Tickhill."

"Why did you not come in under a flag of truce, then?"

"The other justiciars do not know of this offer, my lord," Justin said, and then held his breath, waiting to see if John would take the bait. Something flickered in those tawny gold eyes, too quickly to catch. Justin ate some of his chicken; even under such stressful circumstances, it tasted delicious. If this was indeed his last meal, at least it would be a good one.

"That is a generous offer," John conceded, but he did not sound happy about it. "Why is she suddenly so eager to settle this siege without bloodshed?"

Justin had decided to tell John the truth, or as much of it as he dared. "She has two reasons, my lord. It would be more difficult to collect King Richard's ransom in a realm beset with strife."

John showed no surprise, confirming Justin's suspicions; he'd wager John had known about the ransom long before Eleanor did, courtesy of his conniving ally, the French king. "God forbid," John said dryly, "that there should be difficulties in collecting the ransom. What was her other reason?"

"She fears for your safety if the castle is taken by force."

"Does she, indeed?"

The words themselves were innocuous, but John invested them with such an ironic edge that Justin stared at him. At first glance, a comparison between John and Daniel Aston seemed ludicrous. What did the worldly, sardonic, and unscrupulous queen's son possibly have in common with the callow, wretched youth huddling in sanctuary at St Paul's? And yet they were both second-best, less-loved sons who had been overlooked and outshone by bedazzling elder brothers. Jealousy might not be as lethal as hemlock or henbane, but it could poison, too. Justin leaned forward, saying with a husky, earnest intensity that John could not ignore:

"The queen's fears for you are very real. When I expressed doubts that you'd be at risk if the castle fell, she was quite vexed with me and dwelt at length upon the dangers you'd be facing. If you need proof of that, my lord, I can offer no better proof than my own presence within this castle."

John frowned. "What do you mean?"

"The queen has been generous with her praise since I entered her service. She has told me that I've earned her trust and I do believe she is even fond of me, in her way. I am sure that she would not want to see harm befall me. I am sure, too, that she knew full well the risks I'd be taking. Yet she did not hesitate. You see, my lord, my life is expendable to her. Yours is not."

John said nothing. His lashes had swept down, veiling his eyes. Beside him, his sultry bedmate continued to eat with gusto, oblivious to the currents swirling around her. Justin could not imagine Claudine playing so passive a role. He reminded himself that he had no proof that Claudine had ever bedded John, and finished his chicken leg. He had said all he could; the rest was up to John.

"You claim the justiciars know nothing of my mother's offer?"

"No, my lord, they do not."

"Who helped you, then, to get into the castle? Who staged that raid upon the gatehouse?"

"I did confide in one man, my lord, telling him that I hoped to convince you to yield up the castle peaceably. He was more than willing to offer his aid once he heard that."

John's smile was skeptical. "And the name of this Good Samaritan?"

"Your brother, Will Longsword," Justin said, and sensed that he'd gotten through John's defenses, however fleetingly. He wished he could think of a way to learn if John had been the one entering the tower chamber as Durand struck him down. He was unwilling, though, to ask outright, for John's imagination was already tangled with suspicions and doubts; Jesú forfend that he plant any seeds of his own. John had fallen silent again. When he could endure the suspense no longer, Justin said cautiously:

"Will you at least consider the queen's offer, my lord?"

John studied him impassively and then nodded. "I shall think upon it."

Justin knew the adage about letting sleeping dogs lie, but he could not help himself. He had to ask. "And what of me, my lord?"

John's expression did not change, but his eyes caught the candlelight, reflecting a gleam that might have been malice or mischief, or both. "I shall think upon that, too," he said.

12

WINDSOR CASTLE

May 1193

Durand sauntered into John's chamber with a deliberate swagger. His gaze flashed from John to Justin, back to John. "You wanted me, my lord?"

"Yes . . . come in, Durand." John's smile was nonchalant, his eyes opaque. "Master de Quincy is going to be my guest for a while. See if you cannot find someplace for him to stay . . . more comfortable than his last lodgings."

Durand did a marvelous impression of a man unhappy with his task but much too loyal to object. "I'll see to it straightaway," he said, glancing at Justin with feigned distaste that was, in actuality, quite real. Justin watched the performance, fascinated in spite of himself by the role-playing. When Durand looked in a mirror, did he recognize the man looking back at him?

John gestured for his servant to pour more wine, then picked up another piece of chicken. Taking that as dismissal, Justin rose to his feet. John let them go, waiting until they'd reached the door. "De Quincy and I have been having a right interesting conversation about the art of lying. Any thoughts on that, Durand?"

Durand shrugged. "Whatever gets a man through the day."

John smiled. "Well, that is one viewpoint. A bit more tolerant, mayhap, than the Church's position. I believe it holds lying to be a sin, no?"

Justin was close enough to see the muscles tighten along Durand's jawline. When the other man spoke, though, he sounded quite composed, even amused. "Are you fretting about the state of my immortal soul, my lord?"

"No, I've never been one for lost causes. Sin all you want, with my blessings. But lying to me would be worse than a sin, Durand. It would be a blunder."

Durand's face was blank, utterly without expression. "I'll bear that in mind, my lord."

John smiled again. "That would be wise," he said, and to Justin's surprise, he found himself feeling a flicker of involuntary, unwelcome sympathy for Durand, who diced with death on a daily basis, knowing that his first misstep would likely be his last.

Neither Justin nor Durand spoke until they had emerged out into the keep's inner bailey. By now the sunset was at its zenith and the sky above their heads was the color of blood. "We can put you in a chamber in the south wall tower," Durand said at last. "If it were up to me, you'd be sleeping in the pigsty. Just what did you tell John, damn your soul?"

"That I was no spy. Of course you'd been very helpful in that regard, telling him you caught me searching his chamber. I suppose I should consider myself lucky that you did not forge a confession for me, too."

Their argument was all the more intense for having to be conducted in hushed undertones meant to deter eavesdroppers. They fell silent until a group of soldiers passed by and then Durand launched another sotto voce offensive. "What did you tell John about me?"

"That you used the truth the way other men use whores, or words to that effect. I may have hinted that you'd seen a chance to settle a grudge. That fit for certes with what he knows of your high moral character, and the public brawl we had at the Tower helped, too. He thinks we are feuding over Claudine. Try to remember that in case he asks."

Durand called Justin a highly uncomplimentary name, but after a moment, he conceded, "Well, I suppose it could have been worse."

"Yes," Justin agreed, "we could have been hanged together."

"I still do not think you'd have betrayed me."

"Gambling on my goodwill, Durand, would be a fool's wager."

"Not your goodwill, de Quincy, your loyalty. As you put it in one of your more coherent moments down in that dungeon, we both serve the queen. How would it have availed her to lose her best man?"

Justin laughed incredulously. "So this was all my fault?"

"Well, it was not mine. If I'd wanted you dead, I'd have reached for my dagger, not a candlestick."

"The candlestick was faster," Justin said laconically, "what with John about to burst in the door," and got from Durand his first spontaneous smile.

"Jesú, but you're a cynical one, de Quincy. You're also a better talker than I expected. Whatever you said to John, it saved your skin. Were you able to perform a second miracle tonight and talk him into yielding up the castle?"

"I think so," Justin said slowly, and Durand gave him a look of genuine surprise.

"I see that I've been underrating you, de Quincy. The next time I shall have to keep that in mind."

"The next time," Justin echoed softly. There was no need to say more. They both understood perfectly.

The next day John demanded to see his brother Will, who immediately rode into the castle under a flag of truce. It still took nearly a fortnight before the negotiations were finally resolved, for John was not about to accept a verbal assurance, even if it came from his mother. Promises had to be committed to writing, compromises made, and the justiciars and barons reconciled to the generosity of the terms being offered by the queen. The Bishop of Durham in particular was incensed and had to be placated for the loss of John's castle at Tickhill, which he'd been on the verge of capturing. Eventually, though, a truce was struck until All Saints' Day, and John ordered the gates of Windsor Castle opened to the army of William Marshal.

Justin stood on the steps of the great hall, watching as Marshal's men swarmed into the bailey. John had ridden out shortly before noon, and with him had gone Justin's nemesis, departing in a cloud of dust for parts unknown. Justin harbored no illusions, though, that the queen's son was done with his rebellion. It would now take another form, but it would go on. He never doubted that Eleanor knew it, too.

Hearing his name called, he smiled at the sight meeting his eyes: Luke riding into the bailey, leading Copper behind him. Drawing rein, the deputy slowly shook his head in mock wonderment. "Well, once again you walked into the lion's den and somehow avoided being eaten. How many of your nine lives did you squander this time?"

"Too many," Justin conceded, hearing again the sound that still echoed in his sleep: the slamming of the dungeon's trapdoor. Over a flagon of wine in the great hall, he gave Luke an edited account of his misadventures, seeking—with limited success—to put a humorous spin upon Durand's double cross. Luke responded with gratifying indignation and predictable carping, taking Justin to task for turning his back upon a viper. "Did you learn nothing from your dealings with the Fleming, de Quincy?

So what happens now? I do not suppose you can complain to the queen . . . ?"

"No . . . her man has covered his tracks. He would merely swear that he was protecting himself, and I cannot offer proof to the contrary. Even if I could, I do not know that I'd want to burden the queen with it. She has enough troubles of her own without taking on mine, too."

Luke didn't argue; in Justin's place, he wouldn't have gone to the queen, either. "Let's drink then to the surrender of Windsor Castle," he suggested, clinking his cup against Justin's, "and to an untimely death for the queen's back-stabbing spy. I suppose I will have to go back to Winchester now and face Aldith's wrath. What about you?"

"I leave for London at first light," Justin said, "to make my report to the queen." And to do what he could for a frightened youth cowering in the shadows of St Paul's sanctuary.

"Well, done, Justin!"

"Thank you, Madame." Basking in the warmth of the queen's approval, Justin found it easy to forget how close he'd come to dying on her behalf. He had survived and she was pleased, and for the moment, nothing else mattered.

"Do you know where John has gone?"

"He took the road north, Madame. My lord Marshal thinks he was heading for his castle at Nottingham."

"I assume Durand went with him?"

"Yes, my lady, he did."

"Good," she said, but her tone was preoccupied. Justin was learning to read her unspoken signals, and it seemed obvious to him that her thoughts were not of Durand. He was not surprised when she did not ask about his collaboration with Durand. Eleanor did not ever ask a question unless she was sure she wanted to know the answer. Justin understood that and waited for the question she did want to ask.

"I have good news of my own," Eleanor said. "The French king was forced to abandon the siege of Rouen and retreat. For the moment at least, Normandy holds fast for my son."

"I am gladdened to hear that, Madame."

"Now we must concentrate all our efforts upon raising the ransom." Eleanor paused to sip from a silver goblet of watered-down wine. "My son . . . he was well?" When he nodded, she drank again, her eyes on Justin's face. "What did you say to John?"

"I told him what you'd bidden me, my lady, that he need not yield up all of his castles if he surrendered."

"I know that," she said, with a trace of impatience. "What else?"

"Just that . . . that you were concerned for his safety."

"I see . . ." Eleanor continued to study him, so intently that he shifted uncomfortably in his seat. He'd been sent to Windsor to speak for the queen, instead had found himself speaking for the mother, and he could only hope now that she'd not see his initiative as presumption.

"For one who grew to manhood believing himself to be an orphan," Eleanor said, "you are surprisingly familiar with the weeds found in family gardens."

Justin tensed, for her words were salted with sarcasm. Then she smiled ruefully and he realized that barbed remark was not aimed at him. So even queens harbored regrets. He thought it a pity that John had not been the one to hear that oblique admission. But whatever had gone wrong between Eleanor and her youngest son, the rift was now so deep and so wide that it might be beyond mending. He was not sure how to respond, finally resorting to a lame joke.

"All I know of family gardens, my lady, I learned by looking over fences."

Eleanor smiled again, with more amusement than his weak jest deserved, and told him to take a few days for himself, a well-earned reward, she said, for serving her son so faithfully. Justin dutifully bade her farewell, hoping he could put those days to good use on Daniel Aston's behalf, and managed to depart the Tower without encountering Claudine. It was only later that he wondered which of her sons the queen had meant.

Justin found Daniel sitting on the cathedral's pulpitum steps, eating bread smeared with honey as his aunt hovered beside him, trying to stitch up a tear in the sleeve of his tunic. When he saw Justin, Daniel jumped to his feet. "Where have you been?"

"I told you, Daniel, that the queen was sending me to the siege of Windsor Castle."

"You were gone so long," Daniel cried, so plaintively that Justin realized how much the boy had come to trust his promise of aid. It was not a comforting thought.

"I know, lad," he said, "I know. But it could not be helped." Greeting Agnes, he seated himself beside them, doing his best to summon up a reassuring smile. "Nell tells me that nothing has happened whilst I was gone. I was hoping, though, that you'd had a change of heart, Daniel, with time to think upon your plight. What about it? Are you willing to tell me now about that argument and the pilgrim pledge?"

Three and a half weeks in sanctuary had stripped away much of Daniel's defensive belligerence. His eyes were red-rimmed, his tunic badly wrinkled, his nails bitten down to the quick, and he'd developed a hacking cough. He ducked his head, not meeting Justin's gaze, and finally mumbled, "I would if I could . . ."

Justin hadn't the heart to berate him. What good would it do? Getting to his feet, he said, "I'll go now to seek Jonas out, will stop by again later if I find out anything from him."

Daniel nodded mutely and Agnes announced that she, too, must go, leaning over to kiss his cheek. Their last glimpse of him was not reassuring; he'd drawn his knees up to his chin, rocking back and forth, a forlorn figure of such abject misery that tears blurred Agnes's eyes. "I must know," she whispered. "Is there any hope for the lad?"

Justin hesitated. Which would be worse, to give her false hope or to take away all hope whatsoever? "Yes . . . there is still some hope, Agnes. If we could locate that Flemish mercer and learn who bought the patterned silk found under Melangell's body, that might well point suspicion away from Daniel and toward someone else."

Agnes daubed at the corner of her eye with one of her hanging sleeves. "He is innocent, Justin, may the Almighty strike me dead here and now if he is not. We cannot let him hang."

"We will not," he assured her, with far more confidence than he really felt. They both took care not to mention that Daniel's time was fast running out, with only a fortnight remaining until his right of sanctuary ended.

Justin's meeting with Jonas was brief and unproductive. The serjeant had nothing to report, no other leads to pursue. The Flemish mercer was still missing, no new eyewitnesses had turned up, and Tobias had convinced the sheriff that they ought not to waste any more time on a case already solved, with the killer sure to hang or abjure the realm. Jonas looked fatigued and sounded harassed, having been routed from his bed before dawn to break up a brawl between feuding neighbors, and he could spare Justin neither time nor encouragement. "Find me a more likely suspect than the Aston lad," he flung over his shoulder, "and I'll do my part. But I've unearthed nothing in my investigation and with all due respect, I doubt that you can do better."

So did Justin, but he had to try. He paid another visit to the Aston shop, where the atmosphere was stifling, suffused with such tension that the very air seemed oppressive. Humphrey ordered Justin from the shop, shouting that he'd done enough for the family with his meddling and his bungling. Justin didn't bother to argue. Within moments, though, Geoffrey hastened out into the street after him.

Daniel's ordeal was clearly taking its toll upon his brother. His sleek blond hair was rumpled and unkempt, his clothing was mismatched, as if he'd thrown on the first garments at hand, and that favorite-son armor appeared dented beyond repair.

"Thank God you're back," he said. "You seem to be the only one who does not think Daniel is guilty. Even my father . . . he has not visited Daniel, not once! He says Daniel's fate is in God's hands and we must do whatever we can to keep the scandal from tainting us, too."

"And your mother?"

Geoffrey stared down at his shoes. "My father forbade her to go to St Paul's and she is too fearful to defy him."

"But you did?" Justin said quietly, and Geoffrey nodded.

"I never had defied him before, at least not openly. But I could not abandon Daniel, I could not!" His voice cracked and he seemed to be blinking back tears. "The whole world has gone mad, for nothing makes sense anymore. At first Melangell's death did not seem real to me. I'd wake up in the morning and for a moment, I'd forget . . . and all was as it had been ere that accursed night . . ." He swallowed, then mustered up a wan smile. "I suppose that sounds crazed, for certes!"

"No," Justin said, "not crazed at all."

"But Daniel's danger is all too real. I live with it day and night. What will happen to him? Tell me the truth, Justin."

"In a fortnight, he must come forth from sanctuary or be starved out. If he is indicted, as seems likely, he must then stand trial for Melangell's murder, and if found guilty, he will hang. Or . . . he may choose to confess and abjure the realm. If so, he will have to make his way, barefoot and in sackcloth, to a chosen port, where he must set sail on the next ship, swearing never to return to England."

"Oh, God . . ." Geoffrey whispered. His eyes were glassy, unseeing. Turning abruptly, he fled back into the shop. Justin waited to see if he would reemerge and then walked away slowly, feeling a great sadness for all those who were caught in the spider's web spun by Melangell's death. Daniel, Geoffrey, Agnes, Cati, her luckless father, even the pitiful, browbeaten Beatrice. No matter what happened to Daniel, their lives would never be the same again.

Justin spent the rest of the day in the neighborhood where Melangell had died, talking to people he'd already interrogated, prodding sluggish memories in vain. He even lingered in the churchyard for a time, mourning both the reckless, lively spirit of a girl he'd never met and his inability to catch her killer. The afternoon had become blustery and damp, with a chill more common to March than May, and he hastened to take shelter under a towering yew tree as a sudden, soaking rainstorm broke over the city. Wet and cold and thoroughly disheartened, Justin gave up and headed for home.

Darkness was blotting away the last traces of daylight by the time he reached Gracechurch Street. He stopped by the smithy to retrieve Shadow and check on his stallion, then continued on to his cottage, where he lit a fire in the hearth and changed into a dry tunic. Like most of his neighbors, he'd gotten into the nightly habit of dropping in at the alehouse, as much for the company as for the ale, and he knew Nell would be expecting him. But the rain was still pelting the darkness beyond his door, the wind was rising, and his spirits plummeting. After feeding Shadow, he dragged out the whetstone he'd borrowed from Gunter and began to sharpen his sword.

Gnawing zestfully upon a pork bone, Shadow gave a muffled bark, chewed some more, and then barked again, clearly torn between hunger and duty. Justin set the sword down. At first he heard only the sounds of the storm, but the dog was now sniffing at the door, tail whipping about in eager welcome. Justin still did not hear anything but the rain and gusting wind. Trusting Shadow, though, he lifted the latch and a slim, hooded figure stumbled through the doorway, into his arms.

He reached out to steady her, assuming it must be Nell. As she raised her head, her hood fell back, and he froze. "Claudine!"

"Justin . . . oh, Justin . . ." Her voice faltered and tears began spilling silently down her cheeks. She was trembling so violently that he steered her at once toward the hearth. Her mantle was sodden and as soon as he removed it, he saw that her gown was, too. "I'm so cold," she whispered, clutching his hand with fingers of ice, "and so wet . . ."

"You're soaked through to the skin. You'd best get out of those wet clothes ere you catch your death." Hobbling his curiosity until he could get her thawed out, he found one of his shirts for her to wear and a blanket, which he draped over her shoulders as she stripped off her stockings. They fell into the floor rushes, puddles of brightly colored silk. Her little leather slippers were caked with mud. He stared at them in disbelief. "Claudine, you did not walk all the way from the Tower?"

"Yes," she said, "I did," and sneezed. "I need help with these laces," she entreated. "My fingers feel frozen."

Loosening the laces, he pulled the gown over her head and spread it out on a coffer to dry by the fire. When he turned back, her chemise had joined her stockings in the floor rushes and she was squirming into his shirt. It billowed about her like a white linen tent, reaching to her knees, and she shivered as the air hit her bare legs. Clutching the blanket closer, she sneezed again and began clumsily to free her wet hair from its pins. Justin handed her a towel, then crossed to the table and picked up his wineskin. Filling a cup to the brim, he carried it back to Claudine, resisting the urge to drink himself. He suspected that he would need a clear head for whatever was coming.

"This will warm you," he said, and watched warily as she drank in gulps. Why was she here? What new game was this? "You truly walked here from the Tower . . . by yourself? Christ Jesus, Claudine, whatever possessed you to do something so dangerous?"

"My mare went lame last week and if I'd asked to borrow another horse, there would have been questions. It seemed easier just to walk. It was not raining when I started out," she said, somewhat defensively. "And by the time the storm broke, it was too late to turn back."

"But to go out after dark and alone . . ." He shook his head incredulously. "Why would you take such a risk?"

She was toweling her hair vigorously, her face hidden by a dripping black curtain. "I did not find out till Vespers that you'd returned to London last night. I could not wait till the morrow, had to see you straightaway." Shaking her hair back, she glanced toward him, and then away. "Justin, I am in such trouble . . ."

"What is wrong? Tell me," he urged, and she regarded

him with enormous dark eyes, almost black against the
waxen whiteness of her face.

"I am pregnant."

Later, he would wonder why he'd not seen this coming. But he'd trained himself to see her as John's spy first,
and only then as his sometime lover. He was expecting
another ruse, possibly even a conscience-stricken confession, although he thought the former was far more likely
than the latter. It took him a moment to absorb the full
impact of her words, and when he did, he sat down
abruptly on the edge of the bed. This was no trick. Not
even Claudine could fake the fear he saw in her eyes. She
was telling the truth. She was with child. But was it his?

"Justin . . . for God's sake, say something!"

"Are you sure?"

"Sure enough to be out of my wits with worry," she
said tartly. "You cannot imagine what these past weeks
have been like, once I began to suspect. You were gone,
and I did not know where, or when you'd be coming
back. I did not draw an easy breath until the queen finally told me that you'd been at Windsor Castle and that
you were safe."

Justin tasted blood in his mouth and realized that he'd
bitten his lip. "The last time we lay together was mid-
April, I think . . ." A Tuesday, the thirteenth day, soon
after Compline. "That is . . . what? Four weeks? Is that
time enough to tell if you're with child?"

She shook her head impatiently. "I was already pregnant then, although I did not realize it yet. I'd missed my
April flux, but every woman misses one now and then.
And since I'd failed to get with child during the years of
my marriage, I'd thought I might be barren, so I did not
worry over-much about pregnancy. But then I began to
get queasy of a sudden, and when I missed May, too, I
knew. . . . Mayhap it was the night we were together at

that riverside inn, or that afternoon in your cottage, ere I was stricken with one of my headaches, remember?"

"Yes," he said, "I remember." If that were indeed the time, the Devil must be laughing fit to burst, for it was then that he'd discovered that she'd played him for a fool from the first, bait for John's trap. Yet if she had become pregnant in March, the baby could not be John's, for by then, he was at the French court. If she could be believed. She was curled up in the chair like a kitten in search of warmth, bare feet tucked up under her, damp hair curling about her face, lip rouge gone, kohl smeared under her eyes. She looked more like a lost, bedraggled child than the seductive spy he knew her to be, and when he rose from the bed and reached out to her, she grasped his hand as if grabbing for a lifeline.

"Justin, I am so scared."

"It will be all right," he lied. "We'll figure something out." But what? Marriage was out of the question, for she would consider marrying beneath her to be as shaming as bearing a child out of wedlock.

As if reading his thoughts, she gave him a tremulous smile. "I know you are thinking of marriage, for you are an honourable man. And if our circumstances were different . . ."

"But they are not." Was there relief in that understanding, or regret . . . or both? Better not to know. He could sort out his own feelings later. Right now they must decide what would be best for Claudine and the babe. "I'll not let you face this alone," he said, and saw her eyes fill with tears.

"You cannot ever know," she said, "how much I needed to hear you say that. I do not think I'd have the strength to cope on my own."

"You need only tell me," he said, "what you would have me do," and her fingers tightened in his, clung fast.

"I cannot disgrace my family, Justin. If I were to bear a bastard child, it might well kill my father. And my brothers . . . I cannot shame them like that, I cannot . . ." She shivered and then said in a low voice, no longer meeting his eyes, "I've learned of a woman who knows how to bring on a miscarriage with herbs like penny-royal. But I am fearful of going to her alone. If you could come with me . . . ?"

"Claudine, no!" Justin had been kneeling beside her, but at that, he sprang to his feet. "You cannot do that!"

"What choice do I have? Justin, I cannot have this child . . . I cannot!"

"Claudine, listen to me. Not only would you be committing a mortal sin, you'd be putting your own life at grave risk. I knew a woman who died that way, the sister of a groom on the Fitz Alan manor. She bled to death and suffered greatly ere she died—"

"You said you would help me, Justin, you promised!"

"I will help, but not to kill our child!"

Claudine flinched. "You think I want to do that? You think I'd risk my life and my soul lightly, on a whim? What if God cannot forgive me? If I cannot forgive myself? What if this is my only chance, my only child? But I do not know what else to do. How can I have this baby without destroying my family's honour?" She stared up at him despairingly, then buried her face in her hands and began to sob.

Justin knelt by her side again, gently gathered her into his arms, and held her as she wept. "We'll find a way," he promised. "Somehow, we'll find a way." She was still shivering and he carried her over to the bed, settled her under the covers, and sat with her until her tears finally ceased. Eventually she fell into an exhausted sleep, and only then did he retrieve the wineskin, pouring himself a generous dose, and then another. When the wineskin was empty and the fire had burned down to glowing embers, he quenched the candles, stripped, and slid into bed, taking care not to jostle Claudine.

He lay very still, willing sleep to come. Beneath the surface, undercurrents and eddies continued to ebb and flow, memories mingling with suspicions and misgivings and regrets. He found himself thinking, with a bittersweet ache, of his mother. Had she been as panicked as Claudine, terrified and abandoned and alone? Had she, too, thought of pennyroyal, prayed for a miscarriage? Or had her sense of joy been greater than her shame? Her secrets and soul-searching had died with her, and he knew only that she'd given up her life for his.

It was far easier to imagine his father's fear and rage. A priest whose ambitions burned as brightly as his faith, he was not going to let a village girl and their bastard son hinder his upward climb. Nor had he. The girl had conveniently died, the son hidden away as a charity case, unacknowledged until that December-eve confrontation in an icy, shadowed chapel at Chester. The irony of their respective positions struck Justin like a dagger's thrust. His father had not wanted him, but never doubted that he was the sire. He would that he could say the same.

Could the child be John's? He had no evidence, no proof, only conjecture and conclusions drawn upon what he knew of the queen's son and the woman lying asleep beside him. It had always seemed likely to him that Claudine and John had shared a bed, however briefly. If she was telling the truth about her March flux, the child must be his. But what if she were not? Why would she lie to him? What else could she do if she suspected the child were John's? She'd have no way to get word to him; not even his mother knew for certes where he was at present. And what if she did not know herself which of them was the father? He'd lain with her in February; what if John had, too? Could a woman tell whose seed had taken root in her womb?

He had no answers, only hurtful questions. It served for naught to rake over such barren, unyielding ground, for he had more pressing worries at hand. He'd promised Claudine he'd find a solution for them. How was he to keep that rash promise? Yet he dared not fail, not with two lives at stake.

He'd finally slept, awakening to the drumbeat of rain on the roof. Claudine was sleeping beside him, her hair tickling his chest, their legs entwined. When he moved, she opened her eyes and smiled drowsily up at him. He touched her cheek, a caress as soft as a breath, and her arms came up around his neck, drawing his mouth down to hers. Their lovemaking was wordless, unhurried, as much an act of healing as lust. Afterward, they lay quietly in each other's arms, listening to the rain until the cottage was filled with the greying light of a damp, spring dawn.

As soon as they left the refuge of their bed, though, the day took a downward turn. Claudine's mood was edgy and brittle, and when Justin brought back fried bread and roasted chestnuts from Nell's alehouse kitchen, she took one look at their breakfast and was promptly sick. Nor did his attempts at reassurance go much better. Their conversation was stilted, their intimacy forced. Not lovers, Justin thought grimly, two people caught in the same trap. Once the rain stopped, he saddled Copper and took her home.

They stood awkwardly in the Tower's inner bailey, holding hands but at a loss for words. Reaching out, Justin tucked away a lock of hair that had slipped from her wimple. "Promise me," he said, "that you will not do anything until we've had a chance to consider all of the choices open to us."

"What choices are there?" she asked, almost inaudibly, and heedless of people passing by, he leaned over and kissed her cheek.

"Claudine, there is a path out of this morass and I swear to you that we will find it. If you could go away to have the babe without anyone knowing, there'd be no scandal, no talk to get back to your family."

"Justin, do you not think I've thought of that? How could I go off without the queen's consent? And how could I afford to live in seclusion until the child was born? Neither of us have enough money for that."

Claudine didn't sound argumentative, merely infinitely weary, and that alarmed Justin more than anger. "Promise me," he insisted, "that you'll do nothing without talking to me first."

"I promise. Now I must go in, concoct some excuse for my absence." She squeezed his hand, then turned away, walking briskly toward the White Tower. Justin stayed where he was, watching until she'd disappeared into the doorway of the keep. Only then did he mount Copper, heading in the direction of the Land Gate.

He reined in, though, after just a few yards. Claudine's promise had been given too readily. She was a risk-taker by nature, and now she was desperate, a dangerous combination. For several moments, he sat motionless astride Copper, and then he turned the stallion toward the stables. Soon thereafter, he entered the great hall and pulled Eleanor's chancellor aside.

Peter of Blois greeted him with distracted civility. "I'd heard you were back, de Quincy. Good work in Windsor. Now I must be on my way, for I—"

"I need to see the queen. It is urgent."

After one glance at Justin's face, Eleanor led the way to the chapel. Seating herself upon the window bench, she gestured for him to join her. He did as bidden, but almost at once got to his feet again, unable to sit still. "It was good of you to agree to see me straightaway, Madame."

"You're not one to bandy about words like 'urgent,' Justin. What is it?"

"I am betraying a confidence, Madame. But I fear the consequences if I do not. Claudine is with child."

Eleanor's eyes widened, but she showed no other reaction; she'd had a lifetime's practice at keeping wayward emotions under a royal rein. "Is it yours?"

"She says it is."

"I see . . ."

He'd known she would; she always did. She was quiet for a time, gazing down at the ringed hands clasped in her lap as she considered the far-reaching implications of Claudine's pregnancy. "I assume you have something in mind, Justin. What would you have me do?"

"Claudine is terrified of shaming her family. Surely there must be a way to keep the birth secret, Madame? She did not see how we could do that, and she might well be right. But you could."

"Yes," she agreed, "I could. And after the baby is born, what then?"

"Madame . . . surely a good family could be found to care for the child?"

"Especially with the resources of the Crown to call upon," she said dryly. "And if I agree to help, what of your involvement? Do you want to be a part of this child's life, Justin?"

"Yes, Madame, I do."

She nodded slowly. Their eyes met and held. There was so much that was unsaid between them, so much better left unsaid. "Well," she said pensively, "this might be the best solution . . . for all concerned."

"Thank you, Madame," Justin said huskily, and she gave him a long, level look.

"You were taking quite a gamble," she said, "were you not?"

"Yes, Madame, I suppose I was." Probably the

greatest gamble of his life. Risking all upon faith and a desperate hope and a shared secret.

Eleanor rose abruptly, crossed to the door, and signaled to someone beyond Justin's line of vision. "Fetch the Lady Claudine."

Within moments, Claudine hurried into the chapel, smiling nervously. "You sent for me, my lady? If it is about last night, I can . . . Jesú!"

As the color ebbed from her face, Justin moved swiftly toward her. She backed away, staring at him in horror. "You told her! How could you betray me like this? I trusted you, Justin!"

"Be glad he did tell me, you foolish girl," Eleanor said impatiently, "for I am going to help you."

"Madame?" Claudine sounded stunned. "You . . . you mean it?"

"Come," Eleanor said, "sit down ere you fall down, child; you're whiter than newly skimmed milk. Yes, I mean it. I shall find a quiet, secluded nunnery for you until the babe is born, far from court gossip and rumors. Once you've given birth, you may return to my service and none need be the wiser."

"And . . . and the babe?"

"I shall find a family to care for the child."

Claudine was overwhelmed. Dropping to her knees, she kissed the queen's hand. "Madame, how can I ever repay you for your kindness and generosity?"

"Doubtless, I'll think of something." Eleanor smiled, patted the girl lightly on the shoulder, and then rose purposefully from the bench. "I'll leave you alone now to collect yourself. Justin, make yourself useful and fetch Claudine some wine; she is still much too pale for my liking." Without waiting for their response, she swept out of the chapel and they heard her telling the chaplain not to enter just yet, that they needed privacy for prayer.

Justin slipped out into the queen's great chamber,

snatched up a flagon and cup, then hastened back into the chapel. Claudine was standing by the altar, her back to him, and did not turn as he crossed to her. "Drink some of this," he urged, holding out the cup. "You still look shaken."

"Do I, indeed?" She spun around, dark eyes smoldering, and struck the cup from his hand, spilling wine all over the altar. "How could you go to the queen behind my back? What if you'd guessed wrong?"

"I had good reason to believe the queen would help us. You are her kinswoman, after all, and I'd just done both of her sons a valuable service. And whilst most people judge women more harshly than men over sins of the flesh, that would never be true of the queen, for gossip and rumor have trailed after her for much of her life." Leaving out the most compelling reason of all, that Claudine's baby might be Eleanor's grandchild.

"Even if you were utterly and completely certain that she would agree, you had no right to go to her without asking me. It was my future you were putting at risk, not yours!"

Justin stepped forward and caught her by the arms, holding her tightly when she attempted to pull away. "You are right and I ought to have consulted you first. But I was trying," he said fiercely, "to save your life and the life of our child!"

Claudine stopped struggling. "Does the baby's life mean that much to you?"

"Yes, it does. I was born out of wedlock, raised as a foundling. I will not let this baby grow up as I did, not if I can help it."

Her eyes searched his face. "You've mentioned your father to me. You know who he is?"

"Yes, I know. But he'll never acknowledge me." Reaching out, he tilted her chin so that he could look into her eyes. "I cannot give the baby my name. But we can make sure that this child is wanted and cared for, and I mean to do that, Claudine." *Whosoever the father is.*

13

LONDON

May 1193

The alehouse was as dimly lit and cool as a cave, the only other patron an elderly man snoring at a corner table, his head pillowed on his arms. No sooner had Justin claimed a table than Nell hastened out of the kitchen, flour streaking her face and the bodice of her gown, even coating the tips of her braids. At Justin's silent query, she said, "Lucy insisted upon helping me roll out the wafers. You want an ale?" When he nodded she shook her head disapprovingly. "You look dreadful. But I suppose you did not get much sleep last night."

Still shaking her head, she bustled off to fetch his ale, leaving Justin to frown after her vanishing figure. Her obvious dislike of Claudine puzzled him, for as far as he knew, the two women had met only once. She'd been just as prickly that morning when he'd come over to fetch Claudine's ill-fated breakfast, serving up a snide commentary along with the bread and chestnuts. The memory of Claudine's morning sickness reminded Justin that he'd not eaten any of that unfortunate repast either. He'd better stop off at the cookshop on his way to St Paul's. He doubted that he'd have any stomach for eating afterward.

"Here." Nell slopped a brimming ale down on the table, then disappeared back into the kitchen. Justin unfastened a small sack, drinking absently as he gazed down at its contents. He was so caught up in his own thoughts that he did not at once realize Nell had returned, not until she shoved a pewter dish toward him. "I just took those wafers out of the pan," she said, "so mind you do not burn your mouth."

Justin accepted the peace offering with an ungracious nod, broke off a bit of crust, and fed it to Shadow. Nell wiped her hands on her apron, pulled up a stool, and helped herself to one of her wafers. Justin waited, hoping she would not ask any questions about Claudine. But she was staring at the open sack.

"What do you have there?" She leaned forward to see. "Is that the rock you found in the churchyard?" When Justin nodded, she reached out, her fingers hovering over the dried bloodstains. "Poor little lass," she said softly. "What are you going to do with it, Justin?"

"I am going to use it as her killer did," he said, "as a weapon."

"Why must you keep asking questions I cannot answer?" Daniel had retreated to the High Altar. "And why are you so angry? You said you believed me!"

"I believe you did not kill her. But I think you know who did—"

"I do not, I swear it!"

"Upon what, Daniel . . . Melangell's pilgrim cross?"

Sweat had broken out on Daniel's forehead. "I knew it was her cross," he admitted. "I'd seen it around her neck. I . . . I noticed what she wore, how she looked . . ." Candlelight caught the flush spreading across his cheeks and throat. "When you showed it to me, I recognized it straightaway. But I do not know how it got in our coffer . . . I do not!"

Justin moved closer, too close for comfort. Daniel was backed against the altar and had nowhere else to go. "Would you swear that upon her cross, Daniel?" When the boy nodded mutely, Justin reached out and thrust the rock into his hand. "And upon this?"

"What is it?" Daniel gazed down at the stone in bewilderment. "Why would I swear upon a rock? Is it a relic of some sort?"

"No . . . a murder weapon."

Daniel stared at him and then turned toward the light. When he realized the significance of those dark splotches, he shuddered and dropped the rock onto the altar, wiping his hands hastily upon his tunic. "I do not understand. Melangell died when she hit her head on the churchyard cross. That serjeant, Tobias . . . he told us so. Was he lying?"

"No, that was the truth . . . as far as he knew. Melangell did strike her head on the cross, as he said. But her killer then picked up that rock, stood over her as she lay helpless at his feet, and split her skull open."

Daniel gasped, tried to shrink back, and Justin grabbed for his arm, held fast. "I do not know if she was already dying. I suppose we'll never know that. All I can say for certes is that the man who wielded that rock showed her no mercy, no pity. He wanted her dead . . . and this is the man you are protecting by your silence, Daniel. So pick up that rock again. You'll not get her blood on your hands, for it is dry by now. If you bring it close to the candle, you can see a black hair or two . . . her hair. You look upon that and tell me again how much you cared for her!"

"I did not know!" Daniel wrenched away from Justin's restraining hold. For a long moment, he stared down at the bloodied rock, his lips moving, and then he made the sign of the cross. "Why did you not tell me this sooner, Justin? Christ Jesus, this changes everything!"

"How, Daniel? Suppose you tell me how," Justin said, unrelenting. He was taken aback by Daniel's response, for when the boy looked up, he was smiling through tears.

"I've been such a fool. I thought she'd died by mishap, in a terrible accident, that even if she'd been pushed in the heat of anger, it was not meant . . ."

"And now that you know it was murder?"

"I know it was not Geoffrey," Daniel said, so simply that he took Justin's breath away. "I was so afraid, you see, for I told Melangell about Adela, about Geoffrey's coming marriage. When she was found dead in the churchyard, the place where they always met, I feared that they'd fought over Adela, that mayhap she'd stumbled and fallen back against the cross. . . . That is why I could not tell you about our argument, for it . . . it gave Geoffrey a motive."

Daniel swiped at his wet cheek with the back of his sleeve, then smiled again, a smile lit by genuine joy. "But my fears were for naught. Geoffrey would never have struck her with that rock, never. So whoever killed her, it was not my brother. And now I know I am not to blame, either. I thought it was my fault, that if only I'd kept silent about Adela . . ." He choked up then, and Justin unhooked his wineskin from his belt, silently passed it to the boy, waiting while Daniel drank.

"Why did you tell Melangell about Adela?"

Daniel blushed, averting his eyes in embarrassment. "It does me no credit, I know. Yet Geoffrey did not love her, not as I did. I knew he meant to marry Adela, and I told myself that Melangell had the right to know. I suppose I was hoping that she'd not forgive Geoffrey, that she'd turn to me for comfort . . ."

"But she did not," Justin said, and Daniel shook his head slowly.

"She became furious, would not believe me. She even put her hands over her ears so she'd not have to hear, insisting that Geoffrey loved her. 'He'll marry me now,' she said. When I persisted, she slapped me and ran off." Daniel raised his hand to his cheek, in remorseful recognition of that slap. "I convinced myself that by telling Melangell the truth, I'd be doing her a good turn. But in trying to keep her from getting hurt, I hurt her, too, and it grieves me greatly, that our last words were angry ones . . ."

Tears welled again in Daniel's eyes. Blinking them back, he gave Justin a shy smile, one that was both sad and hopeful. "It is a relief to have the truth out in the open at last. You'll say nothing of this to Geoffrey, though . . . will you? It would shame me beyond bearing if he knew of my suspicions. And I did not really believe it, not in my heart. Melangell must have been killed by a stranger, mayhap someone who saw her enter the churchyard and seized his chance. She was too trusting of men, would have been easy to take by surprise. It seems so cruel that she should have met with such evil in God's Own Acre . . ."

Justin nodded somberly; that, at least, he could agree with. Turning toward the altar, he retrieved the rock. It seemed to have gotten heavier in the time it had taken for Daniel to unburden himself at long last.

Justin had chosen a table where he could watch the alehouse door. An ale sat untouched in front of him, and Shadow lay at his feet, nudging him occasionally in a vain attempt to get attention. Nell had been no more successful than the dog, and had finally withdrawn in a sulk. When Jonas opened the door, letting in a crack of late-afternoon sun, she picked up a flagon and hastened toward him.

"He's been in a foul mood ever since he came back from St Paul's. I've not been able to coax two civil words out of him, so I assume he had no luck in prying answers from the Aston lad."

"Then why," the serjeant asked, "did he send for me?"

Nell swung around to give Justin a probing look, then hurried after Jonas. She reached the table just as he took a seat and sat down herself, her chin raised, shoulders squared, her body's very posture daring either man to object to her presence.

Neither one did. Jonas reached for her flagon, signaling to Ellis for two more cups. "Well?" he said. "I doubt that you summoned me for the pleasure of my company, as charming as it is. What did you find out?"

Justin took a deep swallow of ale, then told them, succinctly and without commentary of his own, letting the facts speak for themselves. Nell was the first to break the silence that followed his revelation. "The boy's loyalty to his brother is admirable. But how sad that no one in that family knows how to share what is in their hearts. If only he'd asked Geoffrey outright, how much misery he might have spared himself."

"You are assuming that Geoffrey is innocent," Jonas pointed out, and Nell set her drink down with a thud.

"You think he is not?"

Jonas gave a noncommittal shrug. "He is what he always was—a suspect. I will question him again, but unless we can dig up new evidence, nothing will come of it. We still cannot prove he met with Melangell in the churchyard that evening, and his motive remains a weak one. So the Welsh girl knew about the betrothal . . . so what? Even if she'd threatened to go to Adela, what of it? It would have been awkward, even unpleasant, but not likely to put the marriage plans at risk. Why would Master Serlo care that Geoffrey had been bedding a peddler's lass? A wink and a nudge for the uncle, a promise to the bride-to-be that the liaison was over, mayhap a few coins for the peddler, and that would be that."

It was a jaded view, but one they could not argue with. London was full of Geoffreys and Melangells and Adelas.

For young men on the prowl for clandestine pleasures, there were always girls willing to accommodate them, and long-suffering wives to turn a blind eye to such straying, provided it was not too blatant.

"Then Daniel's admission has changed nothing," Nell concluded. "It may have eased his mind, but he is still the one in the shadow of the gallows. Little wonder you're so disheartened, Justin. What now?"

Justin was staring into the depths of his drink. At first he didn't seem to have heard her question, but then he said, very low, "I keep coming back to Melangell's own words. 'He'll marry me now,' she said. Why now? What made her think she had the upper hand over Adela?"

"That is easy enough to answer." Nell's mouth turned down. "She believed it because she wanted to believe it, because it was too painful to admit the truth. Girls like Melangell always learn the hard way."

"That makes sense," Jonas allowed. "But I think you have something else in mind, Justin. Am I right?"

Justin nodded. "Suppose she was pregnant?"

"Well, that would be another kettle of fish," Jonas said cautiously. "If the girl was carrying Geoffrey's child, that might well put the cat amongst the pigeons. At best, Geoffrey would have to satisfy the girl and her father, reassure Master Serlo and his own father, placate his betrothed, and make some provisions for the babe. At worst, his hopes of marrying Adela might have gone up in a puff of blue smoke. It would depend upon how determined Melangell was to stir up a scandal, how prideful or unforgiving his betrothed was. So a pregnancy would indeed complicate life for Geoffrey far more than a few moonlight trysts. Passing strange, for we expect— even encourage—young men to plough any unfenced field, then act surprised when there's a crop to be tended. What you're really asking, though, is whether I think

Melangell's pregnancy would give Geoffrey a convincing motive for murder. I'd say so."

Nell had been uncharacteristically silent. When they glanced toward her now, she shook her head. "I do not think so," she said, refusing to meet their eyes. She seemed to hear the lack of conviction in her voice, for she bit her lip and then burst out with the truth. "It is just that . . . that I do not want it to be Geoffrey!"

Justin looked at her bleakly. "You think I do?"

Jonas smiled thinly. "Let's not get ahead of ourselves here. At this point, all we've got is a handful of cobwebs and smoke. What put this idea in your head, Justin?" Getting a shrug in reply, he studied the younger man with an eye that seemed much too knowing for Justin's comfort. "Well, no matter. We might as well pursue it, for what else have we got? This hunch of yours . . . do you have any evidence to back it up?"

"No," Justin said. "Not yet."

Justin waited until after dark, for by then the peddler would be back from his rounds. Cati was sitting cross-legged on a stack of firewood in the communal kitchen, black head bent over a flashing knife. She looked up, startled, at the sound of her name, acknowledging Justin with a hesitant smile.

"Where's your dog?" she asked, her dark eyes shining when Justin stepped aside to reveal Shadow's presence. The young dog proved to be an admirable ally, frisking forward to greet the girl like a long-lost friend, and for the first time, Justin heard Cati's laugh. Fending off Shadow's canine kisses, she giggled and politely made room for Justin on the wood pile. "I am carving a sling-shot," she explained, holding up a forked stick for Justin's inspection. "My old one broke."

Justin admired her handiwork and didn't doubt her when she boasted that she'd once knocked an apple off a tree branch with a well-aimed stone. Watching as she played tug-of-war with Shadow over a stick of firewood, he asked after her father and was startled when she said he was already asleep above-stairs.

"So early? Is he ailing, Cati?"

She shook her head, so vigorously that long hair whipped across her face. "No . . . he is just bone-weary. Ever since our mule died, Papa has been pulling the cart himself."

"That cannot be easy for him."

"Papa is strong," she insisted. But he saw the doubt in those wide brown eyes. "I try to help," she said softly. "I got some goose grease salve from Clara and I rubbed it into the blisters on his hands."

"I'm sure that did help, lass," Justin said, feeling as if he was offering a meagre crust of bread to a starving child. He hated to make use of Cati this way, hated what he might have to do to clear Daniel, hated where his suspicions were leading him, one reluctant step at a time. "I daresay all your father needs is a good night's sleep," he said, as heartily as his queasy conscience would allow. "He is not one to sicken easily. Not like Melangell."

"Why do you say that?" she asked, sounding surprised but not suspicious.

"I'd heard that she was ailing in the weeks ere she died, that her stomach was unsettled a lot," he said nonchalantly, and then held his breath, waiting for her response.

"Who told you that . . . Clara? Melangell did not want Papa to know, saying he'd worry for naught. But I knew she was worried, too, else why would she have sought out a doctor? Doctors are for the rich or the dying, not the likes of us. I do not know where she got the money for it, but she said it was worth every penny and she was so relieved afterward that the doctor must have helped."

"Do you know the name of the doctor, Cati?"

"No, she never told me that." Cati let Shadow win the tug-of-war and grinned when he then tried to entice her into a romp by dropping the stick into her lap. She and the pup were soon chasing each other about the kitchen, while Justin watched with a distracted smile. How had Melangell found a doctor? Who would she have turned to for advice? Who was she likely to have trusted?

"Cati . . . I'd like to talk to you about your sister's pilgrim cross. I think you know something about its disappearance," he said, and saw her face shutter, her body stiffen warily.

"What would I know?" she said evasively, and then cocked her head. "I hear Algar and Clara coming in!" And she was off, with Shadow at her heels, to welcome the landlord and his wife back from Compline services.

Justin's vexation with their inconvenient arrival was fleeting, for it occurred to him that they might be the very ones he was searching for. After an exchange of greetings with the affable landlord, he offered to fetch a bucket of water from their well, and while he was pouring it into Clara's kettle for boiling, he asked if she'd known that Melangell had been ailing.

Clara was utterly unlike her loquacious, expansive husband. The words that spewed out of his mouth in such torrents emerged from hers in thin trickles. She paused to look at him over the kettle, pale eyes appraising. "I suppose it cannot hurt the child now to speak out," she said at last. "Aye, I knew. I had my suspicions what was wrong, too, but I figured it was none of my concern, between the lass and the Almighty."

"Did you suggest she see a doctor?"

"Not a doctor, no. For what ailed her, I sent her to a midwife."

The morning sky was mottled with clouds and a brisk wind was coming off the river. Justin found the dwelling on Watling Street without difficulty, one of a row of wooden houses painted in bright hues of blue or green or red. The midwife's house was the color of spring grass, well kept up, the lower floor rented out to a friendly shoemaker who was more than happy to gossip about Dame Gunilda. She had an ailing husband, he said, sick with a palsy, and a hard row to hoe, for they had no children of their own, dependent upon the rent and what she earned as a midwife. She was out now, he said, called to a birthing at first light, but Justin was welcome to wait for her in the shop.

Justin did, pacing restlessly as customers came and went and the bells of St Antholin's Church rang in the canonical hours. It was nigh onto noon when the shoemaker pointed toward a woman trudging wearily up Watling Street and Justin hastened out to intercept her.

Gunilda was a stout, fair-haired woman in her middle years, her apron splotched with birthing blood, her veil askew. But her disheveled appearance was belied by shrewd blue eyes and a forthright manner. After hearing Justin out, she said briskly, "Come with me. I'll see to my husband, then we'll talk."

The man in the bed was gaunt and grey, his skin and hair bleached of color, his mouth contorted in a ghastly rictus of a grin. Justin's first fear was that he was dead. Gunilda showed no alarm though. Straightening up, she said, "He sleeps. If you keep your voice low, you may ask your questions now."

"I have reason to believe you saw a young woman in early April, slender and dark, with curly black hair and brown eyes and a Welsh accent. Her name was Melangell, although she may have given another. Do you remember her?"

"Yes, quite well. Why? What is your interest in her?"

"I am trying," he said, "to bring her killer to justice." She did not react as he expected, saying only, "I see."

He did not think her callous or uncaring, though. Like Jonas, he thought, she'd looked upon too much suffering ever to be surprised by life's cruelties. "Tell me," she said, and he did. She listened without interruption, and when he was done, she sat back in her chair, shading her eyes with her hand.

"She told me her true name," she said, "for she had nothing to hide. She had no guile in her, God pity her. What do you want to know?"

"Was she with child?"

"She was."

Justin exhaled a pent-up breath. "Would you be willing to swear to that in court?"

"Yes," she said, "I would." She rose then, abruptly, as her husband moaned in his sleep. Leaning over the bed, she tucked the sheets around his emaciated, twisted body, and then turned back to face Justin.

"Do you know why I remembered her so well? I see many girls who've gotten themselves in trouble, after all, and their stories are all alike, their fears the same."

Justin said nothing, thinking of Claudine. Had Melangell wanted pennyroyal, too? He did not ask, for if Gunilda did indeed help desperate girls to end unwanted pregnancies, she would never admit it.

"But this girl was different from the others. She was an innocent, Master de Quincy. No, not a virgin maid, but an innocent, nonetheless. She did not even know what the cessation of her monthly fluxes meant. She'd feared that she'd been stricken with some mysterious malady, an ailment she thought 'city folk' might catch. Poor, ignorant little lass . . ."

"And when you told her she was with child? Was she distraught, fearful?"

The midwife smiled sadly. "She rejoiced, Master de Quincy. She laughed and wept and said that she could not believe she'd been so blessed."

* * *

Justin had no luck in reaching Jonas, who'd been called out to hunt for a missing child. Leaving a message for the serjeant, he decided to stop by and check on Claudine. He found the Tower in an uproar. Eleanor was meeting in private with Hubert Walter, the Archbishop of Rouen, and several justiciars and bishops, and the Great Hall was packed with highborn guests and their entourages. Justin was able to snatch only a few moments with Claudine, who looked pale and seemed tense and preoccupied. The encounter was neither reassuring nor satisfying, and only exacerbated his overall sense of foreboding.

Sunset was still an hour off, and a rowdy game of camp-ball was in progress in the Tower bailey. Justin would normally have lingered to watch. Now he never even glanced toward the game; he was trailed by too many ghosts.

"Justin!"

The voice stopped Justin in his tracks, for it was one he'd not heard for nigh on five months, only occasionally echoing from the depths of unsettled dreams. He spun around, disbelieving, to find himself face-to-face with his father.

Aubrey de Quincy seemed even more stunned than Justin. For a frozen moment, they simply stared at each other. Justin recovered first. "What are you doing here?"

Aubrey was so rattled that he actually started to answer. "All the bishops have been summoned to London for the election of the Archbishop of Canterbury. We convene on Friday to—" He broke off then, remembering that he was the one who ought to be asking the questions. "Where have you been all these months? First you ride off from Chester without a word to me, and then I get a letter from Lord Fitz Alan, saying he dismissed you for contumacy and willful disobedience. What exactly did he mean by that?"

Justin started to explain but his father gave him no chance. "I would hope you did nothing to disgrace yourself. Since I recommended you for a position in Lord Fitz Alan's household, your behavior reflects upon me, too."

"You need not fear. I did not tell him about you." Justin looked away but not in time. The relief in Aubrey's eyes was unmistakable.

"Why did you not let me know what happened? It was most irresponsible for you to disappear like that. It never occurred to you to write a letter, telling me your whereabouts?"

Justin looked at him incredulously. "You expect me to believe you cared where I'd gone?"

Aubrey's jaw tightened. "I made discreet inquiries."

"Of whom . . . God?"

An angry flush rose in Aubrey's cheeks. His coloring was fair; his hair, greying now, had once been sunlit. Justin assumed that his mother had been dark, as he was. He could not bring himself to ask, though; the one time he'd questioned his father about her, he'd been told she was a wanton, better forgotten—words that would come back to haunt them both when he learned the truth about his paternity.

The silence between them was suffocating. Justin's breathing had quickened. He wanted to turn and walk away, but he could not. It occurred to him suddenly that Aubrey might well be a grandfather by year's end—if Claudine carried the babe safely to term, if she'd not lied. What of it, though? Confessing to his father would not even get him absolution. To the Bishop of Chester, he would ever be a shameful secret, never a son.

"This serves for naught," Aubrey said abruptly. "You made your feelings quite clear in our last meeting. So be it, then." He took only a few steps, though, before he stopped. He seemed to hesitate and then half turned, back toward Justin. "You are faring well on your own?"

"Yes," Justin said, "I am."

Before he could say more, a ball thudded onto the ground between them, rolling forward until it hit Justin's boot. Several of the camp-ball players started toward them, only to halt uncertainly once they realized they'd almost struck a bishop. One of the youths, though, was known to Justin, a squire to Nicholas de Mydden. Recognition was mutual and the boy advanced, grinning. "Sorry, Your Grace," he said cheekily. "Master de Quincy, could we have our ball back?"

Justin reached down and picked it up. A pig's bladder, filled with dried beans, it was surprisingly heavy. He threw it into the squire's outstretched hands, and then turned to face his father.

Aubrey was staring at him in appalled disbelief. "You have no right to that name!"

Justin raised his head. "I have a blood right," he said defiantly, "if not a legal one."

Aubrey's mouth thinned, the blue in his eyes turning to ice. Reaching out, he grasped Justin's arm. "This is no game, boy. Heed me and heed me well. If you do anything rash, we'll both be the losers for it. Now tell me the truth. Have you told anyone about me?" When Justin did not reply, Aubrey's fingers tightened and his voice sharpened. "Answer me! Have you?"

"No!" Justin jerked free, so violently that they both stumbled.

Aubrey remembered, too late, that they were in a public place. Lowering his voice, he said tautly, "You are sure?"

Justin's eyes glittered. "I've confided in only one person . . . the queen."

Aubrey's vaunted control shattered and for a moment, his emotions showed nakedly on his face: horror warring with hope that this was a cruel joke. Rallying, he said scornfully, "You expect me to believe that you've become the Queen of England's confidant?"

"Ask her," Justin said, "if you dare." When he saw Aubrey's color drain away, leaving him white and shaken, he knew that his father realized he was speaking the truth, however unlikely. But rarely had a victory left such a bitter taste.

14

LONDON

May 1193

Nell was staring down at the candle wax drippings that spattered the surface of the alehouse table. Her shoulders had slumped, her chin tucked into her chest so that her face was only partially visible to Justin. "This is so sad," she said, in a muffled, melancholy voice that sounded as if she were swallowing tears. "I am beginning to think I've done you a wrong, Justin. If not for my prodding, you'd never have become involved in Melangell's killing. I ought to have known better. For nothing in this life is ever easy or pain free, nothing."

"You're right about that," Justin agreed wearily. "This is bound to end badly, Nell. The only question is how badly."

"That poor little baby," she said softly, "with no one to pray for its soul. . . . Do you mean to tell Godwin and Cati?"

"No . . . why give them another loss to grieve?"

"Will Jonas now look upon Godwin as a suspect? There are men who'd have blamed the girl for shaming their family. If Godwin found out about her pregnancy and confronted Melangell in a rage . . . ?"

"I do not believe it happened that way, Nell. The Welsh do not judge the child to be guilty of the sins of the parents. To be bastard-born in Wales is not the burden it is throughout the rest of Christendom. Whilst Godwin has no Welsh blood, he wed a Welshwoman, lived for

years in the Marches. Clearly he shares some of the views
of his wife's people."

Nell would normally have wanted to know more
about these heretical beliefs of the Welsh, but she hadn't
the heart for it now. "So what will you do?" she asked,
and Justin pushed away from the table, got reluctantly to
his feet.

"There is but one solid piece of evidence linking Daniel
to Melangell's killing . . . her pilgrim cross. St Davydd did
not protect Melangell in her time of need. We can only
hope that he does better for Daniel."

Thames Street was crowded with Danish sailors eager to
sample London's more sinful pleasures. Godwin's hoarse
boasts about the fine quality of his goods earned him
blank looks or jests in a language he did not understand.
Jostled and ignored by the rowdy seamen flowing like a
foreign river around his cart, he succeeded only in attracting the hostile attention of a tailor, who strode from
his shop to demand that he sell his "rags" elsewhere.
Godwin did not argue. He'd rigged up a rope harness between the shafts and by throwing his weight against it, he
succeeded in getting the cart moving again.

Watching from across the street, Justin let the peddler
pass by and then caught the eye of the leggy little girl
trailing after the cart. Cati's long black hair was tangled,
in need of her dead sister's brush, and her skirt was clumsily mended, with uneven stitches and the wrong color
thread. It occurred to Justin that Godwin urgently needed
a wife for himself, a mother for his daughter. But how
could he hope to feed three on the meagre income he was
now eking out?

Falling into step beside Cati, Justin said, "I need your
help, lass."

"You want to buy something?" she asked, with a

disingenuousness that might have been amusing under other circumstances.

"Daniel did not kill your sister, Cati. If I am to save him from the gallows, I need to know how that St Davydd's cross got into his coffer. I think you can tell me."

She gave him a sideways glance, a half shrug. She'd slowed her pace, so that the cart was now some yards ahead of them. "I do not want my papa to know," she said at last. "You promise?"

When Justin nodded, she shook her head. "Swear it," she insisted, "and then spit!" Only after he'd complied with her ritual did some of the tension ease in those narrow little shoulders. "Melangell and I were taking our bath in Clara's kitchen," she said, speaking so softly that Justin had to strain to catch her words. "I noticed that she no longer had the cross around her neck. I thought she'd lost it and berated her for being so careless, for I knew Papa would be sorely distraught. She was vexed at first. But she finally told me the truth, after making me promise that I'd not tell Papa."

"She gave it to her lover," Justin said, and Cati nodded. "Yes," she whispered. "She gave it to Geoffrey."

Justin spent the remainder of the afternoon trying to find Jonas. The gaol by the River Fleet, Newgate Gaol, the Guildhall, the Jewry, and finally the Tower. Each time he was too late; Jonas had been there and gone.

The upper storey of the Tower keep was overflowing with the highborn. The Bishop of Salisbury, Hubert Walter, was the center of attention, and to judge by the deference being shown him, his election to the archbishopric of Canterbury was seen as a foregone conclusion. For Justin, there was greater danger in this conclave of bishops than in the meanest Southwark streets, but he had no choice. Hoping that he'd not run straightaway into his father, he edged into the crowded hall.

Claudine intercepted him almost at once. She was becomingly flushed, in a high temper, and launched into an indignant account of a quarrel she'd just had with another of the queen's ladies. Justin listened with half an ear, his eyes sweeping the hall for that one bishop among so many. It was like looking for a single carp in a pool teeming with fish, difficult to distinguish one from another.

"I am glad you're here, Justin, for I have need of you." She lowered her voice. "I've heard that there is a midwife in Aldgate who offers herbs that ease this accursed morning queasiness. I cannot very well send anyone else on such an errand, can well imagine the rumors that would stir up. Afterward, let's stop by the Eastcheap market. Spending money invariably raises my spirits!"

Justin missed that indirect admission of despondency, heard only the jest about shopping. "I cannot take you to the market today," he said brusquely, "for I've an urgent matter to attend to."

Claudine's eyes sparked. "Jesú forfend that I trouble you with my trifling concerns," she snapped, turning to flounce away, but not so quickly that he could not catch her. Her surprise was considerable, therefore, when he did not even try. Expecting at any moment to feel his restraining hand upon her arm, she was taken aback to find he'd stalked out.

Justin's anger carried him as far as the bailey. There his step slowed. Instead of heading for the stables to retrieve Copper, he turned and reentered the Tower keep. He found Claudine sitting in one of the window alcoves, looking so dispirited that he felt a conscience pang. Moving toward her, he saw her head come up defiantly and gave her no chance to rekindle their quarrel, saying swiftly, "I got some bad news today. Yet that is no excuse for taking out my foul mood on you, Claudine."

"No, it is not," she said coolly, before curiosity won out over pique. "What bad news?"

"I learned," he said, "that someone I like is a murderer."

She stared at him and then gave an abrupt laugh. "I'll say this for you, Justin, that your troubles are never ordinary! But do not dare stop now. Tell me more about this murderer."

He did, using no names. She listened attentively, reminding him again how different she was from John's sultry, shallow Windsor bedmate, and when he was done, she went right to the heart of the matter. "So you think the lover killed the girl to keep her from thwarting his chances with the heiress. Sad, but not so surprising. But did he then deliberately divert suspicion onto his own brother?"

"I do not know," Justin admitted. "For his brother's sake, I would hope not. But I am not finding it easy to give him the benefit of any doubt."

She nodded somberly. "The killing was most likely an act of panic, not calculated. But if he could cold-bloodedly connive to blame his brother, that would be unforgivable. I wish you luck, Justin, for I fear you will need it."

Justin did, too. "I'll take you wherever you want to go once this is settled," he promised, and she smiled. Her next question caught him off balance.

"Justin . . . do you know the Bishop of Chester?"

He stiffened. "Why?"

She didn't miss the evasiveness of his answer. "Well, he has been asking questions about you, discreetly done but too persistent for casual curiosity. And at the moment, he is staring at you with an odd intensity, the way a cat might watch a mousehole."

Justin couldn't help himself. He spun around, saw his father standing by the open hearth. They looked at each other in what was the loudest silence of Justin's life, and the longest. And then he heard Claudine's indrawn breath. Even before their eyes met, Justin knew she'd guessed the truth. She'd always been too clever by half, would need no other clues than their shared surname and her knowledge of his past.

"Justin . . . is he your father?" she asked softly, not at all discouraged when he didn't reply. "I'm right, aren't I? That explains so much!"

Justin saw no point in making denials she'd not believe. "I would be grateful if you kept this to yourself, Claudine," he said, and when she promised that she'd say nary a word to another living soul, he wondered if he could believe her.

Jonas blew on the dice and then flung them onto the table. Two of the dice turned up a seven, but the third one showed a four. Jonas swore and the other man chortled, then reached for the dice, threw, and gave a triumphant shout when he rolled three sixes. "I warned you I was unbeatable at raffle," he boasted as Jonas dropped a few coins into his outstretched palm. "What say you we try hasard now?"

"Let me get another drink first," Jonas said, looking around for the serving maid. He swore again, profanely, at the sight of a too-familiar face, and warned Justin off with a growl. "I'm not on duty now, de Quincy, so tend to your own troubles till the morrow. All I want to do tonight is enjoy a good ale and play a few games of hasard."

"I'll buy the ale," Justin said. "But your dicing will have to wait. Right now we need to plan a hunt."

Jonas glowered at him, but allowed himself to be steered toward a corner table, despite the protests of his dicing partner. "What sort of a hunt?" he demanded. "What quarry?"

"The kind you care most about catching," Justin said grimly. "A killer."

* * *

The morning had begun with a promise of premature summer warmth, but by noon the sun was getting skittish, darting behind every passing cloud, and by day's end, the sky was a leaden shade of grey. Justin and Jonas had spent several hours keeping the mercer's shop under surveillance and by now they were both chilled and tired. So far their vigil had been uneventful. Humphrey Aston had quarreled loudly with a customer, cuffed the ears of one of his hapless apprentices, and fawned over Adela when she paid a brief visit in midafternoon. Geoffrey left the shop only once, trailed inconspicuously by Jonas to the riverside cookshop and back. Eventually the last customer departed and the journeymen pulled down and locked the shutters. As Justin and Jonas watched, Humphrey, his son, and the apprentices disappeared through the gateway leading to the Astons' great hall.

Jonas stood and stretched. "What now?"

"Soon," Justin predicted. "Since he plans to take supper with Adela this eve, he'll go to St Paul's ere Vespers begins."

"And if he does not?"

"He will," Justin said, with a certainty that was justified by Geoffrey Aston's reappearance shortly thereafter. Geoffrey had changed into a dark green tunic—green, the color for lovers, Justin thought bitterly—and brushed his blond hair. Under his arm, he carried the sack from the cookshop and he'd raided his mother's garden for a small bouquet of columbine and primroses, presumably for Adela. But his dapper appearance was belied by his demeanor; there was no spring in his step and he kept his head down as he trudged toward the Cheapside, making it easy for them to follow him, unobserved.

"I cannot believe I let myself be talked into this," Jonas grumbled. "We could have confronted him at first light and been done with it."

"How . . . by beating a confession out of him? It has to be done in his brother's presence, Jonas, for it to work."

"I do not share your faith that an appeal to his conscience will succeed. It has been my experience that killers rarely have consciences."

"Well, I think this one does," Justin insisted and hoped he was right. Ahead of them, Geoffrey was entering St Paul's churchyard and they quickened their pace. Vespers had not yet begun and there were only a few parishioners chatting on the steps of the church. One of Jonas's men was loitering beside the cross, flirting with two girls passing by, although he straightened up and tried to look alert and vigilant as soon as he spotted his serjeant. "Come with me," Jonas said curtly, and he hurried to catch up with them as they entered the church.

They found Daniel and Geoffrey in the nave. The younger boy was rooting in the cookshop sack. "Geoffrey brought me some marrow tarts. You can share one, if you like." Then he saw Jonas standing behind Justin, and his smile faded. "Why is he here? He cannot take me yet!"

"I'm not here for you, lad." Jonas advanced up the nave, keeping his eye all the while upon Geoffrey. "Remember that Flemish mercer? Well, we found him in Stamford. He is on his way back to London with one of my men even as we speak, ready to reveal who bought that fragment of silk, Melangell's last gift."

Even in the subdued lighting of the nave, Justin could see that Geoffrey had lost color. But Daniel was smiling again, tentatively, like one afraid to let himself hope. "Then . . . then Melangell's true killer may soon be exposed?"

"What do you say, Geoffrey?" Jonas's teeth flashed in what was technically a smile. "Think you that the true killer is about to be unmasked?"

Geoffrey went even paler. "I . . . I hope so," he mumbled. "Daniel, I have to go."

"Nonsense," Jonas said heartily. "Adela will wait for you." He cocked his head to the side, with another one of those terrible smiles. "Or will she? Who knows with women, eh, lad? Unpredictable creatures, the lot of them. Take Melangell now, with her tears and threats. She ought to have known better. A man is not likely to look fondly upon a woman who is set upon his ruination, is he? It could even be argued that she brought it upon herself—"

"What are you on about?" Daniel glanced uneasily from the serjeant to his brother. "What threats?"

Geoffrey sucked in his breath. "I do not know. All this talk of threats and ruination . . . it makes no sense. Melangell knew about Adela from the first."

Daniel opened his mouth, but no words emerged. Justin had taken advantage of Geoffrey's preoccupation with Jonas to move closer, much closer. "So you told me," he said, "that first day, out in the street. I was favorably impressed by your candor, as you hoped I'd be. Most people are not good liars. They are either too emphatic or too sly. Not you, though. Credit where due, Geoffrey, you lie well."

"I am not lying! Melangell did know about Adela!"

"No, she did not . . . not until Daniel told her, the day she died."

"Daniel told her," Geoffrey echoed numbly. Daniel said nothing, but he didn't need to; his stricken look spoke volumes. Geoffrey's eyes darted from one to the other; Justin could see sweat now glistening at his temples. "Daniel . . . Daniel was wrong. Melangell *did* know about Adela. Mayhap not about the plight troth, but . . ." He let the words fall away. "I do not understand why this matters. There were no threats, no tears. I do not know what nonsense Daniel may have told Melangell, for I did not see her on that day."

"Of course you did, lad," Jonas said calmly, almost

gently. "You gave her the silk you bought that morning from the Flemish mercer."

"No . . ." Geoffrey's voice had thickened. "No, I did not!"

"Then why," Jonas asked, "did the mercer say you did? What reason would he have to lie?" His own lie, delivered with convincing aplomb and a shrewd sense of timing, dealt a severe blow to Geoffrey's embattled defenses. He bit his lip and took a faltering backward step as Jonas continued, reasonably and remorselessly, "No, lad, you might as well face it; he'll be believed. We already have the motive and his testimony will prove you had the opportunity, too. Men have been hanged on less evidence than that."

Geoffrey tried to laugh in disbelief, but what emerged was a strangled sound of despair. "This is madness, all of it. Why would I kill Melangell? Even if she had threatened to go to Adela, what of it? Master Serlo would not care that I'd been tumbling a peddler's wench. So common a sin would not jeopardize the marriage . . . and what other reason would I have for killing her?"

Jonas smiled again, a hunter's smile. "So you admit that jeopardizing your marriage would be a motive for murder."

"I did not say that!"

"It sounded like that to me. How about you, lad?" Jonas swung around suddenly upon Daniel. "Didn't it sound like that to you?"

"I . . . I do not know! Why are you badgering him like this?"

Jonas was no longer smiling. "Because there is blood on his hands, the blood of two innocents. In killing Melangell, he killed a child, too, his own child."

Daniel choked back a cry. "Melangell was pregnant? Geoffrey, is that true?"

Stunned, Geoffrey could only shake his head mutely, the flowers for Adela falling unheeded to the floor at his feet.

"I spoke to the midwife myself," Justin said, with enough ice in his voice to turn that simple sentence into the most damning of indictments. "She remembers Melangell well, for she was so joyful upon learning she was with child, Geoffrey's child."

Daniel stared at his brother. "Christ Jesus ... Geoffrey!"

"No!" Geoffrey finally found his voice. "No, it is a lie, all of it!"

"Are we all lying, then? The midwife, the Flemish mercer, your brother? If that is going to be your defense, God pity you, lad." Jonas sounded almost fatherly now, no longer accusing. "You'd do better to admit the truth, seek forgiveness from God and the girl's family. It cannot have been easy, living with a burden like this—"

"How can you have sympathy for him?" Justin asked sharply. "He killed that girl!"

"Yes, he did," Jonas conceded. "But I doubt that he meant to do it. There are different sorts of killings, and it is easier to understand one committed in a red-hot rage, one that was not planned and was most likely regretted afterward, once it was too late. That was the way it happened, Geoffrey?"

The serjeant's question was so natural, so disarming, that Justin half expected Geoffrey to confess without even realizing that he was doing so. But Geoffrey stayed stubbornly silent.

"Listen to the serjeant, lad." By now they'd attracted a shocked audience: the priest preparing to say Vespers, several parishioners arriving early for the service. "Repent your sin whilst you still can," the priest entreated. "The Almighty will forgive you, but only if you confess and do penance."

"I ... I have nothing to confess," Geoffrey insisted,

but it was a hollow protest, convincing no one. Realizing that, he repeated loudly, "I've done nothing wrong!"

That was Justin's cue. Clamping down on Geoffrey's arm, he said scathingly, "Look at your brother when you say that—if you dare! Mayhap Jonas is right and you did not mean to kill the girl. But even if the murder was unplanned, you knew exactly what you were doing when you set out to blame Daniel for the killing."

Geoffrey gasped. "No! I would never do that!"

"That almost sounded convincing," Justin jeered. "But we're past the time for denials. All your secrets have come home to roost, Geoffrey . . . the Flemish mercer, Melangell's pregnancy, that bloodied rock, her jealousy of Adela. We know, too, about her St Davydd's cross. She gave it to you, a pledge of her love, and after you killed her, you hid the cross in your brother's coffer so suspicion would fall upon him—"

"No! It was not like that!" Geoffrey tore loose from Justin's hold, spun around toward his brother. "Tell them, Daniel, tell them you do not believe this!"

Daniel stood, frozen, staring not at Geoffrey, but at Justin. "Melangell gave him the cross? You are sure?"

"She told Cati," Justin said, and Daniel shuddered, a soft moan, involuntary and anguished, escaping his lips.

"Daniel, no, that's not the way it happened!" Geoffrey's words were slurring in his haste to get them out. "I never meant to blame you, I swear it!"

"You put the cross in with his clothes," Justin pointed out relentlessly. "And then when it was discovered, you urged him to flee, knowing that flight would be taken as an admission of guilt. Did you hope that he'd be killed resisting arrest? How disappointed you must have been when he managed to reach sanctuary!"

"No . . . no, it was not like that! I never wanted Daniel to be hurt!" Geoffrey reached out to his brother, but Daniel shied away from his touch. His face was ashen in the candlelight, his eyes glistening with unshed tears. Geoffrey's mouth contorted. "Daniel, for the love of God—"

His voice broke and Jonas was suddenly at his side, a hand clasped on one of those quaking shoulders. "Then why did you hide the cross in Daniel's mantle?"

"I didn't . . ." Geoffrey gulped back a sob. "I did not know what to do with it . . . after. I could not keep it, but neither could I throw it away, for it had meant too much to Melangell. . . . So I shoved it into our coffer of winter clothes till I could think more clearly. I never thought about the mantle being Daniel's, I swear I did not . . ."

"A touching tale," Justin said, with a sneer he patterned after Durand's, "but it is one not even your mother would believe. You had your chance to speak up and clear your brother the night we found the cross. Instead, you sent him out into the streets to run for his life, hoping that he'd be cornered and killed—"

"No . . . Jesú, no!" Geoffrey shook his head vehemently, frantically. "I wanted him to get safe away! I know I should have owned up to the truth that night, and I would to God I had . . . Daniel, I swear I do. I never meant for any of this to happen. None of it was planned. Melangell and I were quarreling, she was threatening to go to Adela, I tried to stop her, and she pulled free, tripped, and hit her head on the cross . . ."

"So you panicked," Jonas suggested. "You ripped her clothes to make it look as if she'd been raped and fled, forgetting about the silk until it was too late. Was that how it happened, lad?"

"I never meant to kill her. None of it seemed real. Afterward, I could not believe it had truly happened. It would have been a bad dream, if not for the blood . . ." Geoffrey was visibly trembling by now. As they watched, he slowly sank to his knees by the altar and wept.

Jonas waited until the tear storm had begun to subside, and then got the sagging youth to his feet. "At least you've cleared your brother now," he said, and Geoffrey sobbed again. He seemed to be in a daze, all fight gone out of him. He looked back only once, imploringly, at his brother.

"I would never have let you hang," he said huskily. "I swear that upon Christ's own rood."

Daniel had retreated into the shadows behind the altar. He did not reply and the serjeant prodded Geoffrey toward the closest door. Before they could reach it, Daniel cried out suddenly, urgently, "Jonas!"

The other man turned, still keeping a firm grip on his prisoner. "What is it, lad?"

"You cannot take him." Daniel's face was still wet with tears, but his voice was steady. "You cannot arrest him here. This is a sanctuary."

"You knew this would happen, de Quincy. Admit it!"

Justin met Jonas's accusatory glare composedly. "I thought it might."

Jonas shook his head in disgust. "You've been keeping too much company with Lord John," he said sourly, "for you're picking up his conniving habits." Turning on his heel, he strode from the churchyard, out into a street now dark and deserted. Justin followed, unrepentant, but prudently giving the serjeant's anger time to cool. They continued along Cheapside, and finally Jonas said grudgingly:

"I suppose we could have had a worse ending to this bloody business. But I would like to know why you'd want to protect Geoffrey Aston from the hangman. For all those remorseful tears, he did bash the girl's head in with a rock."

"I was not trying to spare Geoffrey," Justin said hastily, for he, too, was haunted by that bloodied rock. "But I did want to spare Agnes and Daniel . . . and as strange as it sounds, I was thinking of Melangell, too. As much as she loved Geoffrey, would she have wanted to see him hanged?"

Jonas grunted. "I have enough trouble communicating with the living, am not about to start asking after the wants of the dead," he said, and they walked on in silence.

15

LONDON

June 1193

The sunlight was white-gold, shimmering with summer heat. Butterflies floated like feathers on the still air, the Tower gardens in fragrant, vibrant bloom. But the tranquillity was deceptive, a false Eden. In the grassy mead, a stable cat stalked unseen prey and a hawk circled overhead. Claudine watched as the songbirds scattered, alarmed by that lazily drifting shadow, death on the wing. She'd had a bad morning, forced to fast by the queasiness that still unsettled her days. The rose Justin had picked for her now lay shredded in her lap, stripped of all its petals by her restless fingers.

"Well," she said morosely, "if there was any doubt, it has bled away. I missed my third flux."

Justin glanced at her swiftly. "Did you have doubts that you were with child?"

"I tried to," she said, with a rueful smile. Justin wasn't sure what to say, so he plucked another rose and handed it to her. She flashed a more convincing smile, but petals were soon drifting down into the grass at her feet. "I asked the queen if the pregnancy would get easier in time. She said usually so, but that some are vexing to the very end. She said of all her pregnancies, she was the most uncomfortable whilst carrying John. So he was causing trouble even ere he was born!"

The best Justin could manage was a laconic "Not surprising." He doubted that there'd ever come a time when he'd feel comfortable jesting with Claudine about John.

"The queen says she has two nunneries in mind," Claudine confided, "either Godstow outside Oxford or Wherwell, which is near Winchester. You'll take me once we decide, Justin?"

He assured her that he would, but then he rose from the bench. Claudine frowned. "You are leaving already?"

"I must. This afternoon Geoffrey Aston is abjuring the realm."

"So soon? His forty days have not gone by, surely?"

"He chose not to wait. Daniel was hoping for a miracle to clear him, so of course he'd have clung to sanctuary until the last possible moment. Geoffrey had admitted his guilt, so he has nothing to gain by delay."

"Justin . . . take me with you." Claudine put a hand on his arm, looking up at him with a flirtatious smile. "I've never seen a man abjure the realm."

"Jesú forfend you miss an experience like that," Justin said dryly.

Claudine wrinkled her nose playfully at the sarcasm. "Wait here," she directed, "whilst I go tell the queen!" Justin sat down again on the bench, watching as she hastened back into the keep, moving with so light and lively a step that none would have suspected she was with child.

By the time Justin and Claudine rode into St Paul's precincts, Geoffrey Aston had already emerged from the cathedral, blinking uncertainly in the harsh noonday light after several weeks of shadowed seclusion. He wore only a single, simple garment of coarse sackcloth, head and feet bare, clutching his wooden cross in an awkward, white-knuckled grip. Flanked by an impassive Jonas and a preening Tobias, he was kneeling before one of the sheriffs of London, Roger Fitz Alan, and the mutterings of the spectators made it clear that he had just confessed to killing Melangell in the churchyard of St Mary Magdalene's.

Claudine pressed forward to see better, and Justin followed, leading their horses. A large crowd had turned out for the spectacle, and most gave way grudgingly. Searching for familiar faces, Justin soon spotted Agnes, her eyes swollen with weeping, leaning heavily upon her husband's supporting arm. Master Serlo was standing by St Paul's Cross, somberly dressed in black, although there was no sign of Adela. Justin wondered if she'd chosen to stay away, wanting to spare herself this last glimpse of the youth who was to have been her husband, or if she'd been bidden to do so by her uncle. Nell and Gunter were present, as were several of their Gracechurch Street neighbors. But he could not find Humphrey Aston or his wife, nor did he see Daniel, or Godwin and Cati.

The sheriff was proclaiming the rules of the abjuration, warning Geoffrey that he must remain on the king's road, that he must proceed straightaway for the chosen port of Dover, that he could not tarry for more than one night anywhere along the route, that he must take the first ship sailing for France and swear by the Holy Cross that he would not return again to England. Geoffrey's head was bowed, his voice almost inaudible as he promised to obey these strictures. The sheriff then reminded the spectators that Geoffrey was now under the protection of the Church.

Justin was startled to hear murmurings of sympathy rustling through the crowd; pity was usually in short supply when felons were forced to do public penance for their crimes. When he said as much to Claudine, she shrugged, saying that the handsome always fare better in this world. It was a cynical observation, but Justin could not find fault with it; how else explain why people were calling Geoffrey a "poor lad," as if the true tragedy was the ruination of his life, not the loss of Melangell's? Justin stared coolly at Geoffrey's gleaming blond head. He was not sorry that Geoffrey would not hang, but he'd forfeited any right to forgiveness the moment he'd reached for that rock.

As Geoffrey rose to his feet, struggling to pick up his cross, some of the spectators began to drift away, for the high drama of the event was now over. Turning to soothe his restive stallion, Justin happened to catch sight of the figure hovering on the edge of the crowd. Muffled in a hood that was conspicuously out of place on a summer's day, Humphrey Aston looked like a man bleeding from an internal wound, his face grey and drawn, his skin blotched, his grieving so raw that Justin felt an unwelcome twinge of pity. He waited, but Humphrey did not move toward Geoffrey, and when he glanced again toward the mercer, he was gone.

Geoffrey started his halting walk across the churchyard, his feet already stinging from the gravel, for his were not the callused soles of youths accustomed to going barefoot. He'd taken only a few steps, though, before Daniel pushed through the crowd to his side. They stared at each other for a pain-fragmented moment, and then Daniel stepped forward, enfolding his tearful brother in a wordless, healing embrace. Again, the bystanders nodded and murmured approvingly, and Justin wondered if they'd have been as magnanimous if Daniel had been the one going off into foreign exile.

Echoing his thoughts with eerie accuracy, Jonas appeared at his elbow, muttering in a mordant undertone, "Half the fools here think that outer packaging is proof positive of the state of one's soul. I suppose we ought to be thankful that Gilbert the Fleming did not have flaxen hair and a winning smile like the Aston lad, else they'd have been weeping over him, too."

They were soon joined by Nell and Gunter, and Justin's worlds collided as Claudine acknowledged his Gracechurch Street friends. It could have been an awkward moment, but Claudine had polished her social skills in the demanding arena of the royal court, and she was up to the challenge, unperturbed by Nell's obvious hostility, Gunter's discomfort, and Jonas's sardonic, silent amusement. Within moments, she'd adroitly drawn them into a lively discussion of Geoffrey's punishment, even coaxing the taciturn Gunter into confiding that he'd not have wanted to see Agnes's nephew go to the gallows.

"You can thank St Justin for that," Jonas gibed, and Claudine turned her long-lashed gaze upon the serjeant, full power.

"What will happen to Geoffrey now?" she asked, in appealingly accented English, for unlike many at the royal court, she'd taken the trouble to learn the native language of this island realm. "What usually befalls men who abjure the realm? Do they seek to do penance for their sins in monasteries? Or," she added slyly, "do they use those sins as stepping stones to greater crimes?"

Jonas grinned. "More of the latter than the former, my lady. I've heard that the French thank us not for exporting our outlaws to their shores. They have no like custom over there, so they cannot even return the favor by sending us their felons. As for young Aston, I suspect he'll do better than most. I doubt that Frenchwomen are any wiser than ours when it comes to a good-looking lad with an easy way about him. And I'd wager that he has money hidden away under that sackcloth, in addition to what the Church provided for his expenses on the road."

Nell nodded emphatically at that. "I know that Agnes and Odo scraped together what they could, and Agnes told me that Humphrey was—for once in his life—being open-handed, giving her a goodly sum to take to Geoffrey last night. Rumor has it that even Master Serlo contributed some."

"A pity they couldn't have been as generous with Melangell's family," Justin said caustically, and Nell scowled at him.

"You cannot blame them, Justin, for grieving over Geoffrey's plight. He is paying a heavy price for a moment of madness."

Justin couldn't resist making the obvious riposte. "Not as heavy a price as Melangell paid."

It was Jonas who played the unlikely role of peacemaker. "If we are going to fight about this, I suggest we do it over wine. Let's find a tavern. We'll let you pay, de Quincy; from the way your money pouch is bulging, you can well afford it."

"Sorry to disappoint you, Jonas, but this is not worth anything, not even blood money," Justin said, opening the pouch to show them the rock.

Nell grimaced. "Why are you carrying that . . . that thing around with you?"

Justin shrugged. "I had it in mind to get rid of it after the abjuration, mayhap put it back in the churchyard where she died. Out of curiosity, how did Geoffrey explain away the rock whilst he was making his tearful confession?"

"He did not," Jonas said, and Justin turned to stare at the serjeant.

"What are you saying? Doesn't a man have to confess fully ere he can abjure the realm?"

"Supposedly so, but he made no mention of it in his confession. He admitted quarreling with Melangell after she threatened to go to Adela and he admitted panicking and trying to make it look as if she'd been raped. But he claimed that she died when she fell back against the cross. Nary a word about picking up a rock and dashing her brains out with it. I guess the lad is getting forgetful under the strain."

"Why did the sheriff not challenge him on it?" Justin demanded, and Jonas gave a weary shake of his head.

"Ask him, de Quincy, not me. Mayhap Tobias neglected to tell him about that particular detail, or mayhap he decided it did not matter."

Justin was outraged. "It *does* matter," he insisted. "He owes Melangell the truth!" Tossing the reins of their mounts to Gunter, he swung around and began to shove his way through the crowd. He had no difficulty in overtaking Geoffrey, who was already leaving bloody footprints in the dust. Lugging the cross, he was staring straight ahead, resolutely ignoring the occasional jeer or catcall as he plodded along the Cheapside, trailed by several of Jonas's men to make sure he got safely out of London. When Justin caught up with him, he flinched at the sound of pursuing footsteps, his shoulders slumping with relief as he recognized Justin.

"I was half expecting her father to be here to confront me," he confessed, "and no blame to him if he did. How could he not hate me for what I did?"

"And what did you do, Geoffrey? I understand your memory needs prodding, for you omitted the most important part of your confession."

Geoffrey came to a halt in the roadway. "What do you mean? I held nothing back. Why would I?"

His feigned bewilderment only stoked Justin's anger all the higher. "You told only half the truth, the half that works in your favor. The other half you ignored, hoping it would be forgotten . . . like Melangell herself."

Geoffrey shook his head slowly. "I do not know what you are talking about. Melangell will never be forgotten, not by me."

."Well said, Geoffrey; you'd have made a fine actor. I would almost believe you . . . if not for this!" Pulling the rock from his pouch, Justin slammed it into the palm of Geoffrey's hand.

Geoffrey looked down at the rock, then back up at Justin, uncomprehending. "What is this?" he asked. "I do not understand."

Justin stared at him in disbelief. "You truly do not . . . do you?"

Jonas's men were growing impatient at the delay and one of them ordered Geoffrey to move along. Reluctantly, he did, first politely handing Justin back the rock. As the men hustled him away, he looked over his shoulder, making one final plaintive protest. "I would not have let Daniel take the blame, Justin, I swear I would not!"

Justin would later wish that he had responded, given Geoffrey the assurance he sought. Now, though, he was too stunned, unable to do anything but stare down at the rock in his hand. "Jesus God," he said softly, as much to himself as the Almighty, "how can this be?"

"How can what be?" Jonas had muscled his way onto the Cheapside. His gaze flicked from the rock to Justin's face, that lone eye narrowing at what he found. "What ails you? What happened?"

Justin swallowed. "I showed him the rock, Jonas, and it meant nothing to him . . . nothing at all."

"Jesú! Are you sure about this?"

Justin nodded and they turned as one to stare after Geoffrey's slow progress along Cheapside, not moving until long after he had vanished from sight.

"Justin, this serves for naught." Nell set a fresh flagon down on the table, then took a seat across from him. "You're not even drinking," she scolded, glancing toward his brimming cup, "just brooding. For the love of the Lord, let it go!"

"I cannot," he admitted, "God help me, I cannot. How could I have been so wrong, Nell? I was so sure this rock was the murder weapon, so sure!"

Nell regarded the troublesome rock with distaste. "Must you have it out on the table like this? It does have blood on it, after all, even if it is not Melangell's."

"Whose is it, then, if not hers? It makes no sense, Nell. What of the black hairs on it? I keep going around in a circle, always ending up back where I started."

"You're in a rut, not a circle, and getting nowhere fast. Put the rock away, Justin. Not all of God's mysteries are meant to be solved. Curfew will be ringing soon and I do not want to send you out sober into the night . . . so drink up, and let's talk of other matters besides that wretched rock. How is Luke faring these days? Have you heard from him since he returned to Winchester?"

"One letter, saying he'd gotten home safely and complaining at length about that 'four-legged fiend,' Aldith's dog, who ate his best boots whilst he was away . . . or so Aldith claims." Justin mustered up a smile at the domestic discord of his friends, but almost at once lapsed back into a distracted silence.

Nell gave an exaggerated, theatrical sigh. "Like a dog with a bone, you are." Seeing that Justin was not going to drink his ale, she reached over and helped herself to it, taking a deep swallow and then another. "This batch tastes a bit off; I'll be having a word with the brewer. You know what surprised me, Justin? That Melangell's father was not there today to see Geoffrey's public penance. I thought the Welsh put a great store by vengeance."

"Vengeance is a luxury, one Godwin cannot afford, not since his mule died."

"Misfortune does seem to be dogging that poor man'

footsteps. I saw him and the little lass the other day in the Cheapside, and my heart went out to them, Justin. Worn down to skin and bones and blisters, he is, and Cati like a wild creature, as bedraggled and unkempt as any beggar's child. What will befall her if her father drops dead in the mule's traces one day? Has she no other kin at all?"

"Her mother has family back in Wales." Justin reached for the drink Nell had appropriated. Thinking about Cati's bleak future was as troubling as thoughts of that blasted, bloodied rock. "She is tougher than she looks," he said, seeking to convince himself as much as Nell. "Her grieving for Melangell is an open wound, one that will be a long time healing. But she is not one for sharing her grief. Only once do I remember her being on the brink of tears, when she was telling me about her sister's funeral and the red dress she'd set her heart upon . . ."

The image of Cati's stifled sorrow was too vivid for comfort, needed to be washed away with ale, and he brought the cup up with such haste that it slopped over the rim. It never reached his mouth. Setting the cup down with a thud, he gave Nell such a blind, unfocused look that she felt a superstitious chill and plucked uneasily at his sleeve.

"Justin, what is it? You look like you've seen one of God's own ghosts!"

He blinked, like a man coming out of a spell. "Not exactly. But it may be that Melangell just whispered a word in my ear, for I remembered something . . ." Before Nell could question him further, he was on his feet. "I have to go, Nell. There is someone I must see."

"Tonight? Curfew is nigh!" She protested in vain, though; he was already halfway toward the door.

The usually affable landlord was less accommodating after being roused from bed and it took a combination of coins and blandishments to win his cooperation. Grumbling under his breath, he lit a candle and led Justin up the stairs to the room rented by Melangell's father. Godwin awoke at once, sitting up in alarm and fumbling for his clothes. Justin claimed the candle, raising it so that its wan flame would identify them. Godwin squinted up at the shivering light, then gestured for silence, pointing toward the pallet where Cati slept. The men retreated, Justin to wait in the stairwell, the landlord to go back to bed. After a few moments, Godwin emerged, half dressed, to sit beside Justin on the stairs.

"Why are you here? What now?" His voice sounded muffled, sleep-sodden, and the candle's light showed hollows and grooves, his features blurred and flattened by exhaustion and despair.

"I am sorry I awakened you, Godwin, but I needed to speak to you straightaway."

"And it could not wait till the morrow? But men like you are not ones for waiting, are they? Ask what you will, then, and try not to wake up my girl."

It took Justin a moment to realize what Godwin meant by "men like you." Men with power. He almost laughed, for he too often felt like an orphan buffeted by storms beyond his control. He had to remind himself that the bishop's bastard foundling was also the queen's man, and to the peddler, the gap between them must have seemed vast, indeed. "You were not there to watch as Geoffrey Aston abjured the realm."

"What good would it do? I'm glad he was found out, glad that he's paying for what he did to my Melangell. But he could bleed his life away a drop at a time and it would not bring her back, now would it?"

"No," Justin agreed, "it would not. Yet there is more to this than you know, Godwin. Bear with me, for I've a reason for asking. I need to know about Melangell's red dress, the one you bought her ere she died."

Godwin looked baffled, but he was accustomed to obeying orders. "What of it?"

"Cati told me that she'd never had a red dress before. Is that true?"

Godwin was beginning to eye Justin as if he was not quite in his right wits. "Aye . . . 'tis true." His voice stayed steady, but his breathing held a betraying quiver. "We buried her in it."

"So Cati told me. Did she ever get to wear it, Godwin?"

"Yes . . . she was wearing it that Friday, the day she died."

It was the answer Justin was expecting. But he'd needed to hear it from Godwin. Rising, he reached for his money pouch. "I have something for you. We promised you'd get it back once the sheriff was sure it would not be needed at trial. He handed it over to Jonas this afternoon." The candle flame illuminated the tarnished, worn sheen of Melangell's pilgrim pledge. Godwin snatched it up, his gnarled fingers clenching into a fist around the cross. Justin dropped his hand to the older man's shoulder, and left him sitting there in the darkened stairwell, clutching his murdered child's talisman.

Justin slept poorly that night and was up and dressed by the time the sky had begun to lighten. A hazy dawn was breaking over London, the streets slowly filling as the city stirred. There was no sign of life at Humphrey Aston's shop, the shutters still down, the door barred. Justin was turning toward the side gate that led to the mercer's great hall when he saw one of the Aston journeymen on the other side of the street. Crossing over, he hailed the man. "Are you about to open the shop?"

The man shook his head, grinning broadly. "We got the day off! I can still scarce believe it, but the old man said he had work to do on his own and did not want the lot of us underfoot."

"Where is he now?"

"In the shop. If you want my guess, he tried to drink himself into a stupor last night and is dog-sick this morn. I never thought to hear myself saying this, but I can almost feel sorry for him . . . almost. There was room for but one person in that shriveled walnut of a heart of his, and that was Geoffrey."

After the journeyman went off to enjoy his day of liberty, Justin returned to the mercer's shop and began to pound loudly for admittance. The response was a curse-laden warning to go away. Justin continued to hammer on the door until it was wrenched open.

"I am closed, you witless, misbegotten lout!" Humphrey bellowed, but Justin shoved the door back, forcing his way into the shop. It was like falling into a damp, dark hole, for the room was lit only by a sputtering candle and the air reeked of tallow grease, sweat, and wine. Getting his first good look at this intruder, Humphrey growled low in his throat. "You!" Snatching up an empty clay flagon, he swung it clumsily at Justin's head.

His aim was off, though, and Justin had no trouble evading the blow. Before Humphrey could try again, Justin clamped his hand on the other man's wrist, forcing him to drop the flagon. It shattered and the impact seemed to bring Humphrey back to his senses. Rubbing his wrist, he glared defiantly at Justin. "Who could blame me if I'd split your head open? Because of your meddling, I lost my son!"

He did not seem drunk, although not for want of trying; the floor was littered with discarded flagons and his eyes were bloodshot and puffy, his tunic so wrinkled and disheveled that he must have slept in it. Justin looked upon this evidence of a man's disintegration and felt not a flicker of pity. "Where is your wife? Is she above-stairs?"

"No, at her sister's. What is it to you?"

"Nothing to me, but this is a conversation you'll not be wanting her to overhear."

"This conversation is over. Get out!"

"Why not try to throw me out? I think I'd enjoy that." Humphrey tensed to launch himself at the younger man, then thought better of it. "What are you doing here? Have you not done enough harm to my family?"

"Let's talk about that, Humphrey, about family. Growing up, I never knew my father and I felt that loss keenly. Looking at you now, I see that I was the lucky one. Your sons would have fared better as orphans."

It had been many years since anyone had dared to talk to Humphrey like this and his face flooded with color. "I want you out of my shop—now!"

"You still do not see it, do you? I know the truth. I know how Melangell died and the part you played in it."

Humphrey scarcely seemed to be breathing, so still was he of a sudden. Only his eyes moved, shifting from Justin's face to the sword at his hip. "What sort of nonsense is this?" he said, sounding more wary now than indignant. "I had naught to do with that Welsh whore's death."

"That is what I once thought, too. Even this did not put me on the right track," Justin said, taking out his money pouch and slowly extracting that broken piece of tombstone.

Humphrey's body sagged and he sank down on a workbench piled with bolts of cloth. Justin held the rock toward the candle's light. "You can see her blood better now. She bled a lot. Was she conscious when you hit her? Had she started to revive, mayhap moaning? Or were you just making sure, finishing what Geoffrey had begun?"

Humphrey said nothing. He'd yet to take his eyes from the rock, transfixed by those brownish stains. Justin leaned back against the door, one hand sliding down to loosen his sword in its scabbard. "You do not want to talk about it? I suppose it is up to me, then. Where shall I start? How about with Melangell's red dress? You were the first one to make mention of it, ranting about her 'whore's scarlet.' I remembered because your outburst was so poisonous, but it took a while to understand its true significance. You see, Humphrey, Melangell had but one red dress, worn for the first time on the day she died. So you lied when you said you'd not seen her that Friday."

Humphrey's face was suffused with heat, with hatred so intense it was almost palpable. "She was a slut," he said harshly, "chasing shamelessly after Geoffrey day and night. I'd warned him away from her, but he kept sneaking around, futtering her on the sly . . . young fool!"

"So you followed him to the churchyard that night, meaning to catch them in the act. Instead you overheard her telling him she was with child. You knew that could wreck Geoffrey's chances of wedding Adela and you were not about to let that happen. My guess is that you hid to hear more. We both know what happened next. Geoffrey pushed her, she fell, and he panicked, thinking he'd killed her. As soon as he fled, you emerged from the shadows. Geoffrey may have lost his head, but not you. No, you saw your chance and took it. Was she already dying when you reached for that rock? I suppose you're the only one who'll ever know that, and you're not likely to say, are you?"

"You've got that right!" Humphrey's lip curled scornfully. "You spin a good tale, de Quincy, but all you've got is a bloody rock and lots of suspicions. You cannot prove a word of this!"

"You are right," Justin admitted. "I cannot prove it. If

I could, I'd have gone to the sheriff. I spent the night trying to figure out how to bring you to justice and realized I cannot. Geoffrey has confessed and the sheriff was never all that interested in the killing of a peddler's daughter, so he's not about to reopen this case without proof. And as you pointed out, I lack proof, at least the sort of proof that would convince a court. What I do have, though, is a remarkably compelling story of greed and guilt and mortal sin. I'm willing to wager that your family, your neighbors, and fellow mercers will be hanging on to my every word."

Humphrey shot to his feet, fists balled. "You cannot do that!"

"I can," Justin said coldly, "and I will. I thought I'd go first to Master Serlo. I think he'll believe me. I think anyone who knows you will believe me—"

"You treacherous bastard!" Humphrey took a threatening step forward, only to halt when Justin let his hand drop to the hilt of his sword. "I'll sue you for slander," he said, and Justin laughed.

"Have you forgotten? I'm the queen's man. Which one of us do you think a court would heed?"

The mercer responded with a curse so profane that Justin was impressed in spite of himself. But he was right about Humphrey Aston; this was not a man to lose his head. There was a long silence and then Humphrey said in a flat, dispassionate voice, "I am not admitting any of this, mind you. I'll deny it with my last breath. I'd rather not have to do that, though, for lies are like mud. They tend to stick. So what will it take to keep you quiet about these ludicrous suspicions of yours?"

"Money."

Humphrey's mouth twisted in an expression of rage, relief, and contempt. "I should have known," he said. "Money is always the answer, even for self-righteous whoresons like you." Crossing to a coffer chest, he removed a key from his belt, and after a moment of fumbling, flung the lid open. "Do not think that you can dip into my well anytime you get thirsty. This one time, you can drink, but no more. Now . . . how much?"

"Enough," Justin said, "to buy a mule."

When the money had been counted out, Humphrey carefully relocked the coffer, then watched as Justin transferred the coins to his pouch. "I'll not expect to see you here again," he warned. "And you can leave the rock."

"I think not," Justin said, glancing down at the dried blood stains and wishing they were the mercer's, not Melangell's. "And we're not done yet. There is one more thing you must do. You're to go to Master Serlo, persuade him to take Daniel on as one of his apprentices."

"What? What sort of daft demand is that?"

"One you're going to meet, if you expect me to keep silent."

"How am I supposed to convince him? Why would he want Daniel in his shop? God knows I do not!"

"Appeal to his better nature. He seems a decent sort, doubtless feels guilty that he was so quick to suspect the worst of Daniel. Offer a very generous bond of surety and a favorable contract. How you do it is up to you. But get it done or we have no deal."

When Humphrey continued to protest, Justin cut him off curtly. "There is nothing more to be said. I'll be back at week's end, so you'd best seek out Master Serlo as soon as you sober up."

Humphrey spat out another oath. "This is extortion, plain and simple!"

Justin halted in the doorway. "No . . . it is retribution." It was a relief to escape the stifling, murky atmosphere of the mercer's shop, and he paused out on the street to savor the sunlight, the clean air. Mayhap Jonas was right and he was taking too many of John's habits to heart. It was easy to abuse power, all too easy. For certes, he'd taken shameless advantage of his position as the queen's man. But after more than five months in the royal service, he felt sure that his queen would have approved of what he'd done. As he walked briskly up Friday Street, he seemed to hear Eleanor's voice echoing on the light summer wind, reminding him again that *There are any number of reasons, Justin, why people are tempted to dance with the Devil.*

The mule was young and sturdy, a pale grey, his mane braided with one of Cati's red hair ribbons. Godwin could not resist running his hands along the animal's sleek hide each time he passed by, but eventually the cart was loaded and the good-byes were said. Godwin clambered up onto the seat and Justin gave Cati a hand up, too. Clara and her husband smiled and waved, and Nell produced a small sack of wafers for their noontime meal on the road. With cries of "Godspeed" and "Safe journey," Godwin and his daughter bade London farewell and began the long journey back to Wales. They'd gone only a short distance, though, before Godwin reined in the mule.

"Justin!" Cati cried, leaning precariously out of the cart. When he saw what she wanted to show him, he nodded and grinned, and the cart lumbered on, accompanied by Shadow until Justin whistled to him.

Nell joined Justin in the street. "What did the little lass want you to see?"

"That she was wearing Melangell's St Davydd's cross."

"Well, St Davydd seems to be smiling upon them these days. How else explain Godwin's new mule?" Nell queried blandly, blue eyes agleam. Justin merely smiled and shrugged, as he always did when the subject of

Godwin's mule was raised. Nell called out a final farewell as the cart turned onto the Cheapside, and then
glanced over at Justin.

"I hope you have nothing in mind for the afternoon.
The Templars' mill offers the best flour and the best
price, but I've need of a strong arm to fetch it home."

"I cannot think of anything I'd rather do than lug flour
sacks back from Southwark," Justin said, and Nell
grinned, linking her arm in his.

The rest of the day was a pleasant one. After picking
up Nell's flour at the Templars' mill, they bought pork
pies from a street vendor and ate by the river, watching
as ships lowered their masts to navigate under the
bridge. On their way home, they stopped in the Eastcheap market so Nell could buy some honey. While she
haggled with the peddler over the price, Justin wandered
over to look at the caged larks and magpies.

"Promise me you're not thinking of buying one," Nell
entreated when she rejoined him. "Not a pie—they never
stop shrieking."

"If I tell you, you'll laugh," Justin said, but he told her,
anyway. "Cati said that Melangell hated to see birds
caged up, and for a mad moment or two, I was actually
thinking of buying one and setting it free . . . for Melangell." He smiled sheepishly. "I realized then that I'd
merely be buying dinner for that ginger tom," he said,
pointing toward a large cat who was prowling under the
cages, hungry green eyes aglow.

"I think," Nell said, "that you've already done what
you could for Melangell," and he let her draw him away
from those wicker cages with their brightly colored cap-
tives, glad that she hadn't caught him browsing at the
booth selling baby rattles and cradles.

With Shadow leading the way, they reached Gracechurch Street in late afternoon. Pretending to stagger
under the weight of Nell's packages, Justin was about to

enter the alehouse when he heard his name being called. Gunter was standing in the doorway of the smithy, beckoning to him.

"A messenger has been looking for you, Justin," he said. "The queen wants you."

AUTHOR'S NOTE

John's conniving is a matter of historical record, as is the siege of Windsor. Justin's participation was, of course, a case of dramatic license. Unlike my historical "sagas," my medieval mysteries have a mixed cast, those who actually lived and those who live only in my imagination. There is no need to document Eleanor of Aquitaine's subsequent history, or that of her sons, but readers might be interested in the fate of one of the secondary characters: Master Serlo of the Mercer's Guild eventually became Mayor of London.

As I explained in my first mystery, *The Queen's Man*, there was no Bishop of Chester. Chester lay in the diocese of Coventry and Lichfield, and although the title Bishop of Chester was used during the Middle Ages, it was an unofficial usage. And as I invariably mention in my historical novels, I use the medieval Welsh spelling for St Davydd, as this is more phonetic. Modern Welsh would spell it *Dafydd*.

In researching *The Queen's Man*, I discovered that medieval detectives labored under certain handicaps, among them, no DNA testing, no fingerprints, no forensics. But in *Cruel as the Grave*, Justin and Jonas did not have to worry about warrants or the admissibility of evidence, so perhaps it all evens out. As long as I get to write about Eleanor of Aquitaine and her fascinatingly dysfunctional family, I have no complaints.

S.K.P.
February 1998

ACKNOWLEDGMENTS

I'd like to thank the following people in particular for their support and encouragement: My parents, the most loving critics any writer could ask for. Valerie Ptak La-Mont, who did so much to keep Justin and me on course. Kyle LaMont, who provided insight on Justin's estrangement with his father. Earle Kotila and Jill and John Davies, who help me to keep the faith. The editor who has been my mainstay from my first book to—hopefully—my last, Marian Wood. My longtime English editor and friend, Susan Watt. And my agents extraordinaire, Molly Friedrich and Mic Cheetham. Lastly, I'd like to thank the readers who welcomed my first venture into the mystery realm, and were generous enough to write and tell me so. Feedback from readers is truly worth its weight in gold.

A CONVERSATION WITH
SHARON KAY PENMAN

Q: As a critically acclaimed author of historical fiction, what inspired you to create this medieval mystery series?

SKP: This was an example of something positive coming out of a negative experience. By the time I'd finished researching and writing *When Christ and His Saints Slept*, I was in danger of burning out. For the first time in nearly two decades, my boundless enthusiasm for the Middle Ages had begun to flag. So I decided I needed a change of pace, and since I am a long-time mystery fan, it occurred to me that a medieval mystery might be fun to write. Once that idea took root, it was probably inevitable that I'd choose to write about Eleanor of Aquitaine, surely one of history's most memorable women.

Q: What aspects of the research and writing of this novel presented the greatest challenges to you?

SKP: In my historical novels, I was constantly trying to keep faith with known historical facts; if I occasionally had to take creative liberties, I made a point of alerting my readers in my author's notes. So the mysteries represent a break with a twenty-year-old tradition. While I strive to stay true to the historical shadows of Eleanor or her son John, I can let my imagination soar with purely fictional characters such as Justin de Quincy or his duplicitous lady love, Claudine. This unexpected freedom is both daunting and exhilarating!

Q: **What initially drew you to work in the genre of historical fiction and what keeps you coming back?**

SKP: I stumbled onto the story of Richard III, probably England's most controversial king, and from that initial fascination with one of history's great puzzles came my first novel, *The Sunne in Splendour*. By the time *Sunne* was completed, I was hopelessly hooked on the Middle Ages. Not that I'd have wanted to live back then; I am much too fond of creature comforts like indoor plumbing and central air conditioning. But the medieval era offers unbounded riches for a novelist.

Q: **How do you balance the demands of crafting a good story with the demands of the historical record?**

SKP: I think I rely upon instinct to a certain degree. I can immediately recognize it when I'm in danger of straying too far afield. For example, I would not feel comfortable creating a character who was utterly at variance with his historical personage, i.e., turning a warrior king like Edward I into a military misfit or depicting the strong-willed Marguerite d'Anjou as a shrinking violet. An exception, of course, is a historical figure whose motives and nature are still being hotly debated, as is the case with Richard III. If I did choose to give my readers a characterization that defies tradition, I would feel obligated to give my readers an explanation, too, for my decision to blaze a new trail.

Q: Are there lines (in terms of historical accuracy) that should not be crossed in the pursuit of a good story?

SKP: Most definitely. I might feel free to switch scenes from one castle to another, or to make a minor change in the time line. But I would not stake out a position utterly unsupported by historical evidence or academic interpretation. I could not create a medieval country that was radical in impulse, democratic in thought, tolerant of dissent. Pacifism, feminism, nationalism—these are all concepts that would have totally different shadings and subtleties in another century. I'd never want to write a book that could be tagged as "the Plantagenets in Pasadena."

Q: While Justin de Quincy is a fictional character of your own creation, is he based on any real-life figure(s) you have encountered in your research?

SKP: No, he has no historical counterpart. I wanted to create a character who has an outsider's viewpoint, one with the skills necessary to survive at the royal court and upon the mean streets of London. From this need came Justin de Quincy, illegitimate son of a bishop, educated above his station in life, not truly belonging in either of his worlds.

Q: Justin has been likened to James Bond. How do you feel about this comparison?

SKP: Bond . . . Justin Bond. No, I don't think it has the

same ring to it. Better that we keep both men in their own times.

Q: **All of your readers and reviewers comment upon the richness and vividness of the historical detail in your books. How do you go about researching your books?**

SKP: After researching and writing seven novels set in the Middle Ages, I feel very much at home there. When I read a novel of another age, I am curious about the details of daily life, wanting to know what the people ate and wore as well as what they believed and feared. So I try to provide that mixture of the mundane and the exotic in my own books.

Q: **Is it difficult to render legendary figures, such as Eleanor of Aquitaine, human and accessible? How do you do it?**

SKP: I think it is definitely more challenging to depict a well-known historical figure, for then readers bring preconceived notions to the book. Someone familiar with the Robin Hood legend, for example, might be surprised to learn that King John was neither an incompetent king nor a moral monster. And mention Eleanor of Aquitaine to anyone who has ever seen *The Lion in Winter*, and Katharine Hepburn inevitably comes to mind! But the process of creating a character remains the same, whether that character comes from the pages of history or my own imagination. When writing a scene, I attempt to get inside the character's head and see things from his or her point of view. Rationalization and self-justification are universal human traits; even outright villains will often see themselves as the ones wronged. Once I take up residence in a character's soul, it is usually fairly easy to identify with his needs or her yearnings. In fact, it was a bit unsettling to discover how readily I could relate to neurotic malcontents like George, Duke of Clarence, or ice-blooded adventurers like the Flemish mercenary William de Ypres!

Q: **Why do you think the stories of Eleanor of Aquitaine and Henry II and their Plantagenet dynasty in Britain remain such a compelling subject for so many writers and artists such as yourself?**

SKP: When I do readings, I often joke that I consider Henry II and Eleanor of Aquitaine and their children to be the ultimate dysfunctional family, and there is probably as much truth as humor in that observation. Henry was one of England's greatest kings and Eleanor probably rivals Cleopatra in her hold upon the public imagination. Yet as parents, they lurched from one blunder to another and have the dubious distinction of producing four of the most self-centered, shallow, or warped sons in the history of the Plantagenet dynasty. We might not be able today to identify with those larger-than-life medieval monarchs, but who couldn't empathize with a father's pain, a mother's regrets?

Q: **What would you most like your readers to understand about the status of women and the human condition in general during the Middle Ages?**

SKP: That the men and women of the Middle Ages are not so alien to ourselves. Obviously their beliefs and superstitions and biases were shaped by factors foreign to us. But I don't believe that human nature has changed drastically or dramatically down through the centuries. Their expectations might have been very different from ours, but their emotions flowed from the same river that runs through our lives today. Also that medieval people were no less complex or contradictory than they are now. Personalities must always be factored into the equation. The most definitive study of the legal status of women in medieval France does not explain a Joan of Arc or an Eleanor of Aquitaine.

Q: The issue of language during this period is a fascinating one which you use to great effect both in this book and its prequel, *The Queen's Man*. Why is French the official language of the English court at this point in time? When does this change?

SKP: French became the official language of the English court as a result of the Battle of Hastings in 1066, in which William the Conqueror, Duke of Normandy, defeated the English king, Harold Godwineson. In the period of my mysteries, English was the language of the conquered, French the tongue of the aristocracy. It would not have been surprising if English had eventually died out under such adverse circumstances. But it showed an astonishing vitality, an unexpected resilience, and over a period of several centuries slowly gained back the ground it had lost. The Norman-French aristocracy engaged English-speaking wet-nurses and caretakers for their children, and by the mid-thirteenth century, many people were bilingual. Edward I is believed to be the first English-speaking king since the Conquest. By the fifteenth century, the setting for my novel *Sunne*,

English had fully regained its supremacy. To complete the linguistic mosaic, Latin was the language of the educated, the voice of the Church, and Welsh remained the mother tongue of Wales, even after the loss of Welsh independence. So I have to be careful in my writings—if Justin de Quincy eavesdrops upon a key conversation, it must be in a language he can comprehend!

Q: Melangell's Welsh heritage figures prominently in this story. Could you discuss the nature of the conflict and tensions between the English and the Welsh?

SKP: Medieval Wales was divided into three principalities, each ruled by its own house. From the time of Henry II, the Welsh accepted the English king as their liege lord, although never willingly, and border skirmishing between the English and Welsh continued to erupt during the twelfth and thirteenth centuries. It was not until the reign of Llywelyn ap Gruffydd that a Welsh prince succeeded in uniting his people against the English. Llywelyn was the first Prince of Wales. After his death in 1282, Edward I appropriated the title for his eldest son and heir apparent, a tradition that continues to this day.

Q: The concept of sanctuary is a fascinating one. Could you talk about the origins of this practice and how widely it was used?

SKP: The concept of sanctuary is an ancient one, existing as far back as the times of the Greeks and Romans. It has equally venerable roots in the Christian religion. The first laws conferring sanctuary upon a church date from 392 a.d., so the tradition was well established by the Middle Ages. The custom gradually lost favor with civil authorities and was officially abolished by King James I in the seventeenth century. Sanctuary's intriguing corollary, Abjuration of the Realm, was of Anglo-Norman origin and peculiar to England.

Q: **For the geographically and historically challenged, could you tell us what region today constitutes Eleanor's beloved Aquitaine?**

SKP: Eleanor's Aquitaine consisted of Poitou and Gascony, a vast, rich region in southwestern France, more than one-quarter the size of modern France. Eleanor's domains were therefore more extensive than the lands under the control of her first husband, the French king Louis VII.

Q: **What are your future plans for Justin de Quincy?**

SKP: I am sending Justin de Quincy into Wales in my next mystery, *Dragon's Lair*, where he'll find himself matching wits and crossing swords not only with John and his personal nemesis, Durand de Curzon, but with the young Llywelyn ab Iorwerth, who figured so prominently in my novel *Here Be Dragons*. And of course the Lady Claudine will continue to complicate Justin's life, as will the father who refuses to acknowledge him.

Q: **Will romance bloom between Justin and Nell?**

SKP: I am not being evasive, but I honestly do not know. I once read a marvelous quote from another writer—I am reasonably certain that it was E. M. Forster—in which he said that his characters were galley slaves, obedient to his will. Mine are less biddable and much more inclined to go off on tangents of their own. A perfect example is Davydd ap Gruffydd, brother of Llywelyn, in *Falls the Shadow* and *The Reckoning*. Davydd was originally intended to be a secondary character, but he would have none of that and was soon stealing scenes with all the panache of a natural-born actor. So even if I reveal my plans for Justin and Nell, they've yet to be heard from.

Q: What will your next project be?

SKP: I am currently working on *Time and Chance*, the next book in my Saints trilogy about Henry II and Eleanor of Aquitaine. If Henry and Eleanor continue to cooperate, always a precarious proposition with that pair, I hope to have it completed in late autumn, with publication scheduled for the year 2000. Then I will do *Dragon's Lair*, Justin's foray into Wales, and after that *The Devil's Brood*, which will deal with Henry's civil war with his own sons.

Q: How does the writing process work for you?

SKP: I do a chapter at a time and don't sit down at the computer until I have it playing out in my head. I don't do numerous rewrites; I stay with a chapter until I am satisfied with it. I also read the chapter aloud to see how it strikes the ear.

Q: What was the best piece of advice you have ever received regarding your craft?

SKP: I think the best writing advice came from my father. He said I should heed my own inner voice and trust my instincts.

Q: **What writers have most influenced you?**

SKP: I am not sure if my writing style has been influenced, per se, but there are a number of writers whose work I admire. Anya Seton's *Katherine* and *The Winthrop Woman* were great favorites of mine. A more recent historical novel that I enjoyed enormously was Larry McMurtry's brilliant *Lonesome Dove*. And anyone who appreciates historical fiction ought to be reading Margaret George.

Q: **What works would you recommend to a reading group?**

SKP: I have eclectic taste in mystery writers: I read James Lee Burke, Sue Grafton, Anne Perry, Robert Crais, Carl Hiaasen, Elizabeth George, Sharyn McCrumb, Joan Hess, Elizabeth Peters, Elmore Leonard, Daniel Woodrell, Sharan Newman, Margaret Frazer, Ellis Peters, Linda Barnes, and Edward Marston, among others. I highly recommend Janet Evanovich's zany mysteries about the star-crossed Stephanie Plum and the Elizabethan mysteries that Patricia Finney writes as P. F. Chisholm. And the top of my list would have to be crowned with Dana Stabenow, whose Kate Shugak mysteries offer such a haunting portrayal, in dark and bright, of Alaskan life and the human soul.

READING GROUP
QUESTIONS AND TOPICS
FOR DISCUSSION

1. What do you predict will be Justin's next adventure? What would you like to see happen to him and the other characters?

2. Which characters did you find to be the most compelling and why? Did you find that you have a preference for either the fictional or real-life characters?

3. What characters would you like to hear from again?

4. Did you solve this mystery or did the ending surprise you?

5. What do you think are the necessary ingredients in crafting a good mystery?

6. If you were to create your own mystery series, what kind of characters would you build it around? Where would it be set?

7. Did the line between the fictional and historically accurate components of this novel seem clear to you? What do you think are the merits as well as

the potential problems of the genre of historical fiction?

8. What aspects of medieval English history did this novel inspire you to learn more about? What did you learn that most surprised or interested you about life in these times?

9. This story raises important questions about human nature and the nature of human society. How has the world changed since the Middle Ages? What do you think has changed (or not), for better and for worse?

10. Discuss the barriers of class, ethnicity, and so forth that thwart many of the relationships in this novel. Do these hierarchies still exist? How did they operate in the Middle Ages and how do they operate today?

11. Discuss the many complicated familial relationships in this novel. Why is the parent-child relationship fraught with so many problems? Do you think human beings have made any progress over the intervening centuries in working out this bond?

12. Eleanor of Aquitaine is a remarkable female figure in history who juggled a whole host of roles as queen, general, prisoner, mother, wife, and so forth. What challenges did she face in trying to balance her duties as a queen with her duties as a mother? In which role(s) would you judge her most successful?

13. Did you find the nature of Justin's parentage to be shocking? Do you think the identity of his father

might be more shocking and scandalous today than it was in medieval England?

14. How do you understand Geoffrey's and his father Humphrey Aston's decisions to remain silent? What are their motives?

15. According to his aunt Agnes, "Daniel has never seemed to blame Geoffrey for being the chosen one." Do you think this is an accurate assessment? Why or why not?

16. What do you think will happen with Claudine and Justin? Discuss the irony of the situation that Justin now finds himself in.

17. Do you find the bond between Eleanor of Aquitaine and Justin de Quincy to be convincing? Why might this queen choose to bond with such a young man?

18. Discuss the impact of a sexual double standard on the characters in this novel. Who benefits and who is punished for their sexual adventures and why?

19. Given the role that unplanned pregnancies play in this novel, what impact do you think the twentieth-century development of safe and effective birth control has had on society?

20. Discuss why Justin came to care so deeply about bringing Melangell's murderer to justice. Why were others, such as Tobias, not so invested in finding the killer? Was justice served in this case? Do you think English and other Western justice systems work more effectively today?

21. Why did your group choose to read this particular work? How does this novel compare with other works your group has read? What are you planning to read next?

THE QUEEN'S MAN
The First Novel of the Queen's Man Series

by Sharon Kay Penman

Epiphany, 1193. Eleanor of Aquitaine sits upon England's throne. Her beloved son Richard Lionheart is missing, presumed dead—and the court is whispering that her younger son, John, is plotting to seize the crown. Meanwhile, on the snowy highroad from Winchester, a destitute young man falls heir to a bloodstained letter, pressed into his hand by a dying man. The missive becomes Justin de Quincy's passport into the queen's confidence—and into the heart of danger, as he pursues a cunning murderer in Eleanor's court of intrigue. . . .

"Full of swordplay, bawdy byplay, and derring-do, *The Queen's Man* is a full-bodied romp, steeped in period detail."
—*The Houston Chronicle*

Published by Ballantine Books.
Available at your local bookstore.

If you enjoyed Sharon Kay Penman's
Queen's Man mysteries,
then discover her other historical novels:

THE SUNNE IN SPLENDOUR
HERE BE DRAGONS
FALLS THE SHADOW
THE RECKONING
WHEN CHRIST AND HIS SAINTS SLEPT

"Penman is an accomplished novelist and certainly
has staked a claim to medieval England
as her literary fiefdom."
—*The Philadelphia Inquirer*

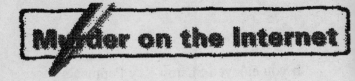

Murder on the Internet

Ballantine mysteries are on the Web!

Read about your favorite Ballantine authors and upcoming books in our electronic newsletter MURDER ON THE INTERNET, at **www.randomhouse.com/BB/MOTI**

Including:

- What's new in the stores
- Previews of upcoming books for the next four months
- In-depth interviews with mystery authors and publishing insiders
- Calendars of signings and readings for Ballantine mystery authors
- Profiles of mystery authors
- Mystery quizzes and contest

To subscribe to MURDER ON THE INTERNET, please send an e-mail to **join-mystery@list.randomhouse.com** with "subscribe" as the body of the message. (Don't use the quotes.) You will receive the next issue as soon as it's available.

Find out more about whodunit! For sample chapters from current and upcoming Ballantine mysteries, visit us at **www.randomhouse.com/BB/mystery**